CELESTIAL CHAOS

THE COMMONS
BOOK 2

JESSICA MARTING

SHADOW PRESS

CELESTIAL CHAOS

Celestial Chaos (The Commons Book 2)

ISBN 978-1-989780-29-9

For Angela—you wanted a starship, I'm giving you a book. I hope that's okay.

CHAPTER 1

A cat-sitter's services would have been a wise investment, Andrew mused. He could have paid someone to come in and feed the furry monsters and his stepmother would have been none the wiser. But no, he had to go and be the responsible stepson and accept her orders to look after the furry beasts while she and his father vacationed in Dublin.

His eyes had immediately welled up when he let himself into his parents' condo, and a fluffy white cat made a beeline for his ankles and draped itself over his shoes. He sneezed, and the sound beckoned to the other three cats that Judith referred to as her "grateful children." He urged the white one off his feet and made his way to the kitchen, the cats weaving in and out between his legs. *They're trying to kill me.* It was the only thing they hadn't done yet that would make Judith proud. He sneezed again as he poured enough kibble into their bowls so he wouldn't have to visit again for another couple of days, and let himself out of the condo while the cats gorged themselves.

Back in his car, he wiped his leaking eyes and slipped on a pair of sunglasses. His car's temperature had soared uncomfortably in the August heat in the ten minutes he had been away, and he turned on the air conditioner as high as it would go and let himself cool down before leaving the luxury condo tower. Once again, he debated whether or not to keep his appointment at Lazarus Cryonics. It was an argument he had had with himself for weeks.

Andrew wasn't a sci-fi fanatic. Nor was he particularly spiritual, paranoid, or afraid of the afterlife. He was simply curious about what he could wake up to in a hundred years or so, and that was the only reason he had made the appointment at the cryonics lab. The technology was available, and he could afford to make it happen thanks to the lab's payment plan. Now all he had to do was make sure he didn't die on safari or someplace where he couldn't be frozen in time.

His phone trilled a few times on his trip to the north-western corner of Toronto, where the lab was located, but he ignored it. A quick glance at the call display when he was stopped at a traffic light revealed it was someone from his office trying to contact him, when he had explicitly told his staff not to while he was taking this brief personal leave. *That will be over soon enough*, he told himself. He had already found a buyer for his small empire of music venues. All he had to do now was sign a few papers at his lawyer's office next week, and his hands would be washed of the whole business.

He was unsure where his life would take him next. He had removed an albatross from around his neck and would be making plans for his demise. Now he had to find something to do for the next forty or fifty years he planned to be alive. He had been tinkering with the idea of joining a few acquaintances in their satellite radio station start-up, and he considered it again as he drove along the highway to the cryonics facility. His potential business partners had been trying to sell him on an alternative station, highlighting independent and up-and-coming acts exclusively, already securing a couple of well-known personalities to host shows and interview artists.

It was the kind of idea with which Andrew had started Tiger Media, and the memories of what it had turned into still left a bitter taste in his mouth. So he was still on the fence about the whole situation.

It was the best idea so far, though. His father and stepmother had been on his case about returning to school. *Ha!*

Lazarus Cryonics turned out to be one of three businesses in a nearly empty office park. The lab shared the property with a kitchen appliance wholesaler and a commercial bakery. The former was closed in the middle of the week, and the bakery had an eviction notice on its door. A Toyota Corolla that had seen better days was the single car parked outside the lab's entrance, and a couple of vehicles sat on the other side of the lot, the drivers taking advantage of the free parking. If it wasn't for the omnipresent sound of construction nearby—probably a new condo tower—Andrew would have thought he had driven into a ghost town.

He was met with a rush of frigid air when he walked into the lab's office. He wondered where the preserved remains were kept. Certainly not here.

Heavy carpeting muffled his footsteps, and a few generic photos of nature graced the gray-painted walls. A couch and table spread with current issues of *The Globe and Mail* and *Maclean's* were to the left of the door. To the right, a young woman peered at him from behind a massive desk. She was dark-haired, green-eyed, pretty in a fresh-off-the-farm kind of way. Wholesome-looking. She tilted her computer monitor off to the side.

"Hey," he said awkwardly. How did one greet an employee of a death merchant? "Why does this place have to be in the middle of nowhere?" he muttered, then silently cursed himself for it. It didn't do to bitch about things hired minions couldn't help.

"Good afternoon. You must be Mr. Claybourne," the receptionist smoothly replied.

He took off his sunglasses and rubbed his itchy eyes. *Damn cats.* He knew he looked like he was back on the hard stuff, and that was embarrassing. She was cute. "I am," he confirmed. "What's your name?"

Well, that came out wrong. He opened his mouth to apologize and explain, but she cut him off.

"Lily," she answered coolly, her voice as chilly as the air conditioning. "May I get you a bottle of water, Mr. Claybourne?"

"No, thank you." So, Lily may already know of him, and not as a name in an appointment book. If she read the alternative weeklies or, hell, even the *Sun*, she would have already heard about Tiger Media's decline and his own downfall. He gave up on small talk and was about to sit on the couch and flip through the newspaper, but a door off reception opened. A pair of very tall men in lab coats stepped out.

"*Min* Claybourne," said one of them. Andrew couldn't place his accent. And what language was this "*min*" salutation? "We have been anticipating your consultation." He held the door open. "Please come in."

They looked like brothers. The one who had greeted him appeared older than his partner, with deep lines bracketing the corners of his eyes and mouth. He had black pupils, but Andrew knew that was probably a trick of the fluorescent light overhead. The younger man had green eyes, a bright, unnatural shade that Andrew suspected was faked with contact lenses. Both were thin, emphasizing their large, bald heads. The look they cast down on him was contemptuous, like he was a bug they could squish between their fingers. When the older one stretched his face into a smile, Andrew saw a mouth full of jagged teeth.

The sight sent a ripple of apprehension through Andrew,

which he tamped down. These guys probably had a genetic disorder or something. He swallowed and nodded, then followed them through the door.

He tried to crack a joke. "I don't want to get suckered into everything. I just want to be alive to see alien ass in a few hundred years." Immediately, he winced.

Very professional, Claybourne. Keep it up. The cute receptionist probably heard that.

He was led down a short hallway, closed doors on either side and one at the end. The one they had walked through slammed shut behind them with an air of finality. Andrew forced away the images of every movie he had ever seen that featured creepy abandoned hospitals and morgues from his mind, concentrating on the manner at hand.

"We can assure you of your preservation only," the older man replied. At the end of the hallway, he opened the door. "I'm Dr. Zadbac," he said by way of introduction. "My associate, Dr. Pitro." He waved his hand to indicate the other man. Dr. Zadbac barked out a harsh command in a language Andrew didn't recognize. "Excuse me," the doctor corrected himself and flipped on a light switch. "I forget the illumination mechanism sometimes."

Uh-huh. Well, smart people tended to have their quirks. "That used to happen to me, too," Andrew said in commiseration. "Then I went to rehab."

The room was small and windowless, with a few chairs pushed against the opposite wall in front of a low table. "You have introduced yourself to our office..." Dr. Zadbac shrugged his shoulders.

"Receptionist?" Andrew guessed.

"Yes, our receptionist. Our assistant, *Minsa* Stewart. She is very helpful in dealing with the people."

"Not so interested in cryonic preservation," piped in Dr. Pitro. His voice was lower-pitched, on the verge of a growl.

"Well, it's not for everyone," Andrew replied. He took a seat in front of the table. A thin tablet computer and a few medical books rested on it.

"What is this *rehab, Min* Claybourne?" Dr. Pitro asked suddenly.

What kind of doctor hadn't heard of rehab? Hadn't they invented the whole process? "It's nothing," Andrew assured him. "I was just being a smartass. I wasn't insinuating that you're a user or anything. Never mind."

Both doctors turned to stare at him. "User?" Dr. Zadbac repeated, his brow furrowed.

Now it was Andrew's turn to feel confused. "I guess you haven't heard those terms in English," he fumbled. God, this was embarrassing. "I used to use illegal drugs."

Zadbac's black eyes widened in understanding. "Drugs. Medication?"

"What I used was once medication, but that was before we knew how bad it was."

Dr. Zadbac thought about this for a minute. Dr. Pitro pinned Andrew with a hard stare, and he fought the urge to squirm.

"I see," said Dr. Zadbac after an uncomfortable pause.

The doctors sat down on either side of Andrew, Dr. Pitro never wavering in his hard stare. Andrew was afforded a view of a large, unframed poster of the human body tacked to the wall next to the door. It had been marked up with a black pen in what he assumed were words in the doctors' native language.

Dr. Zadbac asked him about his medical history while Dr. Pitro made notes on the tablet computer, holding it away so Andrew couldn't see the screen. At least, he presumed Dr. Pitro was taking notes; he would tap away whenever the older doctor said anything. Andrew had had all the childhood diseases and vaccinations, and he didn't have any allergies aside from the one to cats. He hadn't had any children—"Thank God for that"—and aside from a reckless eighteen-month period that resulted in his voluntarily checking into a thirty-day program, he hadn't had any major health issues.

"That's something I wanted to ask you about," Andrew said. "I've been clean and sober for almost three years, but I don't know if it can affect the cryonics process or my brain can be revived later on." Some of the stuff he had read about cryonics had mentioned that.

Now the doctors looked confused. "We assume you bathe daily, *Min* Claybourne," said Dr. Zadbac. "Your kind prefers it, do you not?"

What? "No, that's not what I meant." *Why am I even bothering? Something is very wrong here.* "You know, I've changed my mind," said Andrew. "I'm sorry to have taken up your time. I don't think cryonics is for me." He stood up and strode to the door.

Dr. Pitro dropped the computer to the table and grabbed Andrew's arm. "What the hell?" said Andrew loudly. "Let me go!" He tried to pull his arm away, but the skinny bastard was stronger than he looked. The doctor's cold expression didn't change, and Andrew suppressed a shudder at the bright green eyes staring at him.

Andrew struggled again. "You treat all your clients like this?" he shouted to Dr. Zadbac.

"We do not get many clients here."

"That's not the point." Using all of his strength, he was finally able to pull away from Dr. Pitro. "*Damn it*, that hurts!" He put his hand on the doorknob, but before he could turn it, something stabbed him in the side of his neck.

An unearthly roar sounded through the room, and in his shocked state, Andrew realized the noise came from him. He reached for his neck and felt something sticking from his skin. He unsuccessfully tried to tug it out, but the motion only sent pain shooting down the side of his body. He whirled around to face the doctors. "What is this?" he yelled.

Dr. Zadbac was shouting at Dr. Pitro in their language, and the younger man sullenly looked away. He offered a few muttered words, but Dr. Zadbac continued to shout, the veins in his head bulging. Andrew tried again to pull the thing out of his neck.

Fuck it, he could go to the hospital and have a real doctor figure it out. He reached for the doorknob again, but Dr. Pitro bellowed something and Andrew was slammed into the wall. He crumpled to the floor and tasted blood.

Dr. Pitro leaned over him, a wan smile on his face that chilled Andrew to the bone. He made a fist as best as he could and clocked the doctor on the side of the face. Dr. Pitro fell over and snarled, then leapt at Andrew.

The next thing he knew, Dr. Pitro's stale breath wafted in his face, and he felt the doctor's jaws latch on to his face and nose. Andrew screamed for the first time in his life.

A few seconds later, he heard a hesitant tapping at the door. A woman's voice called out, "Dr. Zadbac? Dr. Pitro? Is everything...?"

Andrew reached up to grasp the knob, but a vicious kick from Dr. Pitro sent him sprawling against the door. "Thank God!" he yelled, relief coursing through him.

"Mr. Claybourne?" she said in surprise. "Dr. Zadbac? Do you need me to call 911?"

"Yes!" Andrew choked out. It hurt to breathe. He had probably broken a few ribs in addition to whatever else Dr. Pitro had done. He didn't want to touch his face. He tried to speak again, but another kick, this time from Dr. Zadbac, prevented him from doing so. He felt something crack inside him, and it dawned on him that he might not get out of this alive.

The receptionist was finally able to force open the door. She looked at the scene before her and screamed.

"Humans," muttered Dr. Pitro.

Andrew wanted to tell her to run away for help, but he couldn't form the words. "Help me," he managed.

She took a step back into the hallway. "What the hell?" she shrieked at the doctors. "What did you do?"

Andrew heard Dr. Zadbac try to speak with her, then closed his eyes and tried to will away the pain. It felt like his whole body was on fire. He was vaguely aware of the sound of feet running down the hall, first the receptionist's light footsteps and then the heavy, ominous thuds of Dr. Zadbac's boots. Pitro kneeled over him and touched the thing sticking out of his neck.

"Just do it," Andrew growled. "Just kill me already."

Dr. Pitro made a noise of disgust, and Andrew felt more pressure on his neck where the weapon was lodged. He realized it was a syringe as the doctor depressed the plunger.

Any hope Andrew might have had about dying painlessly evaporated. Agony radiated through his body, paralyzing him and freezing his vocal cords. His eyes bugged open of their own accord until they felt like they were going to pop out of his skull.

His last rational thought violently pulsed through him. *Please, let it be over soon.* Then he felt his lungs take one last deep breath of air and offered a quick prayer for death.

CHAPTER 2

Lieutenant Honora Kharn loved her job. She hadn't joined the Kurran Special Ops to impress other people or prove something; she enjoyed the rigid discipline of Ops combined with the freedom, the *rush* of conducting potentially lethal experiments in high-end fighter craft. While she hadn't shown it, she had been honored and excited about her newest assignment, and it finally stood right in front of her.

Earth, 2017. Her information packet said this particular area was in the middle of a brutal summer heat wave, just past 1500 hours. Humidity shimmered off the crude landing pad visible through her ship's forward viewport. No, not landing pad. *Parking lot.* Those land vehicles sparsely dotting the asphalt were called "cars." Whatever they were, they weren't necessary for this mission.

According to her commanding officers at Special Ops, Nym enemy agents had developed a way to travel back in time and for some strange reason had set up a cryonics laboratory in this inhospitable climate and era. She double-checked the cloaking mechanism on her ship and let herself out into the heat. Honora immediately cursed softly to herself. Her flight suit wasn't designed to protect her from high temperatures.

The building the Nym had appropriated was a short distance from where she had anchored her ship. She walked briskly, hoping no one noticed her. The lab shared space with other residents, all as empty-looking as the parking lot. She couldn't read the signs. There were too many extraneous letters.

She let herself into the building and a blast of freezing air startled her. Her weapon at the ready, she silently crept along plush carpeting through a simple office. A door off it was wide open, revealing a short corridor. She heard someone moving around and cursing faintly in the Nym tongue, and she braced herself, deciding the best moment to take him by surprise. She guessed that whoever was in there was alone and, at best, feebly armed.

Honora barrelled down the corridor and burst through the half-open door at the end. She heard a very surprised shout and more Nym cursing. Before the Nym could react, she landed a kick to his knee and hooked her foot upward, causing him to lose his balance and land on his back. He crashed into a table, and the primitive material crashed to the floor under his weight. His wide green eyes stared at her in shock, and Honora swore she saw a trickle of fear cross his face.

He was stunned for a few seconds before he said in Nym, "How the hell are you here?"

Honora didn't see the point in replying. On the rare occasions she had attended Ops-sanctioned interrogations, she was the one who induced suspects to talk without speaking herself.

The Nym regained his composure and scrabbled to his hands and knees. He looked around the room, presumably for something he could use as a weapon. "Bitch!" he spat in Nym, then again in Kurran to drive his insult home. Lucky for Honora, she spoke both languages.

She didn't offer a retort. Instead, she positioned her laser pistol directly over his heart. She had her orders: *Don't even bother trying to bring in the Nym. Just kill him and get rid of the evidence. And for the gods' sakes, don't change history.*

The Nym blinked his green eyes at her and gasped for breath before rising unsteadily to his feet. Honora slammed her pistol into his ribcage and felt a satisfying crack. He fell back on the broken table and coughed, black blood oozing from the corners of his mouth. She had hit him harder than she thought, and now he was bleeding internally. She didn't want to be around when *that* stink started.

"Before you kill me, I should tell you something," the Nym gasped in his own language.

Honora paused but didn't lower her weapon. He was incapacitated, but she wouldn't put it past the Nym to have access to an explosive.

He simply raised his hand and pointed the door. Beside it, a figure in a dark suit was hunched over on itself, facing the wall. There was blood—dark red, human blood—surrounding its head, smeared on the carpeted floor. There was some drying on the Nym's face, something she hadn't noticed in her sneak attack.

"You... you fucked up," he wheezed. Despite the agony he had to be in, the Nym managed a smirk. "That vortex isn't stable. You are going to be..." He coughed, black fluid dribbling down his chin. "Late."

Honora had already guessed that she had been gone at least six months from her own time, but she didn't care. She also placed more faith in the Kurran Empire than the Nym.

She fired her weapon. The Nym's body nearly split in two from the laser blast, and immediately the room filled with the nauseating stench of blood. She held her breath and felt around her uniform's pocket for one of the Special Ops' tricks she knew the enemy was unaware of. She withdrew a sealed packet of blue dust and upended it over the dead Nym. The powder accelerated decomposition, and in about an hour the enemy agent's remains would disappear.

Next, she withdrew a thin, flat disc and adjusted a dial across its top. She fastened it to the underside of a chair and was reassured by its tinny beeping. Within fifteen minutes, this laboratory would explode, taking away all evidence of the Nym.

The chronometer fastened around her wrist beeped, indicating that she was running out of time before she had to return to her ship and get back into the vortex's maw. If she didn't hustle, she would be either blown up or stuck in this godsforsaken time forever.

She took in a quick breath through her mouth. Already the Nym's skin was slackening against his bones. Her chronometer beeped again. She had to get out *now*.

A moan from the prone figure on the floor stopped her from leaving the room. A hand fluttered in the air. Against her better judgement, she leaned over for a closer look.

"Hey," she said in Kurran, then quickly caught herself. "Hello?" she tried again, in the most widely used Commons dialect, a derivative of the language spoken here in the twenty-first century.

He responded with another moan. She lifted away his hand.

Five years in Special Ops had shown her things beyond her worst nightmares. But she couldn't suppress a gasp at the sight of the human male curled up on the floor. He was unrecognizable beneath the blood. It looked like his nose had been shredded. She checked for a pulse and found it, stronger than she had expected.

She couldn't just leave him here. There had to be a way for her to send for the local authorities and then get away before the lab blew up. Whatever this man told them was his business. No one would believe he had been attacked by alien agents from the future, so she wouldn't worry about that.

A low, inhuman growl sounded from his throat, and she winced. She helped him to a sitting position. "I'll get help," she promised. "I'll figure out a way." How the hell did these people communicate with each other? There had to be some kind of device in the building she could figure out.

The bomb she had set under the chair ticked away, the small pings as loud as thunder in the silent room. Simultaneously, her chronometer beeped again.

Then she noticed the syringe sticking out of the side of his neck and swore. The delivery method was old-fashioned, but she recognized the dregs clinging to the needle's chamber: Plinksmi, a Nym sedative used in torture. The man was in more pain than she thought, and there was nothing available on this planet that would save him.

She had two choices: put him out of his misery or take him where he could be treated.

Her chronometer chimed again. She had to get the hell out of this building in less than five minutes, or she would be just as screwed as the man in front of her.

His head lolled to the side and slumped to his chest. She was stronger than the average Kurran or Commons female, but she couldn't move an injured man to her ship on her own.

She clasped the man's arm in her hand and set transport coordinates to her ship through her chronometer.

———

IT TOOK a few heart-stopping seconds before the tiny transport unit built into her chronometer sputtered to life, but she was able to move herself and the mysterious human back to her ship. She had only enough time to fly it through Earth's atmosphere to the familiar blackness of space and hightail it to the barely visible red waves that indicated the entrance to the Nym's artificial vortex. As she let her ship get sucked into it, she briefly wondered if the Earthers had detected it, then quickly shelved that thought. She had to use a special filter on her ship's forward viewport to identify it; surely that hadn't been invented in 2017.

She tossed a quick glance over her shoulder at her passenger, noticing that he didn't look any worse for wear after having his molecules rearranged for the first time. He was breathing, but it was laborious, and she wouldn't be able to treat him with a field kit until she was sure they were on their way home.

Honora input the coordinates for the time she was supposed to return, giving herself a three-year margin of error. She had been assured by her commanding officers that she would not end up stuck five or ten years in the past, and she hoped they were right. *Of course they were right*, she admonished herself. Special Ops did not make those kinds of mistakes. There was no chance of meeting her past self in training or anything else that belonged in fiction.

She couldn't help but snort at that. Time travel was *still* supposed to be the stuff of vids, and yet here she was. *Damn Nym.*

She made a few more adjustments on the smooth control panel in front of her. She had made it into the vortex in one piece; now she had to find out what time she would land in. Ideally, she would be right back in 2867, but she doubted her luck was that good. A reading from a navigation console confirmed that. She would be arriving at a hypergate to Kurran space between 2868 and 2869.

It was a little better than she had expected. She had told her colleagues that she would see them in a few months, despite having only been gone for what felt like four days. As for her few remaining family members, Special Ops could concoct a story if they asked about her whereabouts. She rarely saw them anyway.

Satisfied with her timing, she swiveled around in her seat to face her new problem. She jumped up and located the field medicine kit under the controls. It had taken only minutes to launch herself from that godsforsaken planet and break through the atmosphere, but it would have felt like days for the poor bastard suffering on her cockpit floor.

She jumped up from her seat and pulled out the syringe. He stirred, and another growl of pain issued from his throat. "I'm sorry," she whispered, pressing a transdermal spray against his neck to administer an antidote. The medication could neutralize any known Nym poison.

Next, she had to do something for his pain. She applied a pain patch to his arm, rolling up the sleeve of his jacket to do so. She felt his muscles contract, and she tried to reassure him. "It's almost over." As though he could hear her—and Honora wasn't positive he couldn't—his fingers groped the air until they landed on her wrist. She laid a palm over his hand in a gesture of comfort unlike her. He murmured something unintelligible. She let him touch her for a moment before she let go to dig through the medical kit.

"I'm doing all I can until I get you home," she said. "I have bone and skin regenerators here, so I can do something about your face."

Honora hated to play the part of chatty, supportive medic, or any kind of role that required her to speak, but desperate times called for desperate measures. She used an antiseptic wipe to clean away some of the blood on his face, and her stomach turned over at the damage. His nose and one cheek were destroyed. Thank the gods she carried the equipment to fix that.

"You'll look a little funny for a few hours, but it's better than the alternative," she blathered. "I don't know if you'll look exactly the same." She fitted the flimsy materials over his face until only his eyes and mouth were visible.

She couldn't leave him on the floor. There was a tiny sleeping area at the back of the ship where he could rest. "I need you to wake up a little," she said urgently. "You don't want to get knocked around if the vortex gets ugly." And it would. She had spent a lot of time strapped into the pilot's seat, gripping the armrests.

He was too groggy to be coherent, although his eyes fluttered to half-mast. They were bloodshot and unfocused, but she could see now that they were a pleasant greenish-brown. Definitely Earth eyes.

"You don't have to get up," she assured him. "Just crawl as best you can, and I'll do the rest. There's a bed you can sleep in until we get home." He obediently helped her slide his body across the small cockpit to the sleeping area. Honora hefted him to the bed and raked safety straps across his body. On second thought, she draped a scratchy Ops-issued blanket over him.

"It will be at least a day before the vortex takes us back to the Kurran Empire," she told him. His eyes slid shut. Within seconds, he was asleep, pain-free if his lack of twitching was any indication.

She laid a hand on his forehead over the regenerators out of some instinct she didn't know she possessed. She caught herself and let her hands fall at her sides. It wasn't her place to offer comfort to refugees.

She returned to the cockpit. There wasn't much in the way of amusements on a modified Ops ship, so she would have a lot of time to stew over the new problem she was bringing to the Kurran Empire.

Honora didn't panic. In her line of work, panicking could mean death. But the impact of what she had done finally hit her. Who was this man? She had been under strict orders not to change history, and she had gone and brought this man aboard. What if he was a world leader? He would certainly be missed.

She brought up the information packet on her control panel and re-read the intelligence reports. The Empire had intercepted coded Nym messages a few weeks prior indicating the enemy's constructing a vortex for the purpose of traveling back through time. There had been reports from the agent or agents posted to Earth in 2017 that something had gone wrong. Why the Nym were involved in time travel and why they had established themselves where they had were still mysteries. The city of Toronto was located in a quiet, middle-power country that wasn't a leader in space exploration, nor had it made a major impact on the interstellar travel that began in 2217.

Honora relaxed a little. Chances were this man wasn't a leader in his community and his absence wouldn't alter the course of history. Still, it wouldn't hurt to check. Maybe her mysterious passenger had an ID badge or something that would identify him.

She went back to the sleeping area and felt around his neck and wrists. He wore a very primitive chronometer on his left arm and nothing else. She sighed. She was going to have to check his person.

He wore a dark suit despite the heat on his home world, and she checked his front pockets. All she found was a set of old-fashioned metal keys and a few credit pieces in different metals. There was a thin, flat instrument studded with buttons in one of his pockets; she assumed it was a communications device. She left everything where she found it. Maybe there was something in his back pockets.

She was careful not to disturb any other injuries he might have sustained in his attack by the Nym agent. She gingerly lifted one side of his body and felt herself blush as she patted his backside. Feeling a lump, she removed a wallet from his back pocket.

Honora took it back to the cockpit to examine more closely. Inside, she found paper currency and a multitude of primitive plastic cards, all of which bore the name *Andrew Claybourne*.

Her passenger had a name.

CHAPTER 3

Between checking on Andrew Claybourne and thinking about how she was going to explain this to her superiors, Honora took a couple of hasty naps in the pilot's seat.

As a Special Ops officer, she was bound to a code of ethics that dictated she care for the well-being of all victims of terrorism and ensure their safety. Her passenger's situation certainly required that. On the other hand, in accepting this mission, she had been sworn to protect history. While his identification didn't appear to be that of someone important on Earth, she couldn't be positive that she hadn't just doomed the Kurran Empire or Commonwealth Space. What if her ship was spit out of this vortex in a day's time and the alliance between the Empire and the Commons didn't exist? For a moment, she almost wished she had simply put Andrew Claybourne out of his misery back on Earth.

He would be gone either way. The thought popped into her mind unbidden. She would have to remember it as a defense.

Her communications console chirped an incoming transmit, and a smile bloomed across her face. It was a written message from the Ops base, pre-arranged for her to receive when the vortex carried her past a hidden communications beacon. She was on the right track, and the Commons and Empire still existed as they had when she had left. Emperor Sarda II was still on the throne, as he had been before. Immediately after she finished reading the transmit, a few scattered news bulletins that the beacon had picked up flowed into her console. It was random pieces, and she recognized names and places. She deduced she had been gone for fourteen months.

A loud groan startled her from the news reports, and she quickly went to the sleeping area. Her charge had been doped up and knocked out for more than thirty-six hours by now, and he was probably hungry. He would also want to know what was going on, and Honora was damned if she could explain it.

Maybe he was only looking for a meal. That would make her life much easier.

He wasn't totally lucid when she peered over at him on the bed. "Hello," she said softly.

He had trouble speaking around the regenerators on his face. They looked like they were loosening; they would fall off when they had done their work. "I think I'm dead," he muttered.

"No, you're not." She considered dosing him up on painkillers again to avoid the inevitable chat about what happened.

He fumbled with the regenerators. "I need this off," he said sleepily.

"No, you need to leave them be," she protested, moving his hands away.

"I don't like wearing masks. If you're going to kill me, just do it."

"I'm not going to kill you," she assured him.

His hazel eyes focused on her with an intensity that made her fidget. "Who are you?"

She told him the truth. "Lieutenant Kharn, Kurran Special Operations."

"Is that like the CIA?"

CIA? It must be a law enforcement agency of some kind. She nodded.

His eyes squeezed shut. "Oh, *shit*," he cursed, and he passed out.

———

A COUPLE OF HOURS LATER, Honora was awakened from a nap by an angry yelp. She bolted back to the sleeping area, where a very awake Andrew Claybourne was struggling with the safety straps around his body. Honora quickly released him, and he sat up, tearing the regenerators off his face.

"What the hell is this?" he demanded, throwing them to the floor. "Who are you, and where the hell are we?" He tried to stand up, but his legs buckled. Honora tried to help him back to the bed, but he swatted her hands away.

"We're on a modified fighter. I rescued you from a Nym agent," she said crisply. "I could either bring you aboard my ship or leave you to die a very painful death on Earth."

He stared at her, then intoned, "You're out of your fucking mind."

No thank you for saving his life? "I'm not," she replied calmly. "When you can get up, you can see for yourself. We'll be dumped out of a vortex within a few hours." She paused. If he didn't believe that he wasn't on Earth, he wasn't likely to take the news of his new era very well, either. "We're on a course for the Kurran Empire, sometime in the year 2868..."

He stared at her, disbelief plainly written on his face. "Uh huh. Look, you're planning to kill me..."

She shook her head. "I'm not going to harm you. I considered it, when you were suffering." Best to get that out of the way. "You needed medical care you couldn't get on Earth in 2017. You may still need treatment, but at least I was able to save your life." She looked closer at him. "And your face."

His nose had been beautifully repaired and matched the pictures on his identification. He still sported bruises, now fading, and the injury on his face would leave scars. She didn't know if the regenerator could have fixed that had he left it on or if he would have to see a specialist.

For a few seconds she forgot she was an Ops soldier and let herself really look at him. He was younger than she originally assumed, in his early thirties. His hair was light brown and speckled with dried blood around his forehead. The glow of his skin spoke of a lifetime on a planet with natural sunlight. He scrubbed at his mouth with the back of his hand, rubbing off more flakes of dried blood, and she saw that his lips were firm. He would be pleasant to look at once he took a shower.

She snapped out of it. "When we get back to the Kurran Empire, you'll have to undergo a medical exam. You've been through a lot."

"No shit," he snapped. "I'd say getting half my face bitten off and then being kidnapped qualifies as 'a lot.'"

"A rescue operation is not kidnapping. And I've treated you as best I can."

He forced himself to his feet and swayed a little. Honora thought back to what she knew about his era and figured he had probably never been in space before. "Let me out," he ordered through gritted teeth.

"I can't. You would die. It's that issue of the lack of breathable air." Sarcasm usually didn't become her, but she couldn't help but be irritated. He was on a ship. There were medical devices that hadn't been invented until several hundred years after he was born lying on the floor. If Honora were in his position, she might assume she was telling the truth.

"Oh, for fuck's sake." He stumbled through the sleeping area to the cockpit. Honora followed, her hand instinctively resting on the laser pistol at her hip.

He stopped and stared through the viewport. He turned back to face her, eyes wide and mouth open.

"I told you," said Honora. It came out more petulant than she had intended.

The view outside was of the vortex, a swirling fog of reds and blues. Every now and then, stars appeared, white and blurred. They were moving thousands of times faster than the speed of light, which she was sure hadn't been accomplished in his lifetime.

"I don't know what your deal is," he managed in a small voice. "But you clearly have too much money and not enough sanity and you've seen *Star Wars* too many times."

"I beg your pardon?"

He stood up straight, finding his space legs. He pointed a finger at her. "You. Are. Fucking. Crazy," he said deliberately.

"No, I'm not, and neither are you."

"What is this? Some kind of ride?"

"It's a heavily modified B-class fighter, so yes, it is a ride. It gets me where I need to go."

He stared at her again. "Look, I don't have nearly as much money as people seem to think, but if you let me go, I'll get you whatever you want."

She shook her head. "I haven't kidnapped you, so I'm not looking for ransom. I've already said that I can't let you go. I'm also not going to kill you, but I have to fly this ship safely, and if I have to drug you again to do so, I will."

He looked her up and down, and she resisted the urge to feel self-conscious. He looked fit and healthy, but he didn't have the advantage of years of military experience. She could easily subdue him if it came to that.

He didn't lunge for her, but instead took in more of the small cockpit. He spied his wallet on top of the control console and snatched it up, rifling through its contents. "At least you haven't taken anything," he groused.

"I hadn't planned to. I wanted to know who you are."

"And now you know. Andrew Claybourne," he introduced himself. "And who might you be?"

"The last time I told you, you were sleeping off some medication I administered, so I'll forgive you for not remembering. Lieutenant Kharn, Special Ops fighter pilot for the Kurran Empire."

"And do you have a first name, Lieutenant?"

Now it was her turn to glare, but she answered. "Honora."

"On-or-ah?" He sounded it out, like he was tasting her name.

She nodded.

"Kharn? Is that Estonian or something?"

"My family name."

He leaned against the back of the pilot's seat and crossed his arms over his chest. "So, Honora, you've kidnapped me and you claim we're in outer space."

"I haven't kidnapped you," she said forcefully. "We *are* in space. And I'd prefer to be called Lieutenant Kharn."

"And I'd prefer that you let me go. I think we should stick to first names. I'm Andrew." He stuck out his hand. Honora was familiar with the gesture, more often seen in the Commons.

She narrowed her eyes at him in suspicion, but held out her hand and shook his. "Lieutenant Kharn."

He grabbed for the weapon at her hip. Instinctively, Honora grasped his wrists and wrenched his arms behind his back. When he struggled, she placed a small kick behind his knee, enough to knock him off balance. She forced him to the deck until he was lying on his back, his eyes angry and surprised. He hadn't expected to her to be so efficient in subduing him. A tremor rocked the ship, and he banged his head against the deck.

Honora put her foot on his chest when he moved to get up. "If you do that again, I'll knock you out," she cautioned. "That was a really stupid thing to do, Claybourne. I have plenty of medication left." She removed a transderm from her utility belt and gripped it, putting as much authority into her voice as she could muster. "This is a high dose sedative. I don't have any issues with sedating you for the rest of our trip if you don't cooperate with me." She held out the slender tube. "Am I clear?"

"No." He wiggled in an attempt to get free. She put more pressure on his chest and he yelped in pain. "Shit! I think my ribs are broken! Let me go!"

"You're not a prisoner, but I'll treat you like one if you do this again. None of your identification indicated you have military training, but I do."

He gave up and lay limp on the floor. Honora removed her foot but didn't put away the sedative. "How do I know that even works?" he asked skeptically.

"I've administered them to you before. Are you in pain now?"

"Just my ribs, where you stepped on me." He sat up and rubbed the back of his head.

Honora gestured to the unused co-pilot's seat. "Sit down and we'll have a talk," she ordered. "I have to start compiling my report for when we get back to base."

"I'm hungry," he complained.

"I'm sure you are. You've been out cold for almost two days." She wished there was a replicator on board, if only to convince him that she wasn't insane and he wasn't in the 21st century anymore. All she had was heavily processed pre-pack-aged meals, and she offered him a tray and spoon.

He set it on the control panel and peeled off the flimsy covering. Honora winced. She didn't even like fingerprints on the panel's surface. He reluctantly poked around the meal tray. "What is this?" he asked.

"It's a pathetic attempt of a common stew in the Empire." Was that a ghost of a smile quirking at his mouth? "It doesn't taste that great, but it's nutritionally balanced."

He nibbled a little off his spoon and made a face.

"Eat," Honora urged him.

"Yeah, I get it. It's good for me. So is kale, and I hate that, too. And I can't be sure it hasn't been drugged."

She sighed loudly and unlatched her datatab from its holder on top of the controls. "I assure you, it's safe to eat. I had one a few hours ago, before you woke up."

He narrowed his eyes at her. "Prove it."

"I have a datacorder that can detect poisons, but I doubt you would believe its readings, so I can't." *What would be the quickest way to administer a sedative to an uncooperative passenger?* "I also have its language set to Kurran. You don't speak it." She held up a hand for silence when he opened his mouth. "The Kurran Empire didn't make contact with Commonwealth Space until a couple hundred years after you were born. As far as you know, I don't exist yet."

His expression didn't waver. "Whatever. Just prove to me it isn't drugged."

They stared at each other for a few seconds before Honora snatched the spoon from his hand and helped herself to a few mouthfuls of stew. She handed it back to him and waited for his reaction.

He looked at the utensil, then her. "Do you have another spoon?" he asked.

"I'd have to open another tray to get it. I don't have any

communicable diseases, Claybourne. Just eat your food. We'll be back in civilized space soon, and you can have all the spoons you want." She opened a program on her datatab to make notes for a report.

"You're pretty uptight for someone who's delusional."

"I'm not delusional." She checked her navigation readings. "In three hours or less, I'll be able to prove it. We'll be dumped out the vortex by then and on our way to a hypergate."

He looked out the viewport, then at the console spanning the width of the narrow cockpit. "I have to give you credit, you know," he said between mouthfuls. "For a crazy person, you go all the way."

She ignored that comment. "I have to start this report. First, what were you doing with the Nym?"

"What's a Nym?"

She gripped the datatab harder than necessary and closed her eyes. *I will not slap this halfwit into the next galaxy.* "The Nym is a very secluded and secretive race inhabiting a planet beyond the Outer Fringes. Before you ask, the Fringes and Outer Fringes are independent republics outside Commonwealth and Kurran space."

"Back it up a little more." He pushed aside the half-eaten remains of his meal, and a few drops of sauce slopped over the tray's side. She sighed and wiped it up with her sleeve. "What's the Commonwealth and this Kurran place you keep talking about?"

She could tell from his tone that he didn't believe her, but she explained. "They're allied territories independent of each other. The Commonwealth is a group of planets and stations ruled by a single democratic government and a mix of people from everywhere in the universe. The Kurran Empire is in its neighboring star system, but most of its citizens are Kurran. The Empire is ruled by elected members of royal families."

"And these Fringes places..." He waved his hand to tell her to get on with it.

"Are completely independent. Most of the planets in the Fringes are tolerant of the Commons and the Empire. The worlds in the Outer Fringes tend to be quite reclusive."

"And these Nym people?"

"Nym," she corrected. "Just the Nym. It's their name, the name of their planet, and their language. The world is very difficult to get to. They are the number-one enemy of civilized space. My orders were to go back to Earth to your time using the artificial vortex they created and ensure they didn't change history."

"You might have," he pointed out. "You took me."

Maybe he was starting to see reason. "If I had left you there, you would have died," she explained. "Whether it was the plinksmi the agent used to drug you or the explosive I planted in the lab, you wouldn't have survived. You weren't going to make it out anyway, so I saved you." He really was being ungrateful about this. "I haven't changed history by bringing you along." *I hope.*

"You haven't done anything except commit an indictable offense." The ship lurched in the vortex, and he slammed his hands on the control panel to steady himself. Honora quickly checked to make sure he hadn't damaged anything.

"Claybourne, I need you to tell me what happened," she said. "The enemy agent established a cryonics facility in your city. What were you doing there?"

He pinched the bridge of his nose. "I was planning my funeral."

She started. "Are you ill?"

"No. Like I told the doctors there, I just wanted to see alien ass in a few hundred years."

Oh, this man was just *charming.*

Honora knew a little about cryonics and had read about

the mass graveyard of preserved remains unearthed on a tiny, uninhabited Commons planet called Darcan-2 a couple of years back. No one had ever been successfully revived. "Cryonics didn't work," she informed him.

"Says you. I was just curious and had some money saved up for doing something stupid after I sold my business."

"I think it was just an office," Honora interjected. "There wasn't any indication of remains being preserved on site."

"Yeah, they were a brand-new outfit, only a few weeks old. I don't think any of their clients died yet."

"Who did you speak to about the lab?" she asked, fingers poised over the datatab's screen.

Instead of replying, he fixated on the small machine. "I didn't know they made tablets that thin. Is it a new model?"

"It's a datatab."

"Whatever you want to call it." He continued with his story, "I booked my appointment for a consultation with Lazarus Cryonics's doctors through their website. I went there and spoke to their receptionist, and Dr. Zadbac and Dr. Pitro took me to their office."

He had used the word "doctors" to describe the lab's staff, and Honora briefly thought that it might have referred to an Earth humanoid. Two Nym names sent a chill down her spine. "There were two?" she asked slowly. She had only seen one.

"Yeah. Dr. Zadbac went after the receptionist when she heard me calling for help. I guess you left her to die."

There was that, and the fact that she had left a Nym agent alive in 2017. "*Sikiaka!*" she swore.

"Huh?"

Honora barely heard him. Bile rose in her throat at the realization of what she had done. She, who had a perfect service record and had been hand-picked to go back in time, had botched the most important mission of her career. "I left one of them alive," she said softly to herself.

"One of them?"

Shock, then fear, crossed Claybourne's features. He rose from his seat and backed away, looking around the cockpit, no doubt for a weapon of some kind. "You killed Dr. Pitro?" he said. Honora heard the fright in his voice.

She couldn't see why he was so put out about it. "If you've forgotten, he did try to kill you."

"You *kill* people?"

Honora couldn't understand his consternation. The Nym had tried to take his face off. But she didn't move from her seat, not wanting to terrify the man any further. "When I'm ordered to, and it's only people who deserve it."

"Who are you to decide who deserves it?"

"I don't," she snapped. "I accept my orders to fire when I'm told, and I'm good at it. I have the experience necessary to navigate a vortex alone. I also have the combat training to take down a Nym agent." Or two, had she been smarter about this. She forced herself to soften her voice. "Claybourne, please sit down. Or don't, it's up to you. It would mean a great deal to me if you would answer my questions. Believe me, I'm going to be punished for what I've done with you. You'll get your chance to gloat."

"Hopefully at a trial," he muttered, but he slid back into his seat. He didn't take his eyes off her, like a mouse hoping a cat was just relaxing near his hidey-hole.

"Could you put your gun away?" he asked.

She shook her head and held up her arms, leaving her datatab in her lap and her laser pistol holstered at her hip. "I'm not going to hurt you," she promised again.

"Okay." He moved his knees away, trying to put as much space between him and Honora as he could. "Dr. Zadbac and Dr. Pitro said a few things that made me believe they didn't know what they were doing, and I decided to leave. Dr. Pitro attacked me—he bit my face and shot me up with something." He ran his hand over the wound, confusion registering when he felt the healed skin. He paused. "I called for help, and the receptionist came running to the office to make sure everything was okay. Dr. Zadbac chased her out, and I didn't see either of them again. Then I woke up here." He stopped his story again. "What happened to the receptionist?"

"I don't know. I didn't have time to investigate. The vortex was changing, and I told you about the explosive at the lab."

"You let her die?" he said incredulously. "You know he probably killed her, right? What kind of secret agent are you?"

Honora was asking herself the same question. "I *am* an excellent soldier, which is why I was selected for this mission." She also noted privately that Claybourne didn't appear so convinced that she was insane since he had recounted what happened to him in the lab.

"I don't think she had anything to do with those doctors. She was obviously human and just doing her job." He shook his head, stood up, and began pacing the cockpit. "I must be losing it," he said, more to himself. "I'm acting as though all this really happened, and I've probably just fallen off the wagon. I'm probably passed out in my bedroom and hallucinating."

Honora didn't know what he was talking about except for the hallucinations. "You're not," she assured him. She tapped out the rest of her notes on her datatab, including her own humiliating admission of failure.

A chime rang through the ship, and the vortex dissipated. Through the viewport, the comfort of deep space beckoned. The old, familiar sensation of freedom shoved aside her sense of impending professional doom, her fears sucked out the airlock as the navigation console pinged the location of the closest available hypergate leading to the Empire. This was what she loved doing: going headfirst into the endless expanse of stars, the second of heart-stopping feeling of weightlessness as a ship was sucked into a gate. She would never tire of it.

She hardly heard Claybourne's sharp intake of breath as the ship briefly jostled. "What the hell was that?" he shouted.

Unable to keep the smile off her face, she replied, "We're going home."

CHAPTER 4

Andrew had to give the crazy woman credit. Honora Kharn had to be pretty damn out there to have put together this kind of setup. This had to be a simulator ride or something. He had been on a few at amusement parks as a child, and their realism had scared years off his life.

Despite his earlier quip about being back on the hard stuff, he knew he was sober. He knew he was awake, and *he* wasn't the problem here.

He just had to wait until the ride slowed down enough so he could escape and call the police. He had checked his phone a few times only to find there wasn't a signal. He had considered going against everything he felt was right and knocking her out, but their earlier tussle dissuaded him. She was a hell of a lot stronger than other women he knew, and he was pretty sure she could kick his ass without breaking a sweat.

She was tall, only an inch or two shorter than his six-foot-one, and fit. Her black pants and jacket were a little too loose to closely see her figure, and they were wrinkled from sleeping in them. Evidently, she didn't get outside much because her skin, even with its warm, tan undertones, looked pale, as if she never saw the sun. Her hair fell just past her collar and was a deep blue-black shade in the lights of what she called the cockpit, tousled and a little fuzzy from lack of combing. Her eyes were nearly the same dark shade, a color Andrew hadn't seen before.

And her *accent*. Andrew was good at placing accents—he picked up the skill during a drunken six-month jaunt around the world in his early twenties—but he couldn't put his finger on where hers originated. It sounded like a cross between Londoner and Eastern European, but there was something else he couldn't put his finger on. Maybe it was faked.

She had done a bang-up job perfecting what she passed off as her reality. The box they were in was small, with smooth computer panels running along a counter across the front end. The small room in the back where he had woken up had a narrow bed that he barely fit into. And the outside details were amazing, exactly as he would have pictured deep space, if he cared to ever think about it.

But he didn't. He needed to get home, contact the authorities and press charges, and then finalize the sale of Tiger Media. He had to tell his potential business partners that he wanted in on the satellite radio station. He doubted telling her would make her release him. Better to wait until she thought she had landed her little spaceship and escape from here.

What about your face? How did she fix that? That reminder was discomfiting. Maybe the bite from Pitro hadn't been as bad as he thought. Maybe Lieutenant Honora Kharn had been a medical researcher, a genius, and she snapped under the pressure.

A green light flashed on the corner of the console in front of them, and she turned to him with a smile of his face.

Wow. She needed to do that more often. It made her appear less terrifying and downright attractive. *Focus, you idiot.*

"We're going into hyperspace," she told him. She fastened

safety straps across her chest. "You'll want to buckle in before we go through."

Oh, what the hell. He could tell his friends about this over coffee. He clicked his own straps into place and tested the fastenings. Good, he wasn't going to be locked in here forever.

They sharply tilted upward, and Andrew was thrown back against his seat. The stars around them blurred for a few seconds, and their ride—he refused to think of it as a spaceship —jerked back and forth for a couple of teeth-rattling minutes. The pathetic excuse for food he'd left on the console slid around in its tray before landing on the floor with a slimy plop. Then everything relaxed, and the view out the window changed to dark, shimmering colors, the way it had been when Honora claimed they were in a vortex.

He refused to think of her as Special Agent Whatever. He wasn't going to indulge her delusions that much.

"How much longer?" he asked.

Honora didn't answer but unsnapped her seatbelt and stood up. She opened a cabinet under the console desk and removed a few wipes smelling of disinfectant. She gestured to the floor. "Help me clean this up. Maintenance gets really upset when agents return a dirty ship."

Andrew reluctantly helped her clean up the mess. She shoved the wipes through a small door in the wall, labeled in a language he couldn't identify. "We'll be back in Kurran space in about twenty minutes," she reported, reading something from the touchscreen under her hands. "It's a shorter trip home than away. This is a good hypergate, and there isn't a lot of traffic today."

"What's a hypergate?" he asked casually.

"Claybourne, do you finally believe I'm telling you the truth about traveling to the future?"

"No. But indulge me." He made an obvious show about checking his phone. Still no service. *Damn it.*

"It's a shortcut. Your ship goes into it and gets dumped out somewhere else millions of light years away. If we were doing this the old-fashioned way, it would take weeks to reach the Kurran Empire from here."

"And all spaceships can get where they want to go using these shortcuts?'

"If it has a hyperspace engine, yes."

"I see." He didn't. He stole a glance at her. She was still examining the data scrolling across the touchscreen. She was smiling again, revealing perfect, white teeth. "What is it?" he prodded.

"All the news coming in through the comm beacons looks good. I haven't changed history."

"My family might dispute that."

She turned to him, her expression as alarmed as when she realized she had only killed *one* person at the lab. "Were they space explorers?"

"No, my father is a lawyer and my stepmother a professional widow."

She looked at him blankly. "I don't understand."

"If my story of being kidnapped by someone who thinks *Battlestar Galactica* is real doesn't kill him, his wife feeding him nothing but butter will."

She continued to stare at him.

Andrew sighed. "My stepmother has already been married twice. Both of her husbands died and left her everything. My father has already had a heart attack, and she encourages him to eat nothing but the most delicious animal-based products."

He saw that the terms were lost on her. "Heart attack?"

Andrew steeled himself with an internal reminder that he was dealing with the insane. "He had a coronary a few years ago. Um...hardening of the arteries, I think, and his heart stopped."

"I didn't know that was possible."

"Well, when you smoke two packs a day and eat your body weight in red meat on a weekly basis, that can happen." Speaking of smoking, Andrew could really use a cigarette about now. He had given it up six months ago, his last bad habit.

Honora looked at him in puzzlement a moment longer. "You'll have to tell my cousin about that. She's a nurse." Her expression soured and she added darkly, "With the Commons Fleet."

Andrew's curiosity was piqued. "What's wrong with this Commons?" he asked.

"Besides mismanagement of resources and constant time-wasting?"

"Honora, I'm from Earth. I know a little something about waste." *Oh, bravo. Next, why don't you ask for lessons flying this thing?*

"Their military is a joke," she said savagely. "They don't even have an elite division. My uncle—my cousin's father—is an admiral in the Fleet, a rank that should mean something, but there are so many of them that all they do is argue with each other, and nothing gets done." She flicked at a few lines of foreign text on the console and they disappeared. "It's pathetic. And that side of the family thought I was making a mistake when I enlisted with the Kurran Forces instead of Fleet."

In for a penny, in for a pound. "And the difference between the Commons and the Kurrans is..." Andrew held out his hands for a reply.

Honora paused. "Well, we're all humanoids. Are you asking about the difference in physiology, government, or culture?"

"What the hell, I feel like learning. Tell me everything you can before we get out of hyperspace."

Her tablet was in hand. "One moment. I'm transmitting

my notes. They'll send me a response and I can think about what kind of defense I need to make when we get back."

"What kind of defense?"

"My justification for bringing you with me." She turned back to him. "All right. Kurran and Commons are both humanoid."

"No green space monsters, then?"

"Scaled species exist but there aren't many in Commons space. I told you before that the Commons is mostly Earth descendants, but anyone is welcome to apply for citizenship or seek refuge there. The Empire is almost entirely Kurran and has been established for millions of years. Travel and commerce are encouraged between both, but it's much more difficult to establish residency in the Empire."

"So you're the new Switzerland, then?"

She didn't press him for an explanation. "Possibly," she said.

Was that a touch of sarcasm? He grinned.

"And before you ask, all humanoids share some common ancestors, although there are genetic variations. Many Kurrans, for example, have empathic or telepathic ability. Earth descendants don't."

"So you're a psychic, too?" This was getting better and better.

Her glare told him she didn't appreciate his mockery. "No. I'm one of the thirty-two percent of Kurrans who don't. There are a couple of Earthers in my ancestry. Telepathy is a recessive gene."

Andrew nodded, and she continued. "The Commonwealth is a democracy. Politicians are elected and must govern without any ties to religion or industry. It's very difficult to run for office when one has been educated in a religious school, for example, or owns shipyards."

Andrew nodded again and wished that kind of system had

been in effect when he was on Earth. What was he thinking? He was *still* on Earth somewhere. Was insanity catching? He shouldn't have eaten that TV dinner she fed him.

"The Kurran Empire has six royal families, and a different family is elected to govern every eight years," she continued. "That's the last remnant of our class system. The recognition of the rest of the upper classes was abolished three hundred years ago. The ruling royal family doesn't hold absolute authority, though. There's an elected group of regular people who have veto power."

"Parliament," Andrew translated. "Like in England."

"I'll have to assume so," she agreed. "Since everyone in the Commons is equal, they're not enthused about our recognition of royalty, but at least our system works. There's much less corruption in the Empire than the Commonwealth."

"I hate to break it to you, but where there's a politician, there's corruption."

She scowled at him. "You're so cynical."

"You would be, too, if you had been kidnapped." And a whole other host of things Andrew had been through—or done to himself, he admitted.

"You're far too cynical for someone from such a primitive time, and I'm not having this argument with you again." A chime rang though the ship, and the vessel swayed from side to side a little. Andrew gripped the armrests of his seat and looked through the window. "Oh, good," Honora said. "We're exiting the hypergate. That was faster than I expected."

Andrew looked around the ship, his eyes locking on the door. He would soon be able to make his escape.

"Hang on, Claybourne. We're going to Kurran Prime, and we have to break through its atmosphere. Depending on the weather, it can get a little rough."

He didn't relinquish his grip on the armrests and turned his attention back to the window. He wanted to see what illusions she would come up with for her next trick. He inhaled sharply at the sight of deep space before them: clusters of bright white stars and a very green planet that didn't resemble Earth in the pictures he had seen. It was rapidly increasing in size.

Honora's hands flew over her touchscreens, and a disembodied male voice piped up from one of them, speaking furiously in a language Andrew didn't recognize. Honora replied in kind, then flicked at something blinking on the screen. She sighed. "I have good news and bad news."

"It's all bad to me, so let's hear it."

She shot him a withering look. "The good news is the weather's perfect, so we'll be landing without any problems. The bad news is I'm in trouble."

Andrew had already figured that, but knew they had different ideas about her troubles.

The planet grew larger before them, and there was some minor turbulence that made them bounce around in their seats. More special effects. Then he could see a city at night, lights dotting skyscrapers far taller than he had ever seen at home.

Honora spoke something in that language again and a voice replied.

"All right," she told Andrew in English. "We're cleared for landing." There was trepidation in her voice. She was nervous about something. Andrew kept his eye on the door. He was bolting as soon as this thing "landed."

The ship circled one of the skyscrapers and touched down on a landing pad. There was a small tower perched nearby, and a man came running out of it.

"Here we are," Honora intoned. "Pray for both of us, if you're into that sort of thing." She let herself out of her seat and crossed the cockpit to the door, Andrew at her heels. She pressed her hand into a pad next to it, and it opened with a sharp hiss. Cool night air greeted them, and with it, a sense of foreboding. Andrew had no idea where they were or how the hell he was going to get home.

The man who had run out from the watchtower greeted Honora in the same language she had used during landing. He saluted her; she replied in kind. He wore an identical black uniform, a detail that made Andrew uneasy.

"Could you speak in one of the Commons dialects?" she asked. She glanced at Andrew. "C-Two, if you're familiar with it."

"English," Andrew volunteered. His unease grew as he took in his surroundings. The roof of the skyscraper was the size of a city block, lights shining around its perimeter. For the first time, he could see the exterior of Honora's vehicle, and it looked like the spaceship she had claimed it to be: a sleek, compact rectangular box, its exit ramp still extended.

When he looked up, he saw a pair of moons in the sky, bright and full. "Honora, where are we?"

She kept a stoic expression on her face, her voice low. "Claybourne, I'm Lieutenant Kharn."

"Okay, Lieutenant Kharn, where are we?"

"Kurran Prime, in the Empire. I explained this," she said to the man. "Claybourne, this is Lieutenant Hisker. Lieutenant, Andrew Claybourne from twenty-first century Earth."

Andrew ignored the man's proffered hand and instead looked back at the sky. "You have two moons," he said quietly.

"We do," the man introduced as Hisker said, and he dropped his hand back to his side. His accent was far heavier than Honora's. "Lieutenant, you and your passenger have to speak with the commander immediately. A lot has happened since you left."

Honora exhaled noisily. "Tell me the truth. I'm going to be eviscerated, aren't I?"

He shrugged. "Maybe, maybe not. You wouldn't believe

what's gone on in the Commons over the last year. Their government broke down and told us everything a few months ago. It's been hell trying to keep it quiet."

"We're not like the Commons. We don't sensationalize everything."

"True," he agreed and bobbed his head. "But I don't think the commander is going to eat you alive." He gestured to the tower. "Lieutenant, Claybourne, we need to go."

Andrew didn't move. He *couldn't* move. Instead, he tried to process what Hisker and Honora were saying.

"Claybourne?" Honora said curiously. "Are you all right?"

He shook his head, fighting a wave of nausea. "I don't think so."

"Are you unwell?"

"Yes. No." He bent over and held his head in his hands, taking in deep breaths. He thought he might pass out.

I think it's real. Honora isn't insane. I really was in a spaceship, and I'm not on Earth.

He straightened himself. "Is Hon—is Lieutenant Kharn normal?" he asked Hisker.

Hisker looked between them quizzically. "She is perfectly healthy. Special Ops agents must be."

"So you're telling me she's really some kind of deep space secret agent?"

"Not in those terms, but yes. She is an agent with the Kurran Special Ops, the same as me."

"What year is this?" he asked hoarsely.

Honora looked startled, and he realized the she didn't know he hadn't believed her story. "The shared calendar of the Commonwealth and the Empire states that the year is 2868," Hisker replied. "Of course, Kurran traditionalists use their own calendar, which predates the one observed by the Commons."

Honora shot him a look, and Hisker shut up.

Andrew shook his head, causing his vision to swim. He felt himself lurch forward, and Honora and Hisker helped him stay upright. He shook them off, but Honora didn't let go. A wise move on her part, because his knees buckled.

"Claybourne?" she said sharply.

He closed his eyes, swaying. She didn't let go, the warmth of her hand through his jacket an odd source of comfort. "Andrew?" she whispered. "You really didn't believe a word I said." She sounded as shocked as he felt.

It took a moment for him to register her words, form a response. Blood pounded in his ears. "No," he answered. "But I'm starting to."

"Can you walk? We have to go inside."

He kept breathing deeply. "Give me a minute. This is a lot to absorb." He felt rooted to the ground, his feet unwilling to move.

"Of course." But she didn't remove her hand. "Lieutenant, can you go inside and inform the commander we'll be there in a few minutes? Claybourne is in shock."

"I'm not," he argued. "I am."

Hisker's footsteps were nearly silent as he walked away. "Honora," Andrew said.

"Yes?"

"Can you take me back?"

She paused, and his heart sank. "Tell me the truth," he urged her.

Honora could have pointed out that she had been telling him the truth the entire time aboard her ship, but didn't. "I don't think so," she said softly. "The scientific particulars about my mission weren't explained to me, but time travel is outlawed in the Empire and the Commons."

"So we can't get back in your ship and go home?" He squeezed his eyes shut and looked away. He already knew the answer.

"No. I'm sorry, Andrew." Her hand slid around his back, a gesture of support he was unused to receiving. "We have to go inside. If you're not up for it, you don't have to speak with my commander now. I can arrange for a room for you in the barracks, if you prefer."

"It doesn't matter." He let her guide him across the roof to the lookout tower.

When the door slid open automatically, he and Honora stepped in and he saw it was an elevator. Honora barked out a command in her language, and they began a smooth descent. Andrew stepped away from her and cleared his throat. "What are you going to do to me?" he asked.

She stared straight ahead at the doors. "You won't be harmed," she said. "I assume you'll begin a new life here."

Andrew contemplated this for a moment. The elevator halted, and the doors opened.

CHAPTER 5

Honora was nervous for herself, outright terrified for Claybourne. He moved mechanically, his steps carefully measured, as he walked through the corridor to the briefing room, a dazed expression on his face.

It hadn't occurred to her until she saw him staring at Kurran Prime's twin moons that he hadn't really believed her when they were on board her ship. She replayed their conversations in her head and now saw he was only playing along, convinced that she really was crazy. Her training hadn't prepared her for that, nor had her own life experience given her much in the way of social skills to offer him comfort.

"Where are we going?" he asked.

They passed by closed doors, all leading to areas a mere lieutenant didn't have clearance to. Honora rarely visited Kurran Prime and knew only the briefing room. Her apartment was on the base a short trip away from the planet, and she worked from there.

"Briefing room," she replied. "When we're there, don't speak until you're spoken to first." She halted at the end of the corridor. A tiny green light blinked at the center of the doors, reading her DNA, before they noiselessly slid apart. The room was set up with a table and chairs, and its windows offered spectacular views of Kurran Prime's perpetual nighttime. Its moons glowed as brightly as its buildings' lights.

She wasn't surprised to see Kakos, the Special Ops's commander, present. His short-cropped blue hair was a little thinner than the last time she had seen him, and there were pronounced circles under his dark eyes. She was taken aback by the sight of a Commons Fleet officer, an admiral, if she wasn't reading his insignia incorrectly. He looked to be nearing retirement age. A short fringe of white hair ringed his head. She immediately saluted and groaned inwardly. She hated dealing with Fleet. If she had to deal with anyone from her Commons counterparts, she would have preferred her uncle.

Kakos greeted her in Commons. "Welcome back, Lieutenant Kharn."

"Commander," she returned.

"Sit," Kakos ordered. She moved for the table, but Claybourne was immobile.

"Claybourne," she whispered gently, and pointed to a chair. He snapped out of his reverie and they took seats next to each other, across from the officers.

"Lieutenant, this is Admiral Donn Kentz of the Commonwealth Fleet," Kakos said by way of introduction. Honora suppressed a groan. She had heard about Kentz through her cousin, Mora, and her uncle. His ignorance was legendary, his rise through the ranks inexplicable to anyone with half a brain. Judging by the disdain on Kakos's face, the commander didn't much care for the man either. "Admiral, this is Lieutenant Kharn. Lieutenant, would you care to introduce your passenger?"

"Andrew Claybourne." She paused, unsure how to proceed. "Of twenty-first century Earth."

Admiral Kentz glared at her, then Claybourne. Honora returned it; Claybourne looked at the table.

"Lieutenant, we received the report you sent us when you were dumped out of the vortex," Kakos said, breaking the silence. "I understand Mr. Claybourne was suffering the effects of a plinksmi dose."

"I realize that my orders were not to change history, but he was dying."

"And your justification was sound, as was the destruction of the lab. However, you didn't eliminate the agent's partner."

"Zadbac's dead," Admiral Kentz announced flatly.

The revelation slammed into Honora with the impact of a laser rifle set to stun. "He is?" Her mind worked, trying to figure out what had happened.

Kakos didn't let the admiral offer his version of the events. "Zadbac was rescued by a Nym crew shortly before the lab exploded. There is evidence that they continued to play with the time continuum, but we have determined that it was brief and didn't incur any lasting damage. Zadbac died during a skirmish with a Fleet ship last year." The commander leaned back in his chair in an unusual display of relaxation. "A lot has happened in the time you've been away, Lieutenant."

"It appears so, Commander."

"Fourteen months. Two years, depending on whose calendar you're following."

Honora nodded.

"Admiral Kentz is here because of the same issue we have here," Kakos said, looking pointedly at Claybourne.

"Our governments have been exchanging information about the Nym for years," Kentz interjected. "We are aware of their advances in time travel, and your passenger is not the first to arrive here from the twenty-first century."

Claybourne straightened, his gaze fixed on the admiral.

"What I'm about to tell you is highly classified and cannot

be repeated outside of this room," Kakos said. "The Commons picked up a time traveler just over a year ago on one of their patrol ships. It occurred within days of your leaving on your mission to Earth. She had been kidnapped by a Nym agent on Earth in 2017."

Claybourne clutched the side of the table until his knuckles turned white. "The receptionist," he breathed.

Honora's heart skipped a beat.

"That how she described herself," Kentz answered.

"You're telling me she survived? Where is she?"

"It's a long story, but she was found on Darcan-2 a few years ago," the admiral explained. "She had been drugged by the Nym agent and left there. Zadbac is now dead, but our theory is that the Nym stopped there on their way back to our time and left her to die of her own accord. She was discovered by archaeologists a few years ago and was a display in a traveling museum exhibit until she woke up."

"Back it up a minute," Claybourne interrupted. "I don't know what Darcan-2 is."

Kentz waved his hand. "It was a planet that was used to inter thousands of remains preserved with cryonics and was excavated a few years ago. The woman in question was in stasis and disguised as a dead body. She woke up in the cargo hold of a ship when the seal on her casket disintegrated."

"Where is she now?"

"That's classified, Mr. Claybourne." There was a touch of smugness in the admiral's voice that made Honora want to shake the information out of him.

Kakos cleared his throat. "My understanding from your intelligence led me to believe that she wondered the same thing about our guest. I don't think it's unreasonable to tell him."

Kentz steepled his fingers.

Claybourne looked at both men frantically. "Is she okay?"

The admiral nodded reluctantly. "She is, and settled in the Commons."

Honora suspected there was more to this story, but didn't press for details.

"Can I meet her?" Claybourne asked.

Kentz and Kakos exchanged glances. The admiral opened his mouth, but Kakos spoke first. "I don't see why not, once you're settled. The admiral knows her partner quite well, and I'm sure he can arrange something." Kentz looked a little put out at this idea, but he smiled tightly and nodded.

"Her partner?" Claybourne looked aghast.

"She lives with a Fleet commander on one of the stations. She seems happy enough," Kentz replied, a note of irritation in his voice. Again, Honora knew they weren't hearing everything. "She works in a pharmacy."

"Seriously?"

"Similar concessions may be made for you, if you choose," Kakos offered. Honora didn't like the way he said "may be." She doubted that a man even as powerful as Commander Kakos could make that kind of offer.

"Can't I go back home?" Claybourne pleaded.

"No." Kentz's answer was blunt.

The look on Claybourne's face tore at Honora, but she forced herself to remain impassive. A dark bubble of fury roiled in her stomach at the admiral's insensitive and cavalier treatment of Claybourne. There had to be better ways to deliver bad news.

Kakos's voice sounded a little strained. "Mr. Claybourne, time travel is outlawed for reasons I'm sure you have already deduced. The Nym developed the means of building an artificial vortex in an attempt to go back in time and destroy the Commonwealth before it started and annex their space. Their technology was faulty, and a pair of agents ended up in your city in 2017, two hundred years before interplanetary colonization began."

Honora could appreciate the history lesson, but a quick look at Claybourne told her he didn't care.

Kentz jumped in. "Fleet and the Empire had exchanged information about strange vortex activity before we knew it was an aid to time travel and sent Lieutenant Kharn back in time." He shot a look of pure malevolence Kakos's way. To Honora, he said accusingly, "We were not informed of your mission until well after our time traveler showed up."

"It wasn't necessary for me to be informed of the politics behind it," she said civilly. Kakos gave a tiny shake of his head, and she shut up.

"It's hardly politics, just common courtesy," the admiral retorted.

Common courtesy? This was what Honora loathed about the Commons Fleet: They were stubborn; slow to react; never admitted wrongdoing; and every mission, every decision down to the most minute detail, involved a committee. Every time a Fleet soldier went on a mission, he had to have a partner with him, something that was rarely done in the Empire. If Fleet had decided to investigate the vortex, they would have sent in an entire godsdamned battleship. Her mother often repeated an old Kurran expression to her when she was a child: *Kerrsha ento plesti stelle vaan,* or "Your mind and the stars are your only companions." She never forgot it.

No one in the Empire made decisions as a committee.

"We will see about making concessions for you," Commander Kakos finally said.

Honora leaned forward. "What sort of concessions? Surely the other Nym victim didn't enroll in a career program on her own."

"She didn't," Admiral Kentz confirmed. With a childish air of defiance, he added, "We're not at liberty to offer the same to Mr. Claybourne, since the *Empire* is responsible for him."

The situation just got a little muddier. The Empire had never been particularly hospitable toward Commons citizens settling in this corner of the galaxy. Honora was at a loss as to what Andrew could really do here.

She again looked at Claybourne, who still looked numb. And exhausted; if anything, the circles under his eyes had become more pronounced. For the first time in days, she felt weariness pull at her, and she longed to go home and sleep.

Kakos noticed this, raising a knowing eyebrow at Honora. The commander had never said so explicitly, but Honora suspected the man was at least empathic. "Lieutenant, you're dismissed," he ordered. "I expect to see you back at Stappic Station at seven hundred hours tomorrow morning."

She nodded and rose. Claybourne remained in his seat. "What about him?" she asked, keeping her eyes trained on Claybourne. He turned soulless, bloodshot eyes to her. "I don't think he's up for more questioning. He still needs medical care." He also needed a sympathetic ear and a punching bag, but Honora didn't know anyone who could provide that.

"Understood," Kakos agreed. "I want to see him at seven hundred hours tomorrow, too." Kentz looked as if he might argue, but didn't. "Lieutenant, your shuttle is still in the bay on deck seven."

She nodded and touched Claybourne's shoulder. "We're leaving," she said quietly.

"Where are we going?" He hadn't truly heard a word of their exchange.

"Stappic Station. A lot of Ops soldiers live there. There's an infirmary I'm going to take you to."

He stood up and woodenly followed her to the door. They walked a few paces in the corridor before he fell behind and leaned against the wall for support. Honora lightly touched his arm, unsure of what to say.

"I'm stuck here," he breathed.

She nodded.

"There's no chance at all of going back to that vortex?" He turned beseeching eyes to her.

"I don't think so," she said softly. "I'm not sure how manipulating it works. It's dangerous. I knew when I went in that I might not come back."

"Why did you do it?"

A little voice in the back of her mind urged her to collect Claybourne and go back to Stappic, get him to the infirmary, but she waited. "I had to," she explained. She tugged lightly on his arm. "Come on. We have to go to Stappic."

He obeyed, a far cry from his behavior on her ship, when he had thought she was making up everything. Once again, guilt slammed into her. Her lack of social skills be damned, she should have tried harder to make him see his new reality. Already, she missed the irritating, sarcastic smartass Andrew Claybourne had been.

They stepped on the lift, and she gave the Kurran command for deck seven. He watched her warily. "You know English," he said.

She was grateful for the change of subject. She shook her head to his statement. "No, I speak a Commons dialect. I couldn't read anything on Earth. Your language has too many letters."

He didn't say anything else until the lift stopped. This deck was home to agents' private shuttle bays. She led him to her own dock and breathed a sigh of relief when the palm pad accepted her handprint. At least she hadn't been totally forgotten in the last fourteen months.

It was chilly in the bay, but she hardly noticed when she laid eyes on her shuttle, a rare source of joy for her. She had bought it her first year in Ops, her first new craft. It was smaller than the fighter she had used in her Earth mission, with only a cockpit and a foldout bunk, but it was hers. Its locks responded to her retina and fingerprint scans without a hitch, and its small ramp descended to the floor. She beckoned to Claybourne. "Get in," she ordered.

"What's this?" he asked.

"My shuttle." Pride tinged her voice. They walked up the ramp, and she ordered its systems online. "There aren't a lot of places to sit, but we're only going to be traveling for a few minutes." She pulled out the bunk and patted it. "Take a seat."

A quick check through the shuttle's systems told her everything was online and no one had been on board in the time she had been away, save for a scheduled mechanic's visit six months prior. She took her seat and initiated launch sequence, the airlock smoothly opening at her command. Automatic airlocks—a necessity of life that the Commons refused to embrace. As far as Honora was concerned, someone stupid enough to hang around shuttle bays and working airlocks deserved to die. She guided the shuttle into deep space.

Claybourne immediately shot to his feet. "Holy shit," he said. "I didn't believe everything before, so..." He groped for words. "I know you see it every day, but this is..." He fumbled again. "Amazing."

"I grew up here," Honora confided. "I still think that."

"What about my home? What did you think of it?"

Honora had disliked the planet as soon as she stepped out of her fighter. It was too hot, it smelled awful, and its sun nearly blinded her. But even she wouldn't say anything so tactless. "I was only there for a few minutes, really. It was very different," she said carefully. "It wasn't just the language. The buildings were so small, and the sun was so bright. We get very little of it in the Empire." She spotted a few other shuttles heading toward Stappic and checked her chronometer. Seventeen hundred hours. The first shift was heading home.

"How do you guys live without the sun?" Claybourne asked.

"We manage." Then Honora had to admit one of her major failings. "Don't ask me how. Environmental science isn't my strong point."

"It isn't mine, either. I lasted less than two semesters in university."

"You're still ahead of me. I didn't even go." Her shuttle was stuck in a long line of traffic. She broadcast her ID and waited for the go-ahead to land.

"How did you end up a secret agent then? Isn't education a requirement?"

Honora was relieved to hear shades of the Andrew Claybourne she had had on her ship. She wasn't naïve enough to expect it to last. "It is for some positions in Special Ops. Not necessarily for a fighter pilot. I barely finished the minimum educational requirements, and I enlisted when I was seventeen. My commanding officers saw I was a good pilot and hand-to-hand combatant, and I was drafted into Ops. And here I am." Honora was surprised with herself at how freely she offered this information. Personal conversations were rare events for her. "What about you?" she asked.

"What about me?" He looked out the viewport. "How come we're not moving?"

"Traffic."

"Oh." He looked at a couple of shuttles idling side by side ahead of them. "I dropped out of university and started my business. Then I did a bunch of stupid crap and nearly lost it, and I've spent the last couple of years rebuilding my life. It was all taken care of, and you know the rest."

"What did you do?"

He paused. "I'd say it was better said over a drink, but I don't drink anymore."

"I don't drink either." The shuttles ahead weren't moving. It was just her luck to come home after fourteen months away and end up snarled in traffic. "What was it? Did you kill someone?"

"No." He said that last word with a touch of incredulousness. "I'm a lot of things, and not all of them are good, but *I've* never killed anyone," he said emphatically.

Honora remembered his horror when he had found out she shot Pitro. "I'm sorry," she offered.

He grunted in response.

"I should clarify," she said. "I'm not sorry I didn't leave you to die or finish you off myself, but I'm sorry there weren't more options."

"You could have stayed on Earth," he pointed out.

Ugh. She pretended to mull that over that for a moment. "I could have," she agreed. "But it wouldn't have been safe for you or Earth. Someone may have come back to look for me, and it wouldn't have just been the Empire. What if the Nym returned? The Kurran Empire wasn't supposed to make contact for hundreds of years." She took her eyes off traffic to look at him.

He was still staring out the viewport, tight-lipped, knuckles gripping the edge of the bunk. She wished she had a shred of empathic sense, anything to give her an idea of what he was thinking right now. "What do you care if history changed?" he asked in a low, dangerous voice. "Strange things happen every day. Do you know how many people wanted to make contact with aliens?"

"It would have been a disaster if the Nym had been the first."

"Why?" he said, his voice rising. "Your precious fucking Empire wouldn't have existed?"

"I don't know." She kept her voice neutral and non-threatening.

"You can't control everything. I had a lot of time on my hands when I was in treatment. I read a lot. There's a lot of stuff about karma and cosmic realignment out there if you pulled your head out of your ass and bothered to look. It would have balanced out in the end."

Great, Andrew Claybourne was a religious nut. Or a philosopher. Honora had little patience for both. And what treatment was he talking about? "No, it wouldn't," she snapped. "You don't know the Nym."

"Why should I care what you have to say? All you do is what you're told."

The shuttles ahead cleared, and Honora moved hers forward. She bit back a hot retort, reminding herself that he had every right to be as upset as she was. She should just be grateful he wasn't trying to attack her again. "You're right," she acquiesced. "That's what I do."

The traffic controller's voice crackled through the shuttle comm, giving her clearance to land at the station. Her usual spot on the fifth deck opened, and she expertly maneuvered her way into it. Safety lights inside changed from red to green when the airlock hissed closed, but Honora and Claybourne didn't move from their seats.

"I'm taking you to the infirmary," she finally said and rose.

Claybourne followed suit. Honora opened the shuttle doors, and they stepped into the dock. "I don't want to go to the infirmary," he groused.

The doors to the station cycled open into a corridor. A few people milled about, some in uniform and others in civvies. "You said before you thought you might have broken ribs," Honora pointed out. Another idea occurred to her. "It should be very different from the kind of medical treatment you've received before."

She heard a couple of surprised greetings from her colleagues, and she half-heartedly waved at a few familiar faces. She wasn't up to sitting down for chitchat and tea right now; what would she say? She had only been gone less than a week by her clock. Claybourne drew curious glances, but he kept his eyes on Honora. "Come on," she urged.

"What are they going to do to me?"

She faced him. He wore a look of misery and, beneath that, defeat. She had seen that before on rescue missions in the Outer Fringes: slaves she had helped free, who had been convinced that an equally dismal fate laid ahead, that nothing could ever get better for them. She had seen it in people whose spirits had been broken, their will to live evaporated.

She softened her voice. "I promise, no one will hurt you. I can stay with you, if you want."

He looked a little alarmed. "What?"

Honora thought quickly. "You'll just stand there and they'll run a datacorder over you and heal the injuries I couldn't when we were in the vortex. Maybe have a bone regenerator applied. It shouldn't take very long."

He contemplated that information and nodded slowly. "That doesn't sound too horrible. I'm not going to get a colonoscopy or anything?"

The term was foreign to Honora. "What's a colonoscopy?"

He shook his head and the corner of his mouth quirked up. "You'll never know how glad I am to hear you say that."

———

HONORA AND CLAYBOURNE were quickly ushered into a private room in the infirmary. He was tended to by Dr. Mal Ralla, a brilliant, arrogant man who had helped develop the Nym antidote, and a long-ago lover of Honora's before she eschewed romantic relationships. Mal had never let Honora forget her Commons ancestry, nor her inability to rise above the rank of lieutenant. As if a fighter pilot cared whether she was a captain or not. Honora certainly didn't.

Claybourne remained still as he was scanned, but Honora could see the curiosity on his face. "What's the verdict?" he asked when Mal was finished.

"Well, you're not dying," the doctor replied. "Lieutenant Kharn took excellent care of you while you were under her protection, so you don't have any permanent injuries, just a couple of broken ribs. I can take care of that. Unbutton your shirt, please."

Claybourne shook his head.

"I would like to apply a regenerator to accelerate the healing process," the doctor explained.

"Will it be a big deal if I don't have one?" Claybourne pressed.

"It will take longer and you will be uncomfortable, but the breaks can heal naturally if you prefer."

"I prefer that."

Mal's finger twitched, a signal at his irritation at being refused and one Honora had seen before. "You do have an interesting medical history. Take a seat." He gestured to the chairs lining the wall of the small room. "You, too, Lieutenant."

When seated, Mal regarded the pair of them, his expression blank. "I've been informed of your status here," Mal finally said to Claybourne.

"News travels fast," Honora muttered. Had the entire Empire fallen into the bad habits of Fleet?

"It does," Mal agreed. "Now, Mr. Claybourne, would you care to enlighten me as to what you have been up to?"

Honora turned to Claybourne. "Do you want me to leave?"

He shook his head. "Hell, no. You're the only person I know here, and this was bound to come out sooner or later."

Mal looked down at the datacorder he still held, at the small screen's readings. "I'm not quite sure where to begin," he said. "I received a transmit from Fleet about the medical care from your time so I'd know what to expect, and a lot of that is showing up, but some of these readings are unusual."

Honora's heart leapt to her throat. "Was it the Nym toxin?"

"No, that's showing up, but I can see you administered an antidote in time. If Kakos didn't already tell you, excellent work."

Four years ago she would have flushed at the compliment. Now she kept her expression neutral and merely nodded.

"I'm referring to what you were put through on Earth," the doctor explained. "I know their medical knowledge was primitive—forgive me for saying so—but I have to ask about a few things."

Claybourne fidgeted in his seat. "I used to have a... substance abuse problem."

"Ah. Recreational drugs? That could account for a few changes in your body chemistry. They wouldn't have been detectable in your time."

Claybourne looked alarmed. "Do I have cancer?"

"No malignancies. But the substance abuse would likely account for a lot of what I'm seeing here. I'm afraid I don't have a lot of knowledge of the illicit drugs of your time. None, actually," he admitted. "But these changes have occurred in other former drug takers. Your brain's neurotransmitters have broken down and rebuilt themselves, for example."

Claybourne ran a hand through his tousled hair. "I used cocaine for a couple of years. It was just an occasional thing at first, and then the last few months of it I went off the deep end. I checked into a program after I nearly lost my business. You know what rehab is?"

Mal nodded.

"Good, because those Nym people didn't. I don't know how to define it—I don't crave it at all, and I didn't really in rehab—but I was getting fu—uh, really wasted four or five nights out of the week the last four months I used it. It was affecting my work, it was making my relationships with my parents worse than they already were, and after I found out that some employees were stealing money, I checked into the program. I'm coming up on three years' sobriety." There was a note of pride in his voice.

"Any other issues?" Mal asked.

Andrew shook his head. "I don't drink. I never had a problem with it, but I don't want to risk it."

"You'll find that a lot of Kurrans don't imbibe, Mr. Claybourne," Mal said, not bothering to hide the smugness in his voice. "That's more of a Commons vice."

All true, Honora mused. She had heard tales from her cousins detailing liberty in Fleet, and she was stunned at what soldiers did to themselves when given a few hours of freedom.

Mal looked back at the datacorder. "What about your lungs? They're regenerating tissue."

"Oh, that. I used to smoke cigarettes. I quit in March." At Honora's and Mal's blank looks, he clarified, "Lieutenant Kharn said you have a different calendar. I quit smoking five months ago." At their continued lack of response, he tried again. "Um, tobacco. Inhaling herbs wrapped in paper tubes. That was brutal."

"I think I have to read some more about ancient Earth habits," Mal commented. "I'm looking at this, and I can't believe you would do such a thing to yourself. Are you aware of what that did to you?"

"I do, and it's common knowledge on Earth."

When Honora and Mal had had their fling, she had been the audience to many of Mal's tirades about the uncouth habits of the Commons, and she was not up to hearing him lecture about something Claybourne knew was bad for him and had already stopped.

Fortunately, her chronometer beeped and a coded message flashed across its screen in tiny letters. Accommodations had been prepared for Claybourne in an apartment on station. "Claybourne," she said. "We need to go. You probably want to rest, and—"

"Figure out how to get home?" he finished. Honora stiffened, and he sighed noisily. "I know, I know," he mumbled. "You keep telling me I can't." He turned to Mal. "Thanks for the check-up, Doc. It's good to know I dodged death once again."

Mal nodded, a wise king bestowing blessings to a commoner. Honora was very, very glad they were no longer involved.

She turned to the other man in her life right now, the one in the wrong era. Dejected, he followed her from the infirmary.

CHAPTER 6

Honora brought Andrew to a simple bachelor apartment. There was a bed across the room from the doorway, a tiny window near the ceiling. In the corner of the room was a desk topped with a computer screen. A small bathroom off the main room was full of devices that Honora had to demonstrate for him, none of which used water. She showed him the kitchenette, which she called a galley, and all that was there was a touchscreen built into the wall and an empty space beneath it. Beside it was a small wall-mounted rack of dishes.

"It's a replicator," she explained. She ran her fingers over the screen, then gestured to the space below. "That's the tray. I'm just going to change the menu's language settings for you." She stood back. "Can you read any of that?"

Andrew tentatively touched the screen. After a moment, he was able to make out a few selections, phonetically spelled. He nodded. "I'll figure it out."

She showed him how to read a selection's ingredients, useful for when he didn't know what a dish was, and useless since none of these foods existed back on Earth. He tried out the unit, ordering a glass of juice. "Wait!" Honora said. She stuck a glass in the space under the touchscreen. "If you don't do that, you'll have a mess on the floor."

"Sorry." He watched, transfixed, as orange fluid filled the glass. He brought the glass to his lips and tasted something unsweetened.

Glass in hand, he sat on the bed and looked around the sterile apartment. "I miss my home," he said. She nodded. "It's just a townhouse in East York. I bought it last year. I mean, about eight-hundred-odd years ago. You know what I mean." She nodded again.

An uncomfortable silence descended over them, and he stared into the glass. "I keep hoping this is a bad dream and I'll wake up," he confessed. Honora didn't reply.

Her silence irritated him. "What do I have to do or say to get a reaction out of you?" he asked.

She thought for a few seconds. "What do you want me to say?"

"I don't know." He slumped over, feeling defeated. The juice sloshed around in the glass.

Honora stepped a foot closer to the bed. "There's nothing I can say or do right now to make this easier on you. I think it would be insensitive if I tried."

Andrew had to concede that she had a point. "So, what now?" he asked.

"Take a shower, get some rest."

"Then what?"

"I don't know."

He was quiet for a moment, trying to form his next question. Finally he asked, "Honora, am I going to disappear?"

She didn't correct his use of her given name. "What do you mean?"

"Well..." Andrew tried to explain. "I'm not a conspiracy

theorist, but I have friends who are, and you know how there are always rumors about government cover-ups."

"That doesn't happen in the Empire, Claybourne."

"Says you. Don't take this the wrong way, but how much classified information do they share with lieutenants?"

Her lips thinned at that question. "I'm not just a lieutenant. I'm a Special Ops agent, and one who was hand-picked to go back in time."

"Touché. But there must be government secrets only your president or prime minister knows." He remembered the society he was now part of. "Emperor, I guess. My point is, no one knows absolutely everything."

"The Special Ops branch is pretty damn close."

Andrew made a mental note to not say anything remotely derogatory about the Kurran Special Ops team. He just couldn't win. He tried another tack. "In the forties, there was this big thing in Roswell, a town in the United States. A UFO crashed and a bunch of people claimed it was a flying saucer from outer space. The American military said it was a weather balloon." His roommate in university, an irritating astronomy major, had an obnoxious interest in all things related to extraterrestrials. Andrew had involuntarily absorbed a disturbing amount of information pertaining to Roswell and Area 51.

"Earth didn't make contact with any other race until the Kurrans initiated it in the twenty-third century."

"That's not my point. You don't know for sure that a bunch of aliens didn't run out of gas and crash-land in the desert."

"I do, actually. The Empire watched Earth for many years before first contact. We were the only ones to do so."

"You don't know that," Andrew insisted again. "There must be things they don't tell you or your boss." He sighed angrily. "Am I going to be hidden away?"

"You heard what my commander said," Honora reminded him. "You'll be resettled."

How could she be so blasé about this? Were Kurrans completely devoid of sympathy? Andrew fought to keep his temper under control. He took a deep breath and counted back from ten, something his therapist had recommended. When he got to five, he was able to speak without shouting, but barely. "Resettled where?"

"I don't know. I presume wherever you want to go. The Empire and the Commons maintain open borders."

"Damn it, Honora—"

Honora's voice rose a few decibels, but it was still even. "I don't know," she repeated slowly. "All I can tell you is you're not going to be staying at Stappic. This is a military base."

"So you can tell me for sure that I'm not going to spend the rest of my life rotting in a cell somewhere?" He stood up and crossed the room, shoving the glass in the dish tray with more force than necessary.

Honora stared at him, a hard look on her face. "I can tell you for sure that you're not going to rot in a cell," she said icily. "Commander Kakos wouldn't lie to me."

"So you're just going to turn me loose?" Andrew hated that he needed help, especially hers, but he simply couldn't see how he was going to manage his life without her.

"You have the right to go where you please."

"Where should I go?" he yelled. "You're acting like this isn't a big deal. I get it—you're this big-shot, ass-kicking fighter pilot who travels back in time and saves the universe and it's just a part of your job description, so you don't give a fuck, and you're pissed off that I'm not falling over in gratitude for your bringing me here. I have a right to be angry. How would you feel if I forced you to live on Earth?"

Honora's expression didn't change, but he saw her body tense slightly, as though she were expecting a potential fight.

That only increased his ire. He still had a tender spot on the back of his head when she had dropped him to the floor on her ship, not to mention his healing ribs. He had no intention of engaging in hand-to-hand combat with her; he never had that inclination to do so with anyone.

He leaned back against the replicator and crossed his arms over his chest, sending a message that he wasn't going to try to kick her legs out from under her. She relaxed.

"This isn't horrible for me," she finally said quietly. "You're right about that. It's a distressing situation, but you're the victim."

"I'm glad to have that acknowledged," Andrew remarked bitterly.

"I promise you won't be left to fend for yourself."

Andrew wanted to believe her. "Uh-huh."

"I know how Special Ops works," she insisted. "I don't see why you wouldn't be treated like any other refugee."

"I'm not a refugee! You took me from Earth!"

"Would you rather be dead? That was the alternative. That toxin hadn't reached its full potency when I rescued you. You would have come to, paralyzed and in excruciating pain, about an hour after you were pumped full of it." Honora fixed her gaze on him. "And before you ask, I've seen it happen before."

Andrew had wondered which was worse, a slow death or finding himself here. "I don't know what I would have picked if I'd had the choice," he admitted. Honora's eyes never wavered from him. To distract himself, he ran his fingertips over the replicator's touchscreen, watching the foreign words blur together without trying to read them.

Honora didn't press him for an answer. Instead, she switched on the computer mounted to the desk. "This is a transmitter," she explained. "You can initiate comms with other people or download broadcasts." Andrew watched disinterestedly as she flicked through the various controls and keyed in commands.

"Just like home," he mused.

"You had this technology?" She looked startled.

"Similar to that, yeah."

"I've programmed my transmit address into it," she said. "In case you need anything."

"I need to go home."

She didn't offer a retort. Instead, she straightened to her full height. "I sent a request for some clothing to be brought to you. It should be here within the hour."

Andrew looked down at his crumpled, bloodstained suit. A stupid ensemble to wear during an August heat wave, but he had wanted to look professional when he planned his funeral. He had forgotten he was wearing it, and for the first time he felt grimy. "Thank you," he said begrudgingly.

"You're very welcome." She looked around the apartment. "Is there anything else I can help you with, besides your time and location?"

"No, I don't think so."

"I'll be returning to my quarters in that case. I need some rest, too."

"Back to the grind tomorrow for you, then?"

He could tell by the expression on her face that the phrase was lost on her. "I suppose so. If you need anything—"

"I can call you," he interrupted. "I should hope so. It's not like I know anyone else here or speak the language."

"Everyone in Ops has at least a basic grasp of the Commons dialects," she corrected him. She strode past him to the door.

Apprehension swept through Andrew. "Wait."

She paused at the doorway. He fumbled for words. "I know you did what you thought was best. I guess I owe you a thank you and an apology."

"Neither is necessary, and I doubt you would mean them. I was only fulfilling my duties, and you're right to be angry about that."

"But still," he tried again, and she cut him off.

"Get some rest, Claybourne," she admonished him. "This has been trying for both of us, and we have to rendezvous with Kakos at seven hundred hours tomorrow." The doors slid open, and she left his apartment with nary a backwards glance.

Andrew scowled at the closed door. What was he supposed to do now?

———

At 0630 hours, Honora felt far more refreshed than she had expected to be after her fitful sleep. She was wracked with guilt and uncertainty over what to do with Claybourne and her treatment of him the previous day. She knew she could have handled it better. She just didn't know how.

Now, she was going to escort him to the Ops main base. She hesitated outside his apartment door, berating herself for not telling him how to open it. She pressed the door alarm and waited.

"*Rorukum!*" he called, in badly accented Kurran. She couldn't help but smile as the doors opened.

Claybourne was wide awake, dressed in plain black pants and a long-sleeved shirt. "Good morning," she greeted him. "Did you find a language program on your transmitter?"

He shook his head and took a sip from the cup in his hand. She could smell the strong black Kurran tea from the doorway. "No," he replied. "A guy came up last night with some clothes, and he had to explain to me how to open the door. These things can't be programmed in English."

Honora winced. "I'm sorry I forgot to tell you. I came by to wake you up, but I see you've managed that."

"Yeah, I figured out the alarm clock."

"You look a lot better." The circles under his eyes had disappeared, as had the dried blood. His face had healed nicely. Honora saw small scars beside his nose and under his right eye that would be permanent, but she thought they added character. She was right in her original assessment of him; he wasn't a bad-looking man. The polar opposite, in fact. She felt herself flush and looked over his shoulder, at the small window near the ceiling.

He didn't seem to notice and shrugged noncommittally. "I'm still pissed off about this whole situation, if that makes any difference."

"I didn't expect otherwise. Have you eaten breakfast?"

"I ate *something*, but I don't know what it was. Tasted kind of like a stir-fry." He took a final swallow of tea and left the cup in the replicator tray. They left the apartment. "I have to say that showering without water is a pain in the ass, though. Do you still use it?"

"Modern stations and ships don't, but you will still find showers and the like on planets and older vessels. Particle cleansing is a cheaper alternative."

Claybourne kept pace with her as they walked through the corridor to the lift. "So, they're charging concert prices for a bottle of water?"

They waited at the end for an available lift to open. "I don't understand," Honora said.

"Water is scarce," he clarified.

A lift opened, and they stepped in. Honora hastily ordered it closed before anyone could jump on with them. "No," she said, feeling a little confused. "Ships have to make more frequent stops at spaceports to refill the supply, and the added weight of the tanks and equipment increases fuel consumption." She ordered the lift to the shuttle bays.

There were plenty of Ops agents around this time of day,

and Honora again exchanged greetings with a few without pausing to chat. Claybourne was quiet until she opened the door to her bay.

"It's cold in here," he groused.

Honora grinned as she opened the doors to her shuttle. "Deep space," she reminded him.

Once in the cockpit, he watched as Honora sat at the controls and started a safety check. "Can I drive?" he asked impishly.

This was closer to the Andrew Claybourne she knew in the vortex. "No," she replied, and thumbed at the bunk. "Sit down."

He didn't listen and instead watched as her hands expertly glided over the controls. He gripped the back of her seat as the shuttle lurched through the airlock into space. "Can you teach me?"

"There isn't enough time today." Kurran Prime was visible from here, and there were few shuttles sharing her airspace, a nice surprise.

"I figured that. I didn't mean today. Some other time."

Honora shrugged. "I don't see why not."

"I'm going to see you again after today, right? They're not sending me off to these Fringes places?"

"Of course not. Claybourne, you really should be sitting when we're in a traffic lane."

He let go of her seat and obeyed, perching on the edge of the bed at the back. "Just call me Andrew," he said. "I think we're on a first-name basis at this point."

"I'd still appreciate it if you would call me 'Lieutenant' in public."

"I'll do that."

They were quiet for the rest of the short ride to Kurran Prime until Honora requested permission to land.

"Aren't you worried about these Nym people getting in?" Andrew asked.

"No. There are a lot of security protocols in place. Better than the Commons." She sighed. "I'm sure I'll hear everything they've screwed up since I've been gone." She was given clearance and turned on the gravity engines that would get them through the planet's atmosphere.

"Your friends didn't tell you last night?" His voice was directly behind her.

"Sit down until we've landed," she chided. "And no, they didn't. I went straight to my quarters and stayed there. I didn't feel like socializing last night."

Or ever. It just wasn't the way Honora operated.

"What about your roommate?"

Why is he asking so many questions? Honora took a deep breath and reminded herself that he was curious and it was her fault he was here to begin with. "I live alone," she replied. "Andrew, please sit down."

"I'm fine. The guy who brought me clothes last night, he said something about having a roommate. I thought that's how things are done in your army." He caught himself. "Special Ops. Sorry."

"I prefer to live alone." They were breaking through Kurran Prime's atmosphere, and Andrew swayed on his feet. "Do you see why I keep telling you to sit down?"

"I can't see from the back." He clutched the back of her seat harder. "I live alone, too."

"So you weren't married on Earth?" The question left Honora's mouth before she could rephrase it. It hadn't even occurred to her to wonder if he was married. There hadn't been any pictures in his wallet, nor did he have a tattoo on his wrist to indicate it. Or a ring, she reminded herself. That was how it was sometimes done in the Commons. He hadn't worn any jewelry save for the chronometer on his left wrist.

Andrew laughed bitterly. "Hell, no. You don't have to feel guilty that you took me away from a wife or kids. Just my friends, my business, my house...you know, my life."

Honora didn't reply, instead concentrating on landing her shuttle.

CHAPTER 7

Andrew followed Honora to the debriefing room they had gone to the day before, unsure of what to expect. She had promised that he wouldn't be left in the lurch, and she really seemed to believe it, but he wasn't counting on that. Years of working in his line of business had taught him otherwise; Tiger Media had been dicked around by everyone from indie musicians to music labels. Promises meant nothing.

The room's doors slid open to reveal her commander and another man sitting at the table. Like everyone else here, his skin looked washed out and anemic due to lack of sunlight, despite his olive coloring. He regarded both of them coolly and gave a regal nod in their direction. Immediately Honora bowed deeply, then poked Andrew in his thigh with her elbow. He took the hint and did likewise.

"What the hell?" he whispered.

"Follow my lead," she hissed. After a few seconds, she stood up to her full height. The stranger stood and greeted her in Kurran, his dark green tunic shimmering under the harsh lights. She replied in kind, crisply saluting, then gestured to Andrew. He assumed he was being introduced and nodded, praying that they would conduct the rest of this meeting in English.

"Sit," the man ordered. He and Honora quickly complied.

"I'm—" Andrew began, but was silenced when Honora jabbed her elbow into him again. He bit back a curse. At least she hadn't poked him in his bad side. His ribs still ached.

"You're Claybourne, the Nym victim," the man said serenely. His voice and mannerisms seemed out of place on this odd military base.

Andrew looked to Honora for guidance. Who the hell was this guy?

She nodded tightly. "Go ahead," she mumbled.

"I am," Andrew confirmed. He shot a quick glance at Honora, but she was looking at her commander.

Kakos cleared his throat. "Mr. Claybourne, this is Emperor Sarda II."

Emperor? He stole another look at Honora, but she stared daggers at Kakos. Andrew realized that she hadn't known they would be having a royal audience.

Kakos took note of Honora's tight-lipped expression and spoke again. "We apologize for not having informed you of the emperor's presence this morning. We didn't expect him to arrive so quickly after we told him about Mr. Claybourne's arrival."

"You should have," the emperor chided Kakos. His voice was even, but Andrew detected the note of irritation under his words. "We are not the Commonwealth, Commander. Incidents such as these are of the highest priority." He looked at Honora thoughtfully. "Your commander has told me what you have done and whether it constitutes a breach of conduct."

"Yes, sir." Hands folded demurely in her lap, she spoke calmly.

"It is rare that I am involved in such matters. The Special Ops unit is self-governing."

Get to the point, Andrew thought impatiently. The emperor raised an eyebrow at him. *Damn it*—he'd forgotten that these people tended to be psychic. *I'm sorry*, he thought back fiercely, and he hoped that would suffice. A smile teased the corners of the emperor's mouth, and he turned back to Honora.

The emperor, Kakos, and Honora began an exchange in rapid-fire Kurran, to which Andrew listened but failed to follow. He heard his name mentioned a few times, and at one point Honora and the commander's voices rose in frustration before the emperor raised his hand for silence. She said something that resembled an apology to both men, then took a deep breath and continued.

Andrew hated being discussed as if he didn't exist. Weren't translators *de riguer* in the future? Maybe something he could wear in his ear? Hell, Google Translate had existed on Earth. The three of them continued to debate, and if he knew his way around this building, he would have snuck out for a few minutes to find a vending machine or this era's version of Starbucks. A double shot of espresso wouldn't be unwelcome right about now. Instead, he forced himself to stare out the window, where the twin moons were still shining. It had to be around eight in the morning, but it didn't feel like it. How did these people live without vitamin D?

Andrew had fixated on the larger of the moons until he felt himself going cross-eyed when the emperor stood up. Honora and Kakos followed suit, and Andrew quickly scrambled to his feet. Honora saluted, then turned to Andrew. "We're leaving," she said in a low voice. She bowed in the emperor's direction once more, but turned for the door before Andrew could as well. He managed to say, "Nice to meet you," before she grabbed his arm and pulled him into the hallway.

"What was that?" he demanded.

"I'll tell you later," she said through gritted teeth. He could hear the fury in her voice, and her hands kept bunching into fists.

Andrew refrained from asking further questions when they boarded an elevator, instead simply watching her.

She stared straight ahead for a few seconds before slamming the palm of her hand against the wall. "*Sikiaka!*" she yelled. "Fuck!"

Andrew's feet moved a half-step away of their own accord.

She turned to him, a stunned look on her face, as though she had forgotten he was there. "I apologize," she said hoarsely. Andrew doubted she was near tears or if she was even capable of crying, but she was angrier than he had seen anyone in a long time.

The elevator stopped at the shuttle bays, and Andrew matched Honora's angry pace through the airlock accessway. Both of them were silent as she prepared for takeoff, and he meekly sat down on the foldout bed. This wasn't the time to gawk at the galaxy through the windows.

She was hunched over the shuttle's controls, stabbing at the consoles with more force than necessary.

"Can I ask what happened?" Andrew asked cautiously.

The shuttle halted, and she leaned back in seat. "Give me a minute," she said. Her voice was low, still tinged with rage. "Let me get out of the traffic lane." The shuttle veered sharply to the left until they stopped by a huge cluster of stars. Andrew stood up to look. The sight really was amazing—stars were so much bigger and brighter than he expected.

"You're not going to like this," Honora said, interrupting his gawking.

He turned away from the starfield and leaned against the wall. "I figured that."

"The good news is you're not going to be carted off and

tossed in a cell," she continued. "You're free to do what you want."

"That's good, isn't it?"

She shook her head.

Andrew opened his mouth to counter that, but her words sunk in. "I'm on my own, aren't I?" Fear bloomed in his chest.

"Unfortunately. The Empire isn't going to treat you like the Commons did your friend. The emperor was quite clear on that. You won't receive any help from the Empire or Special Ops when you resettle." She flexed her hands again, gearing up for an imaginary fight. "The emperor said you're a mistake."

"So I'm being swept under the rug," Andrew interpreted. "I'm going to end up a crazy homeless guy on some planet here talking about how I came from the past."

"No!" she said emphatically. The vehemence in her voice scared him a little. "I won't let that happen. I brought you into this and I'm taking responsibility for you. The emperor doesn't want you in the Empire."

"You're turning me over to those people in the Commons?"

"I didn't say that," she protested. "Although I don't think that's a bad place for you to be. First, their military has experience with time travelers, and second, they're a lot more tolerant than the Empire." She ran her hands through her hair. "I already have a place where you can stay, if you want."

"I don't really have a choice. Where is it?" Andrew was already dreading her answer. It was going to be some kind of cottage in the middle of nowhere, with only slimy, tentacled aliens for company. He knew it.

"My family's home." She took a deep breath. "It's near the border, on the Commons side. I'll send a transmit when we get back to Stappic Station so they can prepare rooms for you. My uncle's an admiral with the Commons Fleet, and he'll be able to offer you more help than the Empire will."

Another idea popped into Andrew's mind. "What about Earth? It still exists, right? I could live there."

"It does, but you wouldn't want to. It's too hot, and I think you a permit to live there."

"Shit." That had been Andrew's only idea. "I guess I'm going to your parents' house, then."

"Not my parents," Honora corrected him sharply. "It's a family home," she emphasized.

"What else did they say in there, Honora?" he pressed. "You can't be that pissed off on my account."

She glared at him. "I can be. But it wasn't only you." Her jaw worked, and she looked at the stars outside. "I've been suspended," she said darkly.

Shock, then unexpected anger on her behalf flowed through him. "Why?" he demanded.

"They're not quite sure what to do with me. Obviously, this isn't a situation covered by Ops regulations. So I've been suspended indefinitely, just so I can remember that a fighter pilot isn't qualified to make the decision I did regarding you."

"But I would have died! If they weren't so concerned with... whatever they're so concerned with, they shouldn't have sent a fighter pilot. Why not a scientist?" He didn't have a clue who was really qualified to go back in time, but a fighter pilot was as good as any.

Honora sighed noisily. "I tried to make those points, but I was told to mind my place. Scientists usually aren't skilled at piloting, and I already told you about my limited education. Besides, fighter pilots, even ones with my skills and experience, are easier to come by than scientists or higher military authorities."

Andrew felt sick, like the gravity had been shut off. "So, they sent you because you're replaceable," he deduced.

She shrugged. "Essentially, yes."

"They wouldn't have missed you if you didn't make it back."

"I knew that going in, and I did it anyway. I *wanted* to go, Andrew. The lifespan of fighter pilots is considerably shorter than the rest of the population."

Outrage colored his thoughts. He had known this woman for only a few days, and he already found himself… well, not quite *liking* her—she was too prickly for that—but he had a lot of respect for her. She was tough, and despite the way her beloved Special Ops treated her, she highly regarded her employers and believed in what they did. Still, that didn't erase his consternation that she accepted she was nothing more than a live body to Ops. She wasn't replaceable.

Andrew wasn't good at being sensitive, but he had to try. "If you're going to cry, I won't tell anyone."

She looked up at him, eyes flashing. Immediately he knew he had made a mistake.

"I am *not* going to cry," she said indignantly.

Andrew held up his hands in a show of defeat. "I didn't mean any offense, but you're really pissed off, and—"

"I am not going to cry," she repeated. "Agents don't do that, no matter what you think about women in combat roles. I know you come from a backward time and you only wanted to be reanimated to 'see alien ass,' as you so delicately put it," she spat.

He winced. "That was a rude thing to say. It was the best excuse I could come up with when people asked why I wanted to be preserved. I also thought you were crazy when I woke up on your spaceship. I wasn't thinking."

Her eyes narrowed. "So you would have spoken to me differently if you believed me? Is that how you treated women 850 years ago?"

"No!" Andrew did not want to get sucked into a debate

between the sexes, and he *had* said something insensitive. "I'm sorry, Honora."

She sighed. "Apology accepted. I'm sorry, too. None of this is your fault. I shouldn't be taking it out on you."

"I don't mind," he said. "Do your worst. If I hadn't gone to the lab that day, you wouldn't be out of a job."

Honora propped her elbow on a console, resting her chin in her hand. She gazed at the stars outside, their light illuminating her face, highlighting her dark blue eyes. For the first time since they rode through the vortex to this century, he remembered how striking she was. "I'm not out of a job. I'm suspended." Andrew refrained from pointing out that where he came from, suspension usually meant that one had to brush up on his résumé. Echoing his thought, she added, "I'm not sure what I'll do if I'm discharged. I don't have any work experience outside the military."

"Bounty hunter?" Andrew suggested.

She turned away from the view outside and faced him, one eyebrow raised. "Do you really think someone could go from Special Ops to bounty hunting?"

"I don't know. I used to promote indie bands and sell their music, and when I stopped doing that, I was going to work at a radio station. Transferring my skills, you know?"

Honora nodded dejectedly. "I don't have much in the way of transferable job skills. If I'm discharged from Ops, my only viable career option is enlisting with the Commons military." She made a face.

With an increased rumble of the engine beneath their feet, she steered the shuttle back into the star lanes. He changed the subject. "So you're taking me to your family home?" he confirmed.

"I'm going, too. Suspended agents can't stay on station."

Andrew was relieved to know he wouldn't be facing her family alone. For some odd reason, a small, unexpected bubble of pleasure welled inside him at the prospect of spending more time with Honora. Even if she would undoubtedly be irritable at not working. What did she do in her spare time?

For that matter, what would he do? He wanted to track down the receptionist from Lazarus Cryonics but didn't have a clue where to start. Then he had to find a way to make himself useful, and he was pretty sure he couldn't transfer his own job skills here. He wasn't even sure music existed anymore.

Well, there was one way to find out. "Honora?"

"Yes?" She kept her eyes focused outside the windows.

"You know what music is, right?"

She turned to face him. "Are you serious?"

"I'll take that as a yes."

"If you're thinking about doing what you did on Earth—"

"I know," he interrupted. "Not possible."

She shrugged. "I was going to say I don't follow it, so I couldn't be of any help." Stappic Station grew closer. "I'm sending a transmit to my family when we get in, then we're leaving, all right?"

Andrew nodded. "Got it."

———

HONORA DIDN'T HAVE MUCH in the way of personal belongings, just enough to toss in a duffel. After Andrew pointed out that he had all of his worldly goods on his person, she let him follow her to her apartment. Unlike other agents, Honora didn't consider Stappic her home. Nor did she consider the Kharn family estate as such. She was mobile and indistinguishable, belonging to no one, without any connections except to Ops. Just one more cog in the machine. Exactly the kind of soldier they preferred.

She sent a quick written transmit to the family home, not

wanting to get into a long, drawn-out conversation over a visual vidlink about her suspension before she had to. She wondered if she would be as pissed off if she could stay on Stappic. Probably, she mused, and then she would have other agents trying to pry information from her. That could be more irritating than her family.

She briefly reconsidered her decision to stay with them. She supposed she could check into a hotel, but she had no idea how long she would be suspended, and there was Andrew to think of. She had some money saved up, but she couldn't afford to spring for two hotel rooms for an indefinite period.

As they rejoined the flow of traffic, she thought that maybe burning through her savings wouldn't be a bad idea if it meant not having to face her extended family. She didn't know who would be around and hadn't waited for a reply before departing the station. Honora was already dreading the inevitable line of questioning.

Andrew, damn him, would not sit down. He stood beside the pilot's seat, watching the stars and other craft fly by. "Are we going into warp space?" he asked.

"I beg your pardon?" Her reply came out more sharply than she had intended, but he didn't seem to notice.

"Hypergates," he clarified. "Sorry."

"Not today." At his slightly crestfallen expression, she added, "Also sorry."

He asked more questions about space travel, subjects she was familiar with, and watched as she maneuvered her craft into the lane that would take them to the Commons border. "Now what?" he asked.

Honora stood up and stretched, but her gaze didn't stray from the viewport. "It's three hours to get there, depending on traffic," she reported. She returned to her seat and from the corner of her eye watched Andrew take in the controls.

"When can I learn?" he asked.

"A major commercial lane isn't the place to learn to fly."

Andrew sighed dramatically. "Well, maybe when we're at your family home, you can find some empty airspace and teach me. Hell, Honora, I have to have *something* to do. I'm so bored I could read—if I could understand your language."

She laughed, releasing a little of the tension that had built up the last few days.

Andrew changed the subject. "So, what kind of snake pit am I walking into?"

Immediately her mirth faded. "The Kharn family estate."

"Is there protocol I have to follow? Is your father a duke? I felt like such a tool when we met your emperor."

Honora understood his sentiment, although she was uncertain why he compared himself to a tool. "That took me by surprise, too." She paused, unsure how to describe her family. "It's complicated," she said lamely.

He nodded. "So is mine."

Honora looked up at him, recalling his thrice-married stepmother. She waited for an explanation. "Oh, no," he said. "You go first."

She bit her lip. "I'm not like my family."

"I need more to go on than that. I'm not like mine, either."

"They're good people," she continued. "They have Kurran ancestry, and they keep the family home tradition, but that's it. They're Commons through and through. I'm the only one who lives in the Empire. Most of my family is involved in the Commons military in some way. I told you about my uncle and cousin. He's an admiral, she's a nurse. My aunt is a researcher with Fleet Medical."

"So all of you live at your house?"

"Everyone has rooms there," she corrected. "It's an estate. It's entirely possible to have everyone visiting and not see anyone unless you want to. Kurran families are very traditional that way. You live at home until you're married."

"So you grew up there?"

She nodded and looked through the viewport to check on traffic. "I did, off and on. My parents enlisted in the Kurran Forces and they died when I was a girl, so I moved there permanently when I was eleven." As was always the case when she spoke about her parents, she didn't feel a twinge of regret. She hadn't been especially close to them, but she had respected them, and they her.

Andrew's eyes were wide. "I'm so sorry."

Honora shook her head. "That's not necessary. They died in battle with the Nym and helped prevent an invasion into the Empire. They and the two hundred other soldiers who gave their lives died honorably." Andrew still looked shocked, and she racked her brain trying to remember any war details on Earth. "Haven't any of your family members served?"

"No. There were wars going on when I was a kid, but I didn't know anyone in the military."

"What about your parents?" Honora countered. "What did they do?"

He shrugged. "Dad's a lawyer, and I already told you about my stepmother. My parents split up when I was a kid, and Mom lives in France with her husband. I'd only recently started speaking to my father and Judith again before I ended up here."

"What happened, if you don't mind my asking?"

Andrew hesitated. "It's complicated," he said, echoing her earlier statement. "And you're going to think I'm a bigger bastard than you already do."

She tried to reassure him. "I don't think you're a bastard." He shot her a look, and she amended, "Well, I would be put out, too, if I found myself in another time."

"Okay, then." He looked out the viewport and steeled

himself. "I told you that I went to rehab for substance abuse. My father never liked what I did with my life. He never saw me as a businessman, just a glorified record store clerk. He hated Tiger Media, and he hated the bands I worked with. He just loathed the whole business. I'm an only child, and I was an embarrassment to him. His grand plan for me was to become a lawyer, and he cut me out of my life for awhile when I applied for a business loan and dropped out of university."

Honora nodded, trying to understand. Her extended family had made a bit of a fuss when she chose to enlist with the Kurran Forces rather than Fleet, but they were still supportive of her in their own ways.

"When I hit rock bottom with the drugs, Dad acted like he was right all along about my life," Andrew continued bitterly. "I'd let a couple of employees run the show when I was out getting high all the time, and they embezzled a lot of funds. The papers found out about the theft and my behavior, and a lot of acts cancelled appearances at locations and withdrew their albums from distribution. I fired a lot of people, apologized for what it was worth, and went to rehab. Then I had to rebuild the business and gain back trust from a lot of people. I did that, and Tiger Media was back on its feet when I decided to get out of it altogether."

"Why?" She was puzzled; his business sounded like something he cared about, and she couldn't see the practicality of abandoning it.

He shrugged. "There are a lot of evil people in the entertainment industry, Honora. I got tired of—well, aside from the coke problem, I wasn't one exactly, but I didn't want to associate with them anymore. I never took advantage of talent trying to get ahead, but I knew of a lot of people who did. I founded Tiger Media to bring attention to indie bands and singers and small labels, give them places to play and promote themselves. I didn't think corruption and greed existed at that level, only with the big corporations." He exhaled noisily. "I was wrong. It was really innocent and naïve of me in retrospect. So I decided to join that radio station, talking about music and plugging the bands. I would still be involved in an industry I cared about, but from a further distance, you know?"

Honora digested this, and guilt continued to eat at her for her part in spoiling his dreams. "Did you play anything?" she asked.

He barked out a harsh laugh. "I failed piano lessons and goofed around on a guitar when I was a kid. Music was my life, but I have zero talent."

Any rejoinder she could have offered was cut off by Andrew's gasp. He pointed out the viewport. "What is *that*?"

Far off in the distance hovered a swath of asteroids. "The Konos Belt," Honora replied. "Asteroids."

"Damn." He fumbled in his pockets and removed the thin, flat communicator he carried with him. He looked at it, crestfallen. "I forgot my phone doesn't work. I was going to take a picture." He returned to the back of the shuttle, and Honora heard him plop to the bunk. "This sucks."

She nodded from the pilot's seat. "I know."

CHAPTER 8

To Andrew's chagrin, Honora remained tight-lipped about her family home, offering one-word answers to his questions.

The Commons-Kurran border was dotted with tall, thin buildings that Honora explained were checkpoints. Shuttles floated in and out of them, carrying border guards between ships. There were dozens of craft of all sizes and shapes on either side of the checkpoints, many in long lines. Honora spoke to someone over her transmitter in rapid-fire Kurran, and they were able to cross without any issues. She explained that the ID broadcasting from her ship identified her as an Ops agent and dual citizen. It helped that she was only piloting a personal shuttle. Larger ships with weapons arrays tended to be stopped and boarded by agents for inspection.

She commented on the long queues of ships waiting to be cleared when they sailed past. "That's unusual," Honora said. "There normally isn't such a long line-up. There must have been a big security breach to bring that on. Andrew, damn it, I'm not going to tell you to sit down again."

He grinned. It was fun rattling her cage. "You could get another seat installed here."

"And have you try to take over the controls and get us sucked in ass-backward into a hypergate? Absolutely not."

To distract her from the fact that he was standing up and holding the back of her seat again, Andrew steered the conversation back to the queue at the border. "Long lines are normal where I come from."

"A lot of irritating things are normal where you come from."

"No need to get snippy. Maybe a lot of people just happen to be traveling today. Maybe there's a rock star and that's his entourage."

"Rock star?" she said curiously.

"Never mind." He watched her hands fly over the controls and for the first time noted the faded scars crossed over their backs. Without thinking, he reached out to touch her. "What happened, if you don't mind my asking?"

She pulled her hand back as if she had been scalded. "Battle in the Outer Fringes," she explained simply. "The ship I was piloting took a direct hit, and one of the consoles exploded. A few pieces caught on fire and landed on my hands."

"Good Lord."

"I was fine," she continued proudly. "They didn't hit anything vital. I just kept going until another ship towed mine away."

How did one respond to that? Andrew complained when he got a paper cut.

"We'll be at the estate in about ten minutes," she announced. There was a note of dejection in her voice.

"Do I have to genuflect in front of anyone?" he asked, only half-joking.

"I beg your pardon?"

He couldn't help but grin. "I'm a lapsed Catholic."

Honora turned a confused face to him. It was almost cute. "Is that some kind of ideology you follow?"

"I *did*, past tense, and it was pretty half-assed at that. Which is why I'm lapsed. Do I have to bow or anything?"

"Oh! No. My family isn't royalty, just regular people." She paused. "I suppose."

Andrew suppressed a sigh and didn't ask her what she meant by "regular people." He'd find out soon enough.

———

As they neared their destination, Honora explained that her home world was constructed around a small planet called Sennethaca that had been enhanced by a joint Commons-Empire team a couple of hundred years prior. Only part of its surface was liveable, and the part that wasn't had a dome constructed over it to support life. The Kharn family estate had been built on the natural part of the planet shortly after the dome enhancement had been completed, along with a handful of homes that had remained in their respective families for generations.

Andrew was knocked to the floor when they broke through Sennethaca's atmosphere. The shuttle jerked from side to side, and a siren briefly wailed before Honora slapped at the console to shut it off. "I told you to sit down," she reprimanded him again. He doubted that would have helped and lay prone on the floor, feeling the ship vibrate beneath him.

The shuttle slowed and its movements smoothed, and he figured it would be safe to stand up again. He rubbed the tender spot where his ribs ached and winced. "Are we almost there?"

"Yes." Honora had slowed the shuttle and was glaring fiercely at the windshield. Rain splattered its surface, and he could see the lush green vegetation of the planet's surface. They were flying toward a large compound, and he saw a sprawling house coming closer. Doors inset into the ground opened up, and Honora steered to them. The rain pounded harder against the shuttle as its speed increased, dipping sharply through the open doors.

It was brightly lit inside, and he could see through the windows that they were in this century's equivalent of a parking lot. There were a few shuttles here and there through the enormous space, and Honora brought hers to a full stop. "We're here," she announced dismally.

When the door yawed open, Andrew picked up her duffel and slung it over his shoulder, ignoring the dull throb in his robs. He really should have listened to her and sat down when they broke through the planet's atmosphere. He walked down the ramp and waited for her.

She eyed him suspiciously. "I can carry my own things, you know."

"I'm trying to be nice. You know what with you saving my life and getting suspended from your job on my account and all."

"Oh. Okay then." The shuttle's door closed; they started walking. "Thank you," she added as an afterthought.

"You're welcome."

They didn't see another soul by the time they stepped into an elevator. Honora pressed her hand into a wall-based palm pad and ordered it to the foyer.

"This is programmed in English?" Andrew asked.

"My family doesn't speak Kurran unless they have to," she replied.

The elevator made a swift ascent and opened its doors to a spectacularly appointed hallway, its doorways branching off in various directions. The ceiling was at least twelve feet above them, the view from the skylights blurred with rain. The floor was veined black and white marble, and there were heavy-looking black enameled chairs and tables casually arranged about. A few lamps with white shades offered some light, and tall, abstract stone sculptures had been settled around the floor. At the very end of the hallway, a good forty feet, Andrew saw a set of glass doors, and beyond that, trees and greenery.

"Wow," was all he could manage to say. The place looked like a magazine feature.

"It's showy," Honora said quietly, distaste creeping into her voice. "Let's go to my apartment before anyone sees us."

What was her issue with her family? Andrew didn't voice the question, but instead followed Honora down the hallway. It was like being a teenager again, sneaking into his girlfriend's house after her curfew, only this time he wouldn't be listening to Weezer on low volume and fooling around.

They made it to a staircase off one of the doorways when an excited squeal stopped them dead in their tracks. "You're here!" said a voice behind them.

Andrew chanced a glance at Honora. She closed her eyes briefly before turning around. "Hello, Ana," she said.

A short, plump woman in her mid-sixties beamed at them. Her hair was iron-gray streaked with blue, her eyes a vivid green. Unlike everyone else Andrew had met so far, she obviously spent some time in the sun, and the sleeves of her olive-drab blouse were pushed up to reveal tanned forearms. "I got your transmit," she said excitedly. "We're all so happy you came here for a holiday."

Honora cracked a smile and didn't correct her. "It's good to see you."

"It's been a year at least! I've missed you!" The woman crushed Honora in a hug and planted a wet kiss on her cheek. "You don't come here often enough," she chastised. Releasing her grip on Honora, she looked at Andrew curiously. "And who is this, carrying your bag like a proper gentleman?"

Without waiting to be introduced, she held out a hand. "I'm Ana, the housekeeper."

Andrew shook her hand. "Andrew Claybourne."

"He's my friend from Ops," Honora volunteered.

Ana scrutinized Andrew's face. "But you're not Kurran."

"It's a long story," Honora explained hastily. "Ana, is anyone else home?"

The housekeeper waved a hand in Honora's direction and gave a dramatic sigh. "She always does this," she said to Andrew in a stage whisper. "Never wants a big show. She doesn't know how much her family misses and worries about her." Louder, Ana said, "The admiral is home in his study and waiting to speak to you, and your aunt is somewhere in the Fringes. Don't look at me like that, Honora, they're your *family*. No one is here just to spite you."

Honora's expression was neutral, as usual. Andrew liked Ana already.

"Your rooms are exactly as they were the last time you were here. I just dusted a little. And it was *me*," Ana stressed. "Not one of the other employees. I've also prepared a space for your... friend." There was a conspiratorial tone to that last statement, and Andrew felt himself redden. Dear Lord, the housekeeper thought they were sleeping together.

"Would either of you like something to eat?" Ana asked. "I have cherry cake ready." She looked back at Andrew. "It's her favorite, you know."

He nodded like he did, and filed away that information. He knew nothing of Honora's likes or dislikes; he'd assumed Special Ops had programmed them out of her.

"Come to the kitchen for a piece when you're settled in," Ana urged. "Coffee, too. Mr. Claybourne, if you're used to Ops food, you'll be happy to know that I haven't let a replicator within twenty feet of the kitchen since I started working here."

Andrew brightened at the thought of real food.

"Go on up," Ana said, flapping her hands at the stairs. "Honora, please speak to the admiral as soon as you're able. He's quite agitated."

"I'll bet," Honora muttered.

"I've put Andrew in the empty apartment in the southwest wing," Ana called. "One door down and across the corridor from yours."

"Thank you, Ana," Honora said sincerely.

At the top of the stairs, a landing led in three directions. Here the floor was carpeted, and windows that spanned the length of the walls offered Andrew a view of the greenery outside. The rainstorm had lessened, and there were a few slivers of muted sunlight peeking through the clouds. It certainly beat the perpetual nighttime in the Empire, and this planet didn't look much different from Earth, he noted sadly. Homesickness tugged at his heart.

This whole house felt almost like a regular home aside from its massive size. He shifted Honora's duffel over his other shoulder and followed her down another hallway. "Here you are," she said, opening a door.

Andrew stepped inside to find a tastefully decorated living room. There were more big windows overlooking a well-maintained garden, and understated furniture in generic beige tones. A few pieces of artwork graced the walls, offering some color. There was a TV screen hanging from the wall, a replicator next to it. An open doorway revealed a bed. It reminded him of a nice hotel and was certainly more welcoming than the sterile room at Stappic Station.

Honora hefted her duffel off his shoulder. "Thanks for carrying this," she said before turning from the apartment. He watched her as she crossed the hall to what he guessed was hers, where she unceremoniously dropped the bag to the floor. He lingered in her apartment's doorway, taking in her space. It was decorated in blues and golds, with a few framed pictures gracing a table beside the couch. It was surprisingly feminine and very unlike the Honora he was getting to know.

She must have sensed his surprise, because she said, "Ana picked the color scheme when I was a kid. I've never had the heart to change it."

Andrew figured it was likelier she didn't care, but he nodded.

A deep male voice lightly tinged with an accent boomed from an intercom built into the wall. "Honora, are you there?" Both of them started.

"Just got in, sir."

"Drop rank, you're with family. I want you and your friend in my study right away."

"*Sikiaka*," murmured Honora.

"I heard that," said the voice disapprovingly.

Andrew had to hurry to keep up with Honora's long strides as she stalked out of the room. "Where are we going?"

"To see my uncle." She looked almost as tense as she had when they met the emperor. "I would have liked to settle in and plan my defense first."

"And have some cherry cake?"

She offered him an uncharacteristic sly look. "Well, yes. Ana's is the best."

They walked through an interminable number of hallways and took several flights of stairs up and down throughout the house. Andrew hoped someone thought to have a map drawn up. *You are here.*

Honora told him that the house had been added on to over the centuries, wings and stories added almost willy-nilly, and it was a confusing jumble to new visitors. She really meant it when she said she could go for days without seeing anyone if she wanted to.

Andrew mulled this over as they ascended yet another

flight of stairs and through an elaborate hallway draped with tapestries. They were embroidered with spaceships locked in battle amid glittering stars. Before he could ask about them, Honora knocked on a door.

"Come in," said the voice from the intercom.

They stepped into an office full of unfamiliar computer equipment and mismatched furniture. A jacket heavy with braid and medals was carelessly tossed over a chair. A replicator unit was mounted into the wall near it, crammed with dirty coffee cups. Behind a dented metal desk sat a man in his fifties, looking very fit for his age. His graying blond hair stood up in tufts around his head. He looked human except for his eyes, a startling blue-black that matched Honora's.

He stood up, towering over both Andrew and Honora, and immediately embraced her. "It's been too long," he said by way of greeting. "You don't know how worried we were when we didn't hear from you for over a year."

"That's what Ana said," she replied into his shoulder before pulling away.

He regarded Honora with warmth for another moment, and Andrew felt a twinge of regret. He had never had the kind of relationship with his father, or any of his family members for that matter. With a shock, he realized he didn't really miss them. Maybe he would later on.

She fidgeted under the man's gaze.

"I know what you've been up to," he said finally. "Fleet has been in touch with your Special Ops. I know about your trip to Earth." He paused. "I'm very proud of you, Honora. We all are."

Honora looked away, clearly uncomfortable with his praise, and turned to Andrew. "Andrew, this is my uncle, Tarek Kharn, admiral of the Fourth Fleet," she said by way of introduction. "Uncle Tarek, this is Andrew Claybourne." She paused, unsure of how to present him.

"I already know," Admiral Kharn said. "Your Commander Kakos immediately informed Fleet of his presence and the actions that brought him here." He raised an eyebrow at Honora. "I said you can drop rank."

"*Sikiaka*." Honora sat down heavily into a faded overstuffed chair.

"I'm not upset," the admiral quickly said to reassure her. "Frankly, Fleet's relieved to know that the other person caught up in the Nym shitstorm wasn't killed. We were given that impression by the woman who turned up last year."

"The receptionist," Andrew said excitedly. "You know her?"

"It's a smaller universe than you think. My daughter is a friend of hers. Mora was on the ship that found Lily in a cargo hold. Lily was always curious as to what happened to you."

"You're fucking kidding me." Instantly Andrew remembered his manners. "Sorry, Admiral."

"Don't worry. I've spent thirty-five years in the military. I've heard it all, in every language. Sit down." He pointed to an ultra-modern chair that looked like it was upholstered in lizard skin. "Do either of you want a cup of tea? Coffee?"

Andrew doubted the crammed replicator was capable of making anything. He and Honora shook their heads. He returned to his seat behind the desk. "Lily Stewart's kidnapping was the talk of Fleet for quite some time. Frankly, it still is. She and Mora are very close, and I understand that Lily is very happy here."

"Where is she?" Andrew asked.

"She lives on a Commons military station with the captain of the ship she was found on. She spent a few years in suspended animation as a museum display before a series of accidents woke her up. Scared the shit out of the poor ensign who found her." The admiral didn't elaborate further but rested his elbows on the desktop, tenting his fingertips. "So,

Honora, I want to hear your version of the events that led you to this suspension." He said the last word with contempt, like he couldn't believe someone like his niece had been tossed out on her ass for saving a life.

Andrew couldn't believe it, either.

Honora relayed their story, leaving out the parts where Andrew had been a jackass. Her voice rose in fury as she ended it with the events of the morning. She forgot herself and switched to Kurran temporarily until her uncle gave her a look. She went back to English or whatever she called it now, and Andrew could see her fighting for control of her temper. It was going to be a long time before she stopped being pissed off.

When she finished, the admiral leaned back in his chair and sighed noisily. "Stories like this remind me of why I enlisted in Fleet instead of the Kurran Forces," he said.

Honora glared at him.

"I didn't mean that in a derogatory way, Honora. Your father took the same path as you and was just as loyal, as was your mother. Neither Fleet nor the Forces are perfect, but you wouldn't have necessarily been suspended for something like this in Fleet. Your duty is to protect the innocent, and you did that. Andrew would have died if you left him there, and there was always the possibility that the Nym could return to tie up that loose end. That would have been a disaster."

Andrew and Honora nodded, thinking of the implications. At least Andrew was. He was still a little fuzzy on what had transpired in the last eight-hundred-odd years.

"Of course you're welcome to stay here as long as you want. This is your home," Admiral Kharn continued. "Both of you. I'll contact Fleet and see about having Andrew resettled on this side of the border."

"That what Kakos said," Honora pointed out gloomily.

"He's likelier to fit in with Commons culture," the admiral said gently.

"It's just—I found him. I don't want him to get hurt."

Andrew felt like a stray cat that had scratched at her door. "I'll be fine," he said, sounding surer than he felt.

"Eventually," the admiral agreed. "Even with the recent influx of Nym refugees in Commons and Fringes space, there are still—"

"What?" shrieked Honora. She leapt to her feet. "There are Nym refugees now?"

"You didn't know." The admiral's voice was flat.

"Of course I didn't. Whose bright idea was it to let them emigrate?" She began pacing the length of the office.

"It isn't how it looks. You've been gone for over a year," Admiral Kharn said, a note of warning in his voice. "A lot happens in that time. Six thousand Nym fled after a massive earthquake on their planet seven months ago. It was horrifying, Honora. We've never really known what's gone on there, and we're finding out now. People were starving; many were dying. They're not hell-bent on taking over Kurran or Commons space. They just want to live in peace."

"But they're *Nym*!" Honora yelped.

"They are, and most Nym aren't evil," the admiral said firmly. "The Commons government and Fleet are working to relocate refugees. There's a large population on Rubidge Station—Mora is posted there now—and Repub-4. They're stranded and traumatized, and they're not a threat."

Honora looked like she was ready to launch into a tirade or at least shoot something, but Admiral Kharn spoke again before she could. "Go get settled in," he urged. "Both of you. You're welcome to stay here as long as you like, but Andrew, if you want help with your new life here, I'm always available. Fleet won't toss you out of their space, I promise." He offered a sincere smile.

"Can I go back home?" Andrew countered.

The admiral's smile faded. "No. I'm sorry, but that's not possible."

Andrew immediately felt like a jerk. "Thank you, anyway."

Honora muttered her own shell-shocked thank you, and they left Admiral Kharn's study. Andrew could feel her seething as they set through navigating the complicated layout of the house, and with it, his own sense of indignation. She really was overreacting. "Are you okay?" he finally dared to ask.

"What do you think?"

His irritation multiplied. "You really want to know?"

She stopped in the middle of the hallway. Its walls and ceiling were glass, and it connected a couple of the house's wings. "I do."

"I think you're being a brat." It was the kindest statement he could think of at the moment.

"Excuse the fuck out of me?" she demanded.

Maybe he could have used harsher language. "It sucks that you're out of a job at the moment, and for what it's worth, I don't think it's right," he said, fighting to keep his temper in check. "But you don't have to be all pissy and self-righteous because some people from another planet are dying and looking to start over somewhere else.

"And you know what else?" he continued, his voice rising a few decibels. "This sucks a lot more for me. At least you still *have* a home. So you're a secret agent. Good for fucking *you*. But that doesn't excuse you from an obligation to be a decent and compassionate human being." Andrew couldn't believe the words tumbling out of his mouth. Except for the F-bombs, his outpatient therapist would have been pleased.

Honora stared hard at him. Andrew stared right back. He wasn't afraid of her kicking his legs out from underneath him; by now he knew she wouldn't do that unless someone else made a move first.

"You don't know what the Nym do," she said frostily.

Andrew felt himself actually roll his eyes. "Yeah, I do. That's how we met. And the country I lived in allowed refugees from places with known terrorists, so I'm not completely ignorant." Honora's glare didn't waver. "You're not an entity unto yourself, you know. You have to get along with other people."

The chill hadn't thawed from her voice when she finally replied, "I'll take you back to your rooms."

CHAPTER 9

Honora felt like stomping around her apartment, maybe throwing something, but she didn't. She didn't have tantrums when she was in the wrong.

She loathed being wrong.

Andrew was right. She *was* being short-sighted and selfish. She had lost her job for the time being, but she still had somewhere to go. Unlike Andrew, who now probably hated her more than he already did.

She looked around the small apartment that was her home but not and sighed. She fought back an uncharacteristic wave of tears and forced herself to breathe deeply. Once she had her feelings under control, she slipped from her apartment to the kitchen.

Ana was filling in a grocery order on a datatab when she arrived. "Hi, love," the housekeeper said brightly. Catching the morose look in Honora's eyes and a few other details someone without empathic talents couldn't see, Ana offered her a sympathetic look. "Is everything okay?"

"No," Honora replied bluntly. She set about making some

tea and cut a big chunk of cherry cake from the pan resting on the counter, placing it on a plate. "I'm an idiot."

Ana set aside the datatab and looked at Honora expectantly.

"I said something stupid and insensitive to Andrew," Honora explained. "Well, a lot of insensitive things. Stuff I had no right saying." She was deliberately cagey around the housekeeper, knowing Ana would understand. She had been in the employ of a high-ranking military family for decades and knew when not to ask questions. Honora dug a tray out of a cabinet and set it with the cake, a teapot, and matching cups while she waited for the kettle to boil.

"And now you're making him a peace offering," Ana deduced.

"A pathetic one. I don't think cake and tea will make up for what I've said and done."

"It's not my place to say anything, but he's not the kind of friend you usually associate with, is he? There's something odd about his aura. Like he's from the Commons but isn't."

Honora's breath caught for a few seconds. "You're right," she said simply.

"I hope you're going to apologize with words, too."

"That's the plan." If he would even speak to her. The kettle started shrieking, and she poured boiling water into the pot.

"Will you be able to manage that tray? I could bring it up."

"No, thank you." Honora carefully picked it up and smiled at the housekeeper before leaving the kitchen.

She found herself at Andrew's closed door, almost as nervous as the moment she had let her ship get sucked into the vortex. Wedging the tray between her hand and the wall, she knocked.

He threw it open, anger still etched on his features. He

looked exhausted and stressed to boot, neither of which surprised her.

"Hi," she said tentatively.

"What do you want?"

Well, it was better than having the door slammed in her face. "I want to apologize," she said. "May I come in?"

He stepped back and held the door open. The tension didn't drain from his features as she set the tray on the coffee table. "I'm not good at this," she admitted. "But you're right about all of this, and I'm sorry." She sat on the couch without waiting for an invitation and poured tea for both them. He sat down heavily beside her and accepted a cup and fork.

Honora could have kicked herself for not bringing along a second piece of cake. She rarely indulged in desserts except when she was here.

"Apology accepted," he finally said, looking out the window. The rain had started up again, a light patter this time. "It's a shitty situation all around." He ate a few bites without commenting further.

He passed his fork to her. "Aren't you worried about germs?" Honora asked, remembering his meal on board her ship.

"No."

He was silent again for a few minutes, and Honora didn't know how to initiate more conversation. She had apologized and could leave, but she didn't want to.

It occurred to her that she had spent more time with Andrew, talked with him more, over these last days than she had with anyone in years. She was almost comfortable with him, but she supposed that was due to their strange circumstances rather than a genuine interest. Still, even with him pissed off at her, she found that she didn't dislike his company.

His voice jolted her out of her musing. "So, any great ideas as to how I should spend the rest of my life?"

No, but at least he wouldn't be alone in that regard if she truly lost her job. "Uncle Tarek said the Commons could help you. They did your friend."

Andrew shook his head. "I only spoke to her a couple of times. Once when I checked into the lab, and again when she came to see what all the screaming was about." He took the fork from her hand and cut off another bite from the cake. "It would just be nice to connect with someone from my own planet and time, you know?"

"Yes," Honora replied before thinking through her answer. "This place doesn't feel like my home."

"You came here when you were a kid, didn't you?"

"I was raised in the Empire," she corrected him. "Even though my father was half Commons. As far as I know, my mother was wholly Kurran. I'm too Commons for the Empire and too Kurran for the Commons."

She had never admitted that to anyone, even though it was obvious to her and her fellow agents. It was the reason she would never rise above lieutenant in Ops; they preferred their own. She had shaken off the subtle jabs at her background when she was seeing Dr. Ralla, but they still rankled her. The Empire might be allied with the Commons, but Kurrans would never see their neighbors as true equals.

"Uncle Tarek is my father's half-brother," she continued. "His family is fully assimilated. Except for him, they can hardly speak the language."

"You're not very close to this side of the family," he stated flatly.

"No." To deflect any other questions about them, she asked, "What about yours? Do you miss your parents?"

He looked out the window for a moment. "My mother, sort of, although we weren't all that close to begin with, especially after my parents divorced and she moved away. I told you

I wasn't close with my father, either. I guess I miss what could have been rather than them personally."

"Yes." Honora felt the same. She still missed them, twenty years after their deaths.

"It's really fucked up that I miss my business more than my family," Andrew admitted.

"It is, But I get that, too. My career is my life."

He nodded and handed her the fork. She finished off the cherry cake before he spoke again. "Are you sure there's no way for me to go back home?"

The heart Honora hadn't known she possessed until recently cracked again. For the second time that day, she had to fight back tears, ones that didn't spring from selfish shame. Over the lump in her throat, she forced herself to reply.

"No, there isn't a way."

———

HONORA WOKE up Andrew the following morning. He scrambled out of bed when he heard her knock, throwing on a robe he had found in the bedroom closet.

She was holding fresh clothes in her hands. "Do you want to go out today?" she asked. "It's short walk to the dome, and I thought you could use some things."

"Don't you have replicators and hover-bikes here?" he asked.

"We don't have hard-goods replicators in the house, and I don't know what a hover-bike is."

"Yet another Disney lie. Do you want some coffee?" His fingers were poised over the replicator's screen. He was getting good at this.

Honora made a face. "I'd prefer it fresh. There's some in the kitchen."

Andrew generated a cup for himself anyway, and unfolded

the clothes she had brought. Plain gray pants and a long-sleeved black shirt that looked about the right size. "It's some of my cousin Zak's stuff," she explained.

Andrew took notice of Honora's outfit. It was the first time he hadn't seen her in a uniform: a round-necked black tunic over slim-fitting black pants, tucked into matching boots that looked like soft leather. Her hair was spiky in places, like she had run her fingers through the strands and left it as is. No makeup. Once again, Andrew was struck by how lovely she was, and how she didn't seem to notice.

"Uncle Tarek wants to speak to us before we go," she added. "We've both caused an intergalactic incident."

"Well, yeah, I thought that was a given." Even during his short time here, he could tell that her behavior and his presence were ruffling a lot of feathers.

"The Empire and the Commons are pissed off because they didn't tell each other that they knew about the vortex," she continued. "I think the Commons actually believes they could have gone through to stop the Nym. And before you ask, they couldn't."

"Is there going to be a war?"

Honora shook her head. "Doubtful. There's a lot of intolerance between us, but no one has ever opened fire in the six hundred years we've been allies. Maybe because the Commons knows the Empire could slaughter them. The Commons has a bigger military, but the Empire has better technology."

Andrew, unfamiliar with the mechanics of war from his own time, had to take her word for it.

When she left, Andrew took a quick shower and dressed. Honora returned to collect him, and they took another labyrinthine route to the kitchen. "Tell me again why this place wasn't renovated in a way that makes sense," he grumbled.

"I didn't have any say about that. My home with my parents in the Empire was a lot smaller."

The kitchen turned out to be a big room that resembled its namesake back at home, full of space-age appliances. Ana sat at a table, a tablet computer and stylus in her hands. The heady smell of coffee was pungent in the air. "Good morning, children," she greeted them. "The grocer was by this morning, and there's fruit in the cooler and muffins in the pantry."

Cooler? Andrew glanced at the industrial-sized refrigerator built into a wall. *Right.* Honora swung open the door and started picking through its contents. Andrew didn't want to stand there like an idiot, and he was pretty sure Honora would make a big deal if he insinuated she should make him breakfast, so he opened the pantry.

Their meal finished, they collected second cups of the incredible coffee Ana had made and began the long trek to Admiral Kharn's office. This time, Andrew noted landmarks and counted the turns he and Honora made.

It turned out that the admiral had received an information packet from Fleet during the night. He obviously hadn't slept much since Andrew's arrival, but he seemed none the worse for wear. "I have good news and bad news," the admiral informed them.

"What the hell," Andrew said. "Let's hear the bad news first."

Admiral Kharn's face split into a grin at that. He quickly wiped it away. "Excuse me, Andrew, I don't mean to be rude. All right, your bad news is that Fleet isn't going to be offering you as many concessions as they did to our last time traveler, and she received those because she came to on one of our patrol ships. The bad news, part two, is that the Empire wants nothing to do with you. The Commons and the Empire are determined to get into a pissing match over this."

Honora snorted.

"And the good news?" Andrew ventured.

Admiral Kharn shrugged. "Well, you're a free man."

Freedom was something Andrew had taken for granted when he was still home. Now, the words sent a chill running down his spine.

"I think you should stay on Sennethaca for now," Admiral Kharn said. "From what I know of Earth, it won't be as big of a culture shock to you. It's ethnically diverse, it's peaceful, and there isn't the reliance on technology here that there is in the space lanes and on the stations."

Andrew nodded, his panic ebbing slightly. "I'll take your word for it."

"What about the Nym?" Honora interjected.

The admiral's expression hardened. "As I told you yesterday, the Nym are being handled."

"But what about the ones who developed the time travel technology?"

Admiral Kharn sighed angrily and rubbed his eyes. "Honora—"

"I went back to twenty-first century Earth," Honora snapped. "I have the right to know."

"And I'm telling you everything I do." At Honora's frosty glare, he held up his hands in defeat. "We haven't accounted for every single Nym known to us. But there's still a very high chance their rulers are dead."

Honora's hands curled around her coffee cup until Andrew was sure it would crack. "So they're still a problem," she spat.

"No one's *in* the Nym system anymore," Admiral Kharn tried to reassure her. "It's a dead planet, a dead system. Right now, Andrew is the bigger issue here."

"Just a minute," Andrew interrupted. "If there could be rogue, insane Nym scientists running around, isn't anyone worried about one of them looking for me?"

Honora shot him a withering look, but the admiral answered him. "No. We doubt they know you're here."

"What if they checked things a little further into the future and found out for sure?"

"Based on Lily Stewart's testimony after she was taken aboard their ship, they don't really care," Admiral Kharn said. "We thwarted their attempt to go back in time and alter the past to prevent the alliance between the Commons and the Empire."

Andrew vaguely remembered hearing about that back in the Empire, but didn't know all of the details.

"What?" Honora said.

"Didn't you ever wonder why the Nym went back in time?"

"I don't question my orders, Uncle Tarek."

"An admirable quality in a soldier, but didn't you ever *think* about it?" Admiral Kharn pressed. "They originally planned to go to 2217, when the Kurrans and the Commons made contact and established their alliance. They miscalculated and ended up stranded in 2017, and the operatives who were sent there took over a cryonics laboratory. Our theory is that another group of Earthers legitimately set up the lab and the Nym took it over. It isn't as though they could have set up a business and not stood out. We have no way of knowing for sure." He stood up. "I need some rest." Honora looked like she was ready to argue some more, but didn't.

The admiral changed the subject. "What do you two have planned for today?"

"Buying a few things," Andrew replied.

"The Commons can help you with job training," the admiral began, but Andrew shook his head.

"No offense to the Commons, but I don't want to sort medication for a living," Andrew said firmly. He didn't think he would be tempted to help himself to any of the pills or patches or whatever was now dispensed, but he didn't think he would ever find himself vaulted 851 years into the future, either. Tempting fate wasn't a good idea.

The admiral looked dubious, but he shrugged. "You're right," he conceded. "It's your future."

———

ANDREW HAD INSISTED he at least try to find work, and after a few hours of trekking through the township around the Kharn estate, he hadn't found a single lead. He could sense Honora's frustration but didn't comment on it.

He wasn't really surprised; he doubted he would have hired someone so obviously out of his element, either. He knew the picture he presented to the café owners, factory managers, and shopkeepers he had spoken to: that of someone who looked a little too fascinated at the gravity-defying manufacturing equipment and replicators spitting out glittering drinks. It had been worth a shot, he told himself; it wasn't as if he had much else to occupy his time.

Honora took him on the promised trip to the domed part of the planet, using a mode of transport that reminded him of the subway back at home. While the organic side of the planet was an odd hybrid of idyllic nature and equipment straight out of an episode of *Star Trek*, the manmade part was bustling with people, crowded with low-rise buildings and open markets. The overcast sky was made darker by the dome, and the area was illuminated with artificial light that mimicked natural sunlight.

"I think I'd rather live here," Andrew said, trying not to stare. "Why don't you?"

"I'm not here often enough to justify renting an apartment," Honora explained.

"Maybe I could find a job here."

Honora didn't reply, but the look on her face told him it was a dim prospect. He sighed.

The train halted every five minutes or so, and Andrew didn't notice any markers at the stops, nor were any announcements made. He followed Honora out at one stop and the train zipped away. "Where to now?"

"This way." She pointed to a street off the main strip, between a pair of buildings. It was so narrow it was almost an alley, forcing them to walk shoulder-to-shoulder. Andrew let his fingertips brush over a building's exterior. The "brick" felt like some kind of heavy-duty plastic.

The alley ended in a square surrounding a small fountain. He blinked at the strange water flowing from it and peered a little closer. No, it wasn't water. Beams of colored lights flowed from the abstract stone structure in a subtle rainbow of hues. "Just a second," Andrew said and walked over to investigate.

The lights pooled into a large basin that reflected his image back at him, mimicking the gentle splash of real water. He dragged his hand through the image, watching in fascination as the light rippled. He half expected his hand to come away wet. It didn't.

Honora's face appeared in the splashing light. "Are you all right?" she asked.

He kept his eyes on her reflection. "We've already established that I'm not. I'm just looking at something I've never seen before."

"Sorry," she said in a small voice.

He looked up and sighed. "Lead the way."

———

Honora brought Andrew to a shop favored by her cousin Zak, a place where she could afford to outfit Andrew on her salary. Some of the merchandise was ready-made, and there were a couple of hard-goods replicators available. She quietly explained to him how everything worked, and he stared at her.

"So I can get whatever I want, custom-made?" he asked.

"Well, I'm not buying you a wedding ensemble," she explained. "Just enough to convince an employer to hire you."

"And keep me from breaking public nudity laws?"

Honora felt herself blush at that comment and distracted herself with a rack of long-sleeved shirts. She picked out a couple in darker colors and draped them over her arm. Andrew was flipping through a catalogue and trying to look bored at the holograms therein. She forced herself not to smile. It was sort of endearing.

"You know that suit I was wearing when the... incident happened?" he asked nonchalantly, mindful of the other customers.

"Yes."

"I think I found a replacement." He paused the catalogue's images, and Honora looked at it. It was a reasonable match for his destroyed clothes. The cut looked a little better, to her unpracticed eye at least, and the fabric would be better quality, but it was the same shade of deep gray, nearly black. She tried not to gasp at the price. The money wasn't as much of an issue as the indulgence. The clothes she owned that weren't uniforms were practical and generic. Fashion had never been an interest of hers, much to the dismay of her cousin Mora.

He caught her look. "That's not in the budget," he surmised.

"Yes, it is," she protested quickly. "If you want it, you can have it." *That's what savings are for.*

He looked at her sharply for another moment, and Honora forced herself to look neutral. She wouldn't argue with him about this. It was obviously something he had liked from his old life. She waved to a passing sales clerk with a data-corder in his hand. "My friend is interested in the suit," she said before Andrew could protest. "With a matching shirt. And some serviceable clothes for every day."

Andrew didn't take his eyes off her. She held out the clothes draped over her am. "Ready-mades," she said uselessly.

He accepted them and didn't appear to notice the clerk discreetly taking his measurements with the datacorder a few inches from him. In a few minutes, his clothes would generate in one of the hard-goods replicators.

"Honora," Andrew began warily.

She cut him off. "When you find work, you can take me out to dinner." The words came out in a rush.

She hadn't been out to dinner with a man in—how long? At least three or four years. But Andrew wouldn't count, would he?

He did, she had to admit.

He tilted his head, the ghost of a smile on his lips. "Okay," he said. "It's a date."

CHAPTER 10

They returned to the Kharn estate a few hours later, packages in their hands. Andrew had let Honora buy him a datatab, and he had seemed surprised to find decks of cards available. "You like those more than the datatab," she remarked. "I thought you would look forward to playing with technology."

He shrugged. "These are familiar, even with the extra suit. Do you know any games?"

"A couple from my training days in Ops. I'm not very good."

Her datatab's light was blinking green when she returned to her apartment, signaling a transmit. She paused when she saw the message was from her commanding officer. Her fingers hovered over the "Accept" icon. Unease churned in her gut. She hadn't been suspended for more than a day; surely a decision regarding her future with Special Ops couldn't have been made so quickly.

Was her suspension lifted? Honora knew she was one of the best fighter pilots Ops had. They needed her.

She hoped they did, anyway.

She finally tapped the icon. The written message was brief: a summons back to Kurran Prime for a debriefing the following morning at 0700 hours. The message specified that she was not yet welcome at the base permanently. Honora gritted her teeth thinking of the long round trip ahead, which she would have to start tonight. Which meant she would have to go to sleep shortly, because she had to be alert when she faced Commander Kakos.

She rummaged around her duffel and swallowed a light sedative she found tucked in a pocket. She had an hour or so before it kicked in, and she debated what to tell her family. She could slip away tonight and come back tomorrow afternoon and no one would be the wiser, thereby avoiding questions and lying about sending updates detailing the situation.

Except there was Andrew to consider. He would notice her absence. Hell, he would probably come looking for her in the next couple of hours when he got bored.

Andrew wasn't her family, and everything that had happened the last few days had been her fault. She had to tell him before she fell asleep.

He opened the door at her knock. "You didn't bring cherry cake," he admonished her.

"No." She stepped into his apartment without waiting for an invitation. "I received a summons back to Ops. I have to be there at 0700 hours tomorrow morning."

"Well, they certainly change their minds quickly, don't they?"

"Ordinarily, no." She shifted on her feet. "I'm leaving tonight."

"Do I have to go?"

She shook her head. "They would have mentioned it."

"Can I go? You know, for moral support and all?"

"I can manage on my own." She didn't meet his eyes.

"I know you can," he replied.

He just wants to help you, Honora reminded herself. *He's trying to be your friend.*

That thought discomfited her more than the transmit. She wasn't used to others outside of her family trying to get close to her. She discouraged it.

Or maybe Andrew didn't really care at all and just wanted to take another shuttle trip. He *had* been asking about when he could learn to fly.

"I'll stay in your shuttle," he promised. "No one will even know I'm there. I just don't want to sit around and do nothing."

"You would be doing that in my shuttle," she pointed out.

"But it wouldn't be here. I have that computer and a pack of cards. I'll find a way to amuse myself."

"All right, you can come with me. But you stay put when I tell you to, you stay on the shuttle, and you don't tell *anyone* about this summons. Not my uncle, not Ana. We're leaving at 0200 hours tomorrow morning."

"Damn, that's early. Or late, depending on how you look at it. I was always a night owl."

"Do you want a sedative? I took one, so I'll be going to bed shortly."

Andrew considered the offer for a second before shaking his head. "No, thank you. I don't take anything stronger than Tylenol these days."

"What's a Tylenol?"

"A mild painkiller that doesn't exist anymore. No, I'm not sure if I should be messing around with tranquilizers. I'll be fine tonight."

Honora shrugged. "That's your choice. You can sleep on the shuttle ride, if you want."

"Or *you* could sleep and I could drive."

A sharp retort was on the tip of her tongue, but Honora

squelched it. He was teasing; it was something friends did. "A tempting suggestion. Maybe another time."

"I'm holding you to that. I really want to learn to fly one of those things."

"You will." She didn't add that if the summons went badly, she might very well have all the time in the world to teach him.

———

ANDREW TRIED TO SLEEP. He undressed, then fiddled with the controls mounted on the wall next to the window, feeling a little proud of himself for looking for them before drawing the curtains. The glass darkened until the room was shrouded in darkness, but it didn't help. Maybe he should have taken that sleeping pill after all.

That's all it was, he was sure of it. If Honora took something, it couldn't be bad. She was a soldier. He had been around her long enough, spoken to her enough, to know that the strongest thing she took was coffee.

He nixed asking the housekeeper or Honora's uncle about sleeping pills or simply staying awake until Honora came to collect him. He dressed again and tiptoed to her apartment across the hall and tapped at the door. When he didn't get a response, he called her name and knocked louder.

Damn it. He let himself in and prayed she would forgive him. He also prayed that bathroom conventions hadn't changed and he would find sleeping pills in the medicine cabinet.

The tiny bathroom was off the bedroom, and he padded along the carpet as silently as he could. The suite was dark as night, and he could barely make out Honora's sleeping form in the bed in the middle of the room. *Damn again*—he should have looked for a flashlight before coming here.

His hand groped along the wall for a light switch, and he belatedly realized that maybe this room had a voice-activated model. Before he could investigate further, a laser split the air and Andrew smelled something burning.

"Shit!" he yelled. Instinctively, he dropped to the floor.

"Lights!" Honora barked. The bedroom ceiling panels slowly illuminated, and Andrew saw that she was sitting up in bed, a gun in her hand and a furious look on her face. Andrew, still crouched on the floor, held up his hands and fell over sideways.

He chanced a look at the place where she had fired. A black smear had been seared into the wall. "Are you insane?" she yelled. She lowered her weapon.

"No, but *you* clearly are. What the fuck?" He stood up and rubbed his side, where his ribs ached in protest.

"You don't go sneaking into a soldier's room at night and not expect to get shot at."

"This isn't nighttime, and I've never sneaked—" He caught her disbelieving glare. "I was invited when I did."

"Don't change the subject."

"All right then. Only an insane person sleeps with a gun!"

She laid the weapon across the bedspread and crossed her arms. "It's a habit. And it was set to stun. You wouldn't have been seriously hurt."

"You sleep in a fortified estate where you don't even bother to lock the door!"

Honora ignored his attempt to reason with her. "Why are you here?" she asked.

"I was looking for one of your pills," he admitted. "I can't sleep."

"Oh." She threw off the covers and got out of bed, revealing her oversized T-shirt and pants, both black. She dug around her duffel in the corner of the room and pulled out a small bag. "Pill or transderm?"

Andrew held out his hands. "I went to rehab for a reason. You tell me."

Honora closed her eyes for a few seconds. When she opened them, her voice was measured and controlled. "Transderm," she chose for him. She removed a small plastic rectangle with a depressor on one side. "Hold still," she ordered and held it against his neck. Andrew caught a whiff of the soap she used—something citrus and feminine—and tried not to notice it.

A small whoosh of air when she activated the thing made the hair on the back of his neck stand up. Honora tossed the device back in the medical bag.

"What the hell was that?"

"A sedative. Andrew, I have a meeting with my commanding officers tomorrow morning. Will you *please* let me sleep?"

A warm, heavy sensation was already spreading through Andrew's body, beginning from his chest and radiating to his limbs. His eyelids drooped, and he sat down on the edge of Honora's bed. It looked inviting, and the side she had been sleeping on was warmer than what awaited him in his apartment.

"What are you doing?" she asked, urgency in her voice.

He leaned back on the pillows and pulled up the blankets. "Taking a nap."

Honora shook his arm. "No, Andrew. You're not sleeping here."

"Why not?"

"Because this is my bed! Get out!"

"I don't think I *can* get out," he replied sleepily. "What was in that thing you gave me?"

"It's just a sedative!"

"What's it supposed to sedate, an elephant?" He forced his eyes open and saw Honora glaring down at him.

"You could at least give me my side back," she seethed.

Andrew heaved a dramatic sigh. "Fine." He forced himself to roll over to the other side of the bed, his heavy limbs protesting. *When was the last time I was this tired?* He felt like he was fighting off a coma. He stripped off his shirt and tossed it to the floor.

"What are you doing?" Honora asked, an obvious strain to her voice.

"Relax, I'm not taking anything else off." He tried to throw off the covers but failed, only exposing the waistband of his pants. "See, I'm still wearing clothes."

"Make sure it stays that way." She ordered the lights off, and he felt the bed sag as she climbed in. There was a rustle of fabric as she rearranged the sheets and blankets around her.

"Honora?" Andrew ventured.

"Good night, Andrew."

"If that's your side of the bed, whose side am I sleeping on?" He didn't know why he was asking, just that it was important he know the answer before lost his fight against slumber.

"Oh, gods. I think I have another sedative in my bag."

"No, no, that won't be necessary. Just tell me whose side I'm sleeping on." He tensed, waiting for the answer.

She exhaled loudly. "Will you stop talking and let me sleep if I tell you?"

"Yeah." He didn't know why he wanted to know; he just did.

"No one's. I always sleep alone, and I happen to prefer the right side of the bed."

Andrew felt a grin stretch across his face at this news, though God only knew why. "Good night, Honora."

———

HONORA WOKE before her alarm could go off. The pleasant heat of a human body next to her reminded her of something she must have dreamed about but had already forgotten, save that it oddly starred Andrew and left her cheeks flaming. She twisted around and made out his outline in the darkness, still sleeping. She groped along the wall next to the bed for the lights' manual override and turned on the illumination to its lowest setting before gently slipping out.

She paused to take in the man still sleeping in her bed. He was on his side, perilously close to her half of the mattress, an arm carelessly flung across the pillows. The sheets pooled around his waist, revealing his shirtless torso, and Honora couldn't help but stare. Despite his lack of military training, he was in decent shape, his shoulders nicely defined.

Honora couldn't remember the last time she had shared a bed with someone. Certainly longer than the last few years she had steered clear of romantic attachments. That awkward feeling she had upon awakening rose again.

Andrew's eyes opened, and he caught Honora looking. She quickly turned away and headed to the bathroom. "Good morning," she called.

"If that's what you want to call it."

She heard the smile in his voice and felt herself flush. "Pack up your things and come back here when you're finished."

Andrew was gone when she emerged from the bathroom, showered and dressed in her black Ops uniform. She packed her duffel and debated whether or not to leave a note for Ana, deciding against it. If she was being reinstituted in Special Ops, she could send a transmit from the base instead of having to go through long goodbyes and an awkward dinner with Uncle Tarek and Ana. She could help Andrew find an apartment, maybe with her cousin Mora's help. According to the admiral, Mora was currently posted to Rubidge Station, a major commercial and military hub, and more than that, she knew Andrew's friend from Earth. If she wasn't being reinstated—her stomach turned over at the idea—she could return to the family estate and no one would be wiser.

Until she told them of her discharge, if it came to that. That would require an escape plan, probably into the Commons, maybe even Mora's station, where she would have to re-establish herself.

She prepared some coffee in the replicator, sealing it into a pair of capped mugs for the trip ahead. He let himself into her apartment, his hair still damp from a shower and a bag of his own slung over his shoulder, wearing some of the new things she had bought for him yesterday. Not his suit, she noticed with a touch of dismay. She would have liked to see him as the businessman he had been in his old life.

If she was facing discharge, what would she do with Andrew?

She pushed aside that thought. She was *not* being discharged today, and she was going to help him settle wherever he wanted. Maybe on one of the border stations or planets, where it would be easier for them to visit. When he wasn't being difficult or questioning everything she said, she liked being with him.

She held out a coffee mug to Andrew. He accepted it. "You snore," he said.

That was the last thing Honora expected to be greeted with. "I beg your pardon?"

"You snore. Not loudly, but you do."

She let that comment slide, and they left the apartment. Andrew wisely kept quiet as they made their way to the underground shuttle bay. The estate wasn't completely dark, but it was silent, and Honora wanted to keep it that way.

She finally replied when they had boarded the shuttle. "I don't snore."

"I thought it was cute." Andrew stood beside the pilot's

chair as she went through a pre-flight safety check. He caught her look and stepped back a few feet. "I'm not complaining."

"Sit down."

He obediently took a seat on the floor and from a pocket removed the cards he had picked up the day before. "Any chance of stopping by a drive-through on the way?"

Safety check completed, Honora activated the controls for the shuttle bay doors. She didn't bother to ask what a drive-through was. "We're going straight to Kurran Prime."

"I thought so, but it doesn't hurt to ask."

A few moments later, they were airborne, the planet's surface shrinking beneath them. She heard something thunk and Andrew curse when they broke through the atmosphere. She took a quick peek over her shoulder. He was cradling the back of his head and wincing. "I'm okay," he assured her.

She keyed in the course for the Commons-Empire border and swiveled her chair around to face him. "How are you feeling?" she asked. "Any effects from the sedative?"

"No, I was just exhausted last night. Uh, yesterday afternoon. I felt like I had been up for days all of a sudden. It was weird."

"It's not going to affect your drug recovery, is it?" The Ops-approved sedatives were designed to be non-addictive.

"No, it was just really odd." He had the decency to color. "I'm sorry if I embarrassed you last night."

"There's not a lot you can do to embarrass me, Andrew. It isn't as though you..." She trailed off. He hadn't made a pass at her.

She wouldn't have minded if he had.

"You didn't act inappropriately," she finished and turned her chair back to face the viewport. At this time of night, traffic in this area was sparse, and she could rely on the craft's autopilot if she wanted to.

"I was an ass," he insisted. "I should have gone back to my own room."

"It's all right." She should have thought things through before shooting him up with that particular sedative. "It was a heavy dose," she admitted. She couldn't bring herself to say that she liked sleeping with him. For the first time in years, she felt a pang of regret at her celibacy.

Her mind flashed back to waking up, how the sight of him sleeping next to her felt natural.

All you did was sleep, she reminded herself. If she was feeling... amorous—which she wasn't, because she was on her way to a career-defining meeting with her superior officers—it was simply because she hadn't had any kind of contact with another person in years. Waking up next to someone had stirred something long dormant within her. It couldn't possibly be Andrew himself. If she had spent the night with Mal Ralla, she would probably feel the same.

She squeezed her eyes shut and conjured up an image of Mal. Tall Mal with his dark bedroom eyes, who spent his waking moments in the gym or patronizing high-end dining establishments when he wasn't expertly laser-stitching soldiers back together. Who had saved countless lives on his operating table. Mal, who was an Ops hero.

Mal, who had treated their relationship like a business partnership, keeping their conversations strictly focused on work and everything wrong with the Commons. Who had viewed her mixed heritage and complete lack of empathic skills as a defect. Who never passed up the opportunity to make a subtle jab at her education, or lack thereof.

Mal, who hogged all the blankets.

No, she didn't miss him.

Instead, she wondered what it would be like if Andrew kissed her. Among other things.

"Honora?" The object of her thoughts was trying to get

her attention. She opened her eyes. Andrew was again holding on to the back of her seat. When she looked up at his face, she saw concern written there, the cockpit's stark illumination highlighting the healing scars on his face.

"Yes?" she said breathlessly.

"Is something wrong? I thought you fell asleep there for a second."

She couldn't meet his gaze. "Nothing that you don't know about," she lied. *I really wouldn't mind breaking this celibacy thing with you, that's all, which would make our situation much more awkward.*

He raised an eyebrow at her. "Are you sure you're okay to drive? Does this thing have a replicator? You look like you need coffee."

She shook her head. "I'm just thinking."

CHAPTER 11

Andrew was unusually quiet for most of the flight to the Empire, sitting on the floor and whiling away his time playing card games. There were parts of the journey where she could have let the autopilot navigate the shuttle's course and taught him to play Stars and Kings, but she wouldn't have been able to concentrate.

Her anxiety only increased when she found that she couldn't access Kurran Prime's shuttle bay using her access codes. "*Sikiaka*," she swore quietly. "I can't get in," she explained. She sent a message broadcasting her ID to the dock, requesting clearance to land. "I've been locked out."

Understanding dawned on Andrew's face. "Oh."

The airlock finally yawed open, and Honora landed her shuttle in a spot reserved for guests. She remained fixed to her seat even after the airlock's safety lights switched to green, staring at the accessway beyond. A lump formed in her throat.

When she was able to speak, her voice was calm and steady. "This is it for me," she announced. She sensed Andrew standing behind her but stared straight ahead, knowing that if she looked at him, she might actually break down and cry. She didn't know which would be worse: Andrew seeing that, or her commanding officers.

Her composure regained, she rose from the pilot's seat and faced Andrew squarely. "I don't know how long I'll be," she said.

"It might not be as bad as you think," he countered, but his argument sounded hollow. He didn't believe that, either.

"I was locked out of the base, Andrew. That's not a good sign." She bit her lip and looked at her duffel stowed in the back of the shuttle, knowing she wouldn't be unpacking it at Stappic Station. "I'm just a civilian now."

He didn't argue. "I could go with you," he offered.

"No." She activated the shuttle's ramp, but before she could descend it, Andrew grabbed her arm. She whirled around, heart in her throat.

"Good luck," he said quietly.

She saw the fear in his hazel eyes, for both of them, and nodded. "Thank you."

Her certainty of what was going to happen only increased as she strode the base's corridors accompanied by an ensign who had to authorize her admittance into restricted areas. Places where, until a few short days ago, she had the right to be. A wave of panic crested over her and she tamped it down, calling on her training to focus on her—what? Upcoming mission? There wouldn't be any more missions for her. She wouldn't even be able to show her face in the Empire because of the shame.

When was the last time a Special Ops agent had been dishonorably discharged? Honora knew of only one case, occurring at least twenty years prior. That one had been assigned to the reigning empress's protection and was discovered to be selling information about her to the Nym. Or who he *thought* was the Nym; Ops had quickly caught on to that and trapped him. In deference to the Commons, necessary allies who didn't support the death penalty, he had been exiled to the Fringes, never to be heard from again.

Now, Honora was about to face a similar fate. Her only consolation was that she probably wouldn't have to find sanctuary in the Fringes, although life in the Commonwealth didn't hold much more appeal.

She was admitted to the briefing room, facing Commander Kakos, who was flanked on either side by a pair of security flunkies. They kept their eyes away from her, focusing on the doorway. *This is a bit much*, Honora thought. *I'm not going to attack my commanding officer.* Former *commanding officer.* She offered a salute; she still respected the man.

"Lieutenant Kharn," he greeted her in Kurran. Honora blinked. She had hardly spoken the language at all since she returned from her mission to Earth.

"Sir," she replied in kind.

"You know why you're here."

"I think so, sir."

"This was not my decision," he began. "You know I have the utmost respect for you as a pilot, soldier, and agent."

She briefly closed her eyes when her vision swam, and Kakos paused. When she opened them, he continued.

"I chose you from the soldiers' ranks to join Special Ops, and I still believe I made the right decision in doing so. You have consistently demonstrated an ability to independently analyze situations and make decisions based on your training while under pressure.

"What happened when you traveled back in time was unprecedented," Kakos continued. "You did what you felt was best. As I'm sure you're aware, the Empire doesn't agree with your decision."

She nodded.

"It's with a tremendous amount of regret that I have to

inform that your discharge from Special Ops is effective imme-diately," he finished. "I argued for an honorable discharge. I lost on that count, too."

Honora thought her legs might give out from under her, but she remained steady. She was expecting this; it was almost a relief to know the final outcome, but it left her feeling like she had been sucker-punched. She shakily exhaled. "I understand."

She didn't. She wanted to march into the Emperor's palace and shake her leader, demand to know what right he had to expel a soldier who had saved the life of someone the Empire didn't think was worthy.

Kakos cleared his throat nervously and averted her eyes. "Your weapon, Kharn," he said, embarrassment tingeing his voice.

Honora removed the Ops-issue laser pistol from the holster at her hip and laid it on the table, feeling like she was leaving a body part there instead. One of the security guards immediately scooped it up away from her.

The commander ordered the security guards to leave. They turned surprised eyes to him. "I know her," he insisted. "She is not a traitor, and I need to speak with her privately. Go."

They obeyed. "We'll be outside the door," one promised.

As soon as they left, Kakos gestured to the table separating them. "Sit," he commanded. As if remembering he couldn't issue orders to her anymore, he softened. "Please."

Honora took a seat across from him. "I assume I'm being exiled from the Empire."

He shook his head. "Not officially. You haven't betrayed us. I would still recommend leaving and resettling in the Commons, however. You have a better chance at restarting your life there."

"I don't know what I'm going to do," she admitted. "You

know my uncle is an admiral in their Fleet, and I could enlist, but I don't want to."

Kakos's reply was blunt. "You're likelier to be accepted among your peers there than here."

Honora knew this, loathe as she was to admit it. Fleet would take just about anyone.

"I find Fleet disorganized and unprofessional," she said, harsher than was necessary.

"You're comparing it to the Empire. The Commons is much larger and is responsible for a lot more than we are. More mistakes are bound to happen in forces of that size. You would be an asset to them."

But she would no longer be independent, at least not for a long time, as she would have to rise through Fleet's ranks. She would be trapped at some patrol ship's navigation panel, not even authorized to apprehend small-time smugglers.

"There is another unit you could join," Kakos said. "One independent of Fleet. It's still in development."

Was Fleet joining the 29th century, establishing its own version of Ops? "Go on," she said carefully.

"I was considering recommending you to this unit before you were sent to Earth. As someone with roots in the Empire and Commonwealth, you would have been an ideal candidate. The Commons is looking to build an agency separate from Fleet to handle law enforcement and free up Fleet to handle larger, more serious issues. Events over the last year revealed corruption in Fleet, and the Commons's government wants a distinct legal entity established, particularly since there's been that spike of Nym refugees."

Honora's heart pounded. "You were going to send me to the Commons?"

"We wouldn't have sent you. We would have *asked* you," Kakos answered sharply. "The Commons Authority was looking for recruits outside of Fleet."

"And they still want me to do this?" she asked.

"You would have to apply," Kakos explained. "And I would be honored to give you a recommendation. You're one of the best agents I've ever worked with, Kharn, but a fighter pilot can only climb so high in Ops. You'll have more opportunity with the Authority, should you decide to join. Opportunities to train others, command a squad. You know you couldn't do that here."

Honora did, but she had never wanted to be a leader. She wanted her fighter craft. She wanted to blow things up.

"May I think about it?" she asked.

"Yes, of course. You're free to get in touch with me if you have any other questions." He drummed his fingertips on the tabletop in a nervous gesture Honora had never seen before. "You're staying with your family on Sennethaca?"

"No," she said, an air of finality in her voice. "But you have my personal transmit address, and I usually carry my datatab with me."

Kakos hesitated before asking his next question. "The man you rescued is still in your care?"

"I'm going to help him resettle. We're going to Rubidge Station. My cousin is a Fleet nurse posted there."

"And she knows the other victim kidnapped by the Nym. We've been in touch with Fleet over this issue. Good choice, Kharn."

Well, she still had to see what Andrew would say about that. "He'll put up an argument. He always does. But I think that's the best place for him to start over."

"You've spent some time with him, then? How is he doing?"

"We talk a lot," Honora said abruptly. "Sort of. I don't think he's given up hope that he can go home, but he's willing to cooperate with me. I think Rubidge will have the most opportunities for him to regain his independence. He's very social. He was an entrepreneur on Earth. I think he's going a little crazy with only me for company."

Kakos offered her the barest of smiles. "I didn't want him to be abandoned," he confided. "You're doing the right thing. I am—*was*—your commanding officer, but I still have to answer to a lot of people above me. Do you understand that?"

She nodded.

He stood up, and she followed suit. "It's no longer my place to say this, but I want you to give serious consideration to joining the Commons Authority," he said. "Dismissed, Kharn."

———

ANDREW HAD PARKED himself in the shuttle's driver's seat and again dealt his playing cards and wished for something to listen to, or hell, even a book to read. As it was, he figured out a way to play solitaire with an extra suit. Neat rows of cards were lined up along the control console, their sparkly graphics of stars, regal profiles, and ornate jewels shimmering in the cockpit's light.

When the shuttle door hissed open, he was startled enough that he knocked over the cards. Honora would kill him if he did anything to damage her shuttle. He had felt the same way about his car, and *that* had been a Honda Accord.

He swept the remaining cards off the controls and scrabbled to the floor to gather them. The door closed and he looked up to see Honora staring down at him.

"I didn't touch anything," Andrew said quickly. "I swear. Nothing started flashing or caught on fire."

Honora bent down and helped him pick up his cards. "That's okay." Lines of tension bracketed her mouth and the corners of her eyes.

"How did it go?" Andrew asked cautiously.

"As I expected. I've been discharged, and we're leaving the Empire," she replied curtly. "I've decided that we're going to Rubidge Station for the time being."

"I take it I don't get a say in this?" He sat back in the cockpit's seat. Honora glared at him and he promptly got up.

"Well, if you know of a better place, I'd like to hear it." She started up the shuttle, and he watched, fascinated, as she flicked through each item on a safety checklist.

"I wouldn't mind going back to your family's house," he admitted.

"I would. I need you to respect that, Andrew." Her voice told him she wouldn't argue. The airlock opened, revealing the massive blackness of space. "My cousin has been posted to Rubidge Station. She might be able to help us. It'll give us time and space to think about what to do next."

"You make it sound like we're stuck together."

She whirled around in her seat. "We are."

Andrew didn't dare contradict her.

Despite the early hour, there was already a steady flow of traffic around the base. He waited until Honora had navigated from it before speaking again. "What are you going to do?" he asked.

Instead of tossing him a biting reply, Honora ran her hands through her hair and leaned back in her seat. There was a defeated air about her. "My former commander recommended that I enlist in the Commons Authority."

"Their army?"

"No, this is a law enforcement agency operating independently from Fleet."

"That doesn't sound too bad."

She sighed. "It's not much better than Fleet."

Andrew sat down on the floor, leaning against the wall. Honora's face was in profile, her eyes on the stars outside. "You really should be sitting on the cot," she admonished, but her voice didn't carry the same level of authority that it usually did.

"I'd rather sit here." He shuffled his cards and built a solitaire spread. He sneezed and idly wondered if a cat had ever been on board.

"We'll be going into hyperspace in just over an hour," she cautioned. "You'll want to hold on to something in case the ride gets bumpy."

Andrew's interest was immediately piqued. "Hyperspace?"

"There's a gate near here that will let us out about half an hour away from Rubidge."

"Will your cousin be okay with us just dropping in like this?"

Honora shrugged. "Mora won't mind. You two will probably get on together very well. She's much more outgoing than I am. More social."

"But she isn't you."

The quiet words tumbled from Andrew's mouth before he thought better of it. Honora turned to face him, shock across her features, and he knew he must be wearing the same expression. For a few seconds, they stared at each other, the only sound the distant thrum of the engine beneath them.

"She isn't," Honora confirmed and busied herself with the controls.

She misunderstood him. He felt like an idiot. "That's not what I meant," he protested. "I like being with you."

She turned back to him, disbelief written across her face.

"I do!" he insisted. "For what it's worth, you're the first friend I've had in a long time." She stared at him, dark blue eyes unreadable. He squirmed under her scrutiny.

"You're mine, too," she finally said.

CHAPTER 12

Mora Kharn had been living on Rubidge Station for the last fourteen months, an assignment that had been excitedly accepted when the patrol ship she had last been posted to was decommissioned and sent to the scrap heap. Now, just over a year later, she was nearly ready to leave. She was on the darker side of thirty, and lately she thought that she might be getting too old to take in the station's nighttime attractions as much as she liked. She told herself that this morning's headache was due to the disastrous date that had ended prematurely the night before and *not* caused by having a couple of drinks at the Solar Flare while she bitched to the bartender about men. If she kept telling herself that, she might believe it.

Her time on station had also sent unprecedented amounts of overtime her way. During her eight years as a nurse, seven of which had been spent with Fleet, she had been in several battle situations on shipboard postings, at least once where she wasn't sure if the crew was going to make it out alive. She had assisted in countless surgeries, seen bodies in all sorts of disarray, and had handled everything with professional efficiency. She didn't think much could surprise her anymore.

But she was shocked to receive a short written transmit from her cousin, whom she hadn't seen in over a year. She had a vague idea what Honora the Hotshot Secret Agent was up to after she had been called to an emergency briefing with Admirals Kentz and Brynon a few days ago. She had longed to get in touch with Honora, but knew her cousin wouldn't be up to chatting over a couple of drinks. Her father had sent a secure transmit to her work inbox at the station infirmary, which confirmed what Kentz and Brynon had been dancing around: Honora had found the man Lily Stewart had been asking about since her arrival in the Commons.

On my way to Rubidge, Honora's message had read. *Hate to impose. Can we meet?* It was short and choppy. Kurran would always be Honora's preferred language.

Could they meet? Mora's heart did a little happy dance, and her headache immediately subsided. It wasn't a hangover after all! She had been waiting for an olive branch from Honora since they were little girls, when her cousin came to live with them. She had always wanted a sister—her brother was much older, and therefore wasn't any fun—but Honora had never seemed interested.

A little nagging voice at the back of her mind warned her that Honora probably saw going to Rubidge as a last resort about something. She had never reached out to her extended family before.

Mora lived in a two-story apartment block populated with Fleet personnel. It was a one-bedroom unit, with the usual array of utilitarian furniture. *Honora can take my bed*, she decided. *I'll sleep on the couch.* She went about changing the bed linens and tabbed in a grocery order for delivery. The replicators here were little better than those available on ships, dispensing soup and beverages.

Her computer chimed another incoming message. *Cleared for docking personal vehicles deck 4D. Where should we find you?*

We? Mora hoped she was using the royal "we." Her apartment didn't have room for "we."

She tapped out a quick message promising to pick up Honora. Why wouldn't she dock at the base? As a member of the Kurran Forces, she would have been entitled to a space.

Mora finger-combed her hair—she was currently growing out an unfortunate red dye job, and half of her hair was its natural white-blond—and dashed out of the apartment. She was feeling a little fatigued, and not only because of the date from hell. *That* had followed a sixteen-hour shift, during which a Nym refugee had gone into labor and no one had been quite sure how to handle it due to the language barriers. But she figured she could pick herself up with coffee when she returned.

She found Honora sitting in a chair in the civilian docks' waiting area. A duffel was at her feet, and while she still wore her black Ops uniform, she had removed her name badge and rank pin, and the shirt's seal was open a few inches, exposing her throat. Mora blinked. It wasn't like Honora to be unkempt. There were circles under her eyes, and she kept clenching and unclenching her jaw.

That odd sight took a backseat to the other surprise. A man sat next to her, light brown hair mussed. There were healing pink scars under one hazel eye and beside his nose, and despite his casual demeanor, Mora saw how he took in his surroundings. This was all new to him.

"Honora," Mora greeted warmly. She couldn't keep a smile from blooming across her face.

Honora rose stiffly, and her companion followed. "Thank you for your hospitality," she said.

No hello, no updates on what the hell she had been up to

these last months, but Mora didn't care. Instead, she let that slide and threw her arms around her cousin and squeezed. Honora tentatively returned the hug, and over her shoulder Mora saw a tiny smile flit across her friend's face. "I'm so glad you're here," Mora said when she pulled away. "How long will you be staying?"

"It's long story," Honora replied, sidestepping the question. She turned to her companion and started a little, remembering her manners. "Mora, this is my friend, Andrew. Andrew, this is my cousin, Mora Kharn."

Mora's suspicions were immediately confirmed. This had to be the man her best friend had been talking about, the poor sap Lily assumed was beaten to death by a pair of Nym doctors on Earth. "Come with me," she urged.

Andrew turned to carry both of their bags, but a sharp look from Honora made him drop it.

"Oh, for gods' sakes, Honora, he's being nice," Mora muttered.

Honora shot Mora an irritated look, but she let Andrew carry the duffels, one over his shoulder and the other in his hand.

The lift that picked them up was empty save for a pair of Fleet officers who stepped out on the first deck of the commercial strip, leaving Mora, Honora, and Andrew alone. "So," Mora began, "tell me what's going on."

Honora's reply was flat. "I've been dishonorably discharged from Special Ops. Just a couple of hours ago. I came here because I don't want to go to Sennethaca and listen to your father try to convince me to join Fleet."

Mora faced her, floored. "How the hell were you kicked out of Ops? You don't even drink."

"There are other ways to be expelled besides conduct unbecoming," Honora replied frostily. "Ops isn't like your Fleet."

"Yeah, yeah, I've heard all of this before. What the fuck did you *do*?"

"She rescued me," Andrew answered for her. "She was doing her job, and the Empire didn't want me there, so they kicked her out."

"Andrew," said Honora softly. She met his eyes and Mora saw the understanding between them.

Huh. *That* was almost as surprising as Honora's dishonorable discharge.

Honora turned back to Mora. "I've heard from a few people that you're acquainted with the other person kidnapped by the Nym," she said crisply, all business once more.

"She's one of my best friends, actually. She always wanted to know what became of the guy in the cryonics lab that day." He didn't look the worse for wear, besides the scars on his face. From Lily's description, everyone had assumed the Nym scientists had killed Andrew. "She lives with a Fleet officer on Kevnar Station. He has furlough right now and they're doing a mountain climbing tour on the outer edge of the Keros Quadrant. She's going to fall over when she finds out about you."

"Everyone keeps going on about how well-adjusted she is," Andrew muttered.

"It gets tiresome," Honora said.

Mora started rethinking letting them stay in her apartment.

The lift stopped at deck twenty-two, one of four decks devoted to housing, and it felt miles away from the stark civilian docks. The foliage and benches spread around the graveled sidewalks almost gave the illusion that one was planetside, were it not for the artificial lighting that was hell on a hangover. Rubidge Station was home to five thousand permanent residents and a Fleet base on its lower decks, and saw tens of thousands of tourists annually. Its botanical gardens and zoo were renowned throughout the Commons, as was its nightlife. Each deck truly felt like a different planet, and that was what Mora loved about living here.

Honora didn't seem too impressed, however. Maybe Mora could have called in a couple of favors and arranged for her to stay in the Fleet barracks. Honora seemed to prefer things a little on the dismal side.

Andrew's eyes darted from place to place, taking in his surroundings. He didn't possess the same wide-eyed wonder Lily had, but he didn't appear to be as accepting of his new circumstances as she was, either. Lily had had a small support network to begin with. Andrew had only Honora.

The front door to Mora's apartment block slid open with a press of her thumb into the keypad. Her unit was on the first floor, and she apologized when she let them in. "I don't have much room," she said sheepishly. An idea struck her. "You two stay here, and I'll stay in the overnight quarters at the infirmary," she suggested.

"I don't want to impose," Andrew protested.

"You don't have much choice," Mora replied with a smile. "Unless you have a credit chip to pay for a hotel room." She regretted the words as soon as they flew from her mouth. His expression darkened at the reminder that he was unable to provide for himself for the time being. "I'm sorry," she quickly apologized. "That was uncalled for."

"No, you're right. Honora said I have a better chance of finding work here, anyway."

Mora knew that it would take more than a job to help someone resettle. She sincerely hoped that Honora wasn't going to drop him off here and take off for parts unknown. Outside of her Special Ops career, Mora didn't really know what her cousin did in her spare time. The realization made her sad.

"Andrew, Fleet has handled a time traveler before," Mora reminded him gently. "I'll help to make sure you're not left out in the cold here."

Andrew nodded, but she knew he didn't believe her. Mora didn't blame him. He had already seen everything she detested about the Kurran Empire.

He sneezed into his arm, and Mora's nursing training took over. "Have you had the Coll vaccine?" she asked.

He looked at her blankly, and Honora had the grace to look embarrassed.

"I take it that's a no," Mora replied smoothly. She crossed the room to her desk and rooted around a drawer for the emergency kit she kept there. She removed a transderm spray.

Andrew spotted it and backed away. "No way," he said. "You're not knocking me out."

Mora turned to Honora. "What the hell have you done to him?" she demanded. "How many times did you dope him up?"

"Twice," Andrew answered before Honora could, warily eyeing the unit in Mora's hand. "Three times if you count when she did her field medicine on that ride off Earth."

"And no one thought to give you the Coll vaccine?"

"What's a Coll vaccine?"

Instead of answering his question, Mora glared archly at Honora. "I know how superior the Empire is, but no one at any time thought to give him the thing he needs most for space travel?"

Honora shot a sulky look her way.

Mora turned her smile to Andrew; she had learned early on in her career that it put patients at ease, especially men. She used her most reassuring voice. "This won't hurt or incapacitate you," she began. "This is a one-time vaccine against Coll particles. They're generated by air recyclers on stations and ships. The particles themselves aren't toxic, but people who don't get the vaccine end up with a never-ending low-grade flu. You'll keep sneezing and feeling unwell as long as you don't have it."

"Do you and Honora have it?"

She nodded. "It'll only take a minute. I just have to administer this on a pulse point."

Andrew looked to Honora for guidance and she nodded. He held out his wrist and Mora activated the transderm on his skin.

Despite her own exhaustion—which wasn't a hangover—Mora was going to contact her father to see about getting Andrew identification and somewhere to stay. Then she was going to take a well-deserved nap in the infirmary's quarters. She packed a few things into an overnight bag and showed Honora and Andrew where everything was in her apartment. She made up the couch with pillows and blankets and accepted her grocery order when it was delivered.

"I'll be out of here," she promised as she tossed a couple of plasticans of stew in her bag. "Can I get you anything else?"

Honora shook her head. "You've already been so helpful," she said appreciatively.

Mora's heart soared. Before she could reconsider the notion, she dropped her overnight bag and threw her arms around her cousin. "Anytime," she said. Honora stiffened, and Mora let her go. "Promise we'll go somewhere and get caught up," Mora urged her.

Honora looked to Andrew, who wore an amused expression on his face. "Yes?" she said, but it was a question. That was good enough for Mora.

———

"YOU TAKE THE BED," Honora ordered Andrew. She sat on the couch, her duffel at her feet, listening to Andrew putter around the kitchen.

He had insisted on making something to eat. "I'm going to go out on a limb here and guess that pizza doesn't exist anymore," he said by way of reply.

"I've never heard of it, but that's not the point. You should take the bed."

"What about peanut butter? I could really go for peanut butter right about now."

"Andrew..."

"Honora, it's a *bed*. It doesn't matter to me. The couch looks comfortable enough." He emerged from the kitchen with a couple of plates and set them down on the table in front of the couch. He plunked down next to her. "I'm not going to ask what kind of animals these cold cuts came from, but I hope these are okay."

Honora studied the sandwich in front of her. She wasn't worried about the preparation. The ingredients in Mora's kitchen were her concern. Her cousin had always had atrocious eating habits, nursing career aside. It was sheer genetic luck that she managed to stay as slender as she did.

Andrew noticed her apprehension and swallowed a mouthful of food. "I didn't spit in it."

Honora laughed and tasted it.

When their meal was finished and the dishes put away, Honora shooed Andrew away to the bedroom and settled on the couch for a nap. Exhaustion pulled at her, but she was unable to sleep. The day's events kept replaying over and over in her mind.

Unemployed. Exiled. With her hard-partying cousin and a man nearly a millennium out of his time for company.

But Honora had never had any sort of company before.

She closed her eyes, but the questions of what to do with

her life kept tumbling through her head. She would *not* enlist in the Fleet, nor did joining what would likely be a shaky, ineffective law enforcement agency hold much appeal. She did not want to track down small-time freighters transporting the occasional case of untaxed liquor so they could make ends meet, nor did she want to help Nym refugees settle in the Commons. *That* was what this Commons Authority was for. Fleet didn't want to deal with the Nym, and neither did she. The Nym had murdered hundreds of thousands of people.

They had killed her parents.

They had nearly killed Andrew.

She didn't know which made her angrier. Involuntarily, her hands balled into fists beneath her blanket.

The Empire didn't care about her parents or Andrew. Or her. Honora had given her entire life over to the Empire, flown where she was ordered to fly, killed whoever she was ordered to kill. She immediately accepted a mission to go into an artificial, highly unstable vortex to maintain the course of history, knowing full well that she might not make it back. She had done it with pride. And because she saved a victim, like she had done countless times on missions to the Outer Fringes, she had been discharged, all because he wasn't the *right* victim to rescue.

Angry tears gathered in her eyes, and she scrubbed them away. It wasn't just the loss of her career or looking after Andrew. It was the rejection from her culture that also mattered. Honora had always been aware that she would never have the social standing a full-blooded Kurran enjoyed, despite being only one-fourth Commons by way of her half-Commons father. If things had gone differently, if her father hadn't followed her mother back to the Empire and pledged their allegiance to the reigning empress at the time, Honora might feel as if she belonged in the Commons instead.

She sniffled quietly, and for the millionth time since her

modded fighter craft was spit out of the vortex, she felt selfish and petty. She didn't have the right to feel sorry for herself.

Soft footfalls on the carpeted floor snapped her out of her wallowing. A dark shape tiptoed across the room. "Andrew, I'm awake," she announced. She willed him not to order on the lights for fear he would see her reddened eyes.

He paused. "Oh. I can't sleep. I was going to look around the station."

Honora bolted upright. "No."

"I'm a free man, Honora."

"You can add ignorant to that, too. You have no idea what's out there. I'll take you later."

"If you're not sleeping, we could go now."

She sighed and rubbed her eyes.

"Lights," Andrew said. The apartment's illumination immediately glowed. He was picking up things quickly.

Like her tear-stained face. "Are you okay?" he asked, eyes wide.

What was the point in lying to him? "No," she admitted.

He cautiously took a step toward the couch, like he was approaching a feral animal. Honora tossed aside the blankets and straightened so he had room to sit.

"I wish there was something I could say or do that would make you feel a little better," he finally said after a moment of silence.

Honora snorted a little. "I don't think I deserve a lot of sympathy."

"No, you do. I've told you before that you've done every-thing right and it's the Empire who's at fault here. You know I'm grateful to you for saving my life." His voice was uncharac-teristically quiet and serious. He reached for her hand clenched around the corner of a blanket and ran his thumb over the old burn scars there.

Honora's breath stuttered at the contact, a spark flaring

where he touched her, sending jolts of electricity up her arm. "Um," she squeaked. When he mistook that as a sign that she didn't want to be touched and loosened his grip, she clasped his hand to keep him from moving away.

When he did let go, it was only to loosely envelop her in a hug. While she knew consciously that it was as much for his benefit than hers, what began as sparks ignited, and warmth flooded her body. She could tell herself it was because she was unaccustomed to physical contact, but she would be lying. It was Andrew.

And oh, gods, it would be awful and awkward if... she didn't want to contemplate his reaction if he found out.

No, she didn't want to contemplate how she would feel if he found out and rejected her. She couldn't see him laughing about this newfound infatuation—now that she had gotten to know him, he seemed like the kind of person to let her down easily—but she would feel the sting of it more acutely than she was prepared to deal with.

She relaxed against him, and she felt his sigh ruffle her hair. "You're a lot stronger than you give yourself credit for," he murmured. "You don't need a stupid Empire to give you orders."

His lips pressed against her temple in a gesture of affection. Honora's head buzzed, bringing up a memory of the lone time she got drunk. Tipsy, really. She felt heady and giddy, and if she didn't move right now, she was going to do something stupid.

She disentangled herself and stood up. "I can't sleep either," she confessed. Her heart hammered in her chest, and she forced herself to keep her expression... not neutral. Friendly. She and Andrew were friends. "Why don't we look around the station?" she asked, the brightness in her voice sounding fake even to her.

He looked puzzled but quickly recovered. "Sure."

CHAPTER 13

Andrew had been curious about the station since seeing it from space aboard Honora's shuttle. Through the windows, it had looked like a squashed sphere of rusty metal, tilted to one side by a couple of turrets, which Honora informed him were Fleet-controlled security towers. The station had been bright with lights, ships clinging to its underside, with constant traffic flowing in and out of its airlocks.

It felt much larger inside, and Honora explained as much of the layout as she could, detailing the tourist attractions and which decks catered to which clientele. The station was jointly run by the Commons government and Fleet, and was the largest in this quadrant. There were apartment buildings, hotels, a couple of casinos, a zoo, a botanical garden, and a museum. Andrew would have had neither the faintest idea of where to start exploring, nor what to do if he got lost.

The commercial strip, full of bars and shops, was alive with activity. Music flowed from pubs and storefronts, and shouts from jewelry and game vendors filled the air. While it was early in the afternoon, the yeasty tang of beer teased Andrew, mixed with the scent of perfume and frying food. He had never been dependent on alcohol, but he found himself longing to sit down and have a drink for the first time since he had become sober.

Over the noise, he heard Honora gasp and grip his hand. "*Sikiaka*," she cursed quietly. She halted and stared straight ahead.

A small group of people were making their way across the strip, headed in their direction. Nym, Andrew realized. They looked just like the doctors back on Earth, except they were offering polite, toothy smiles to others who were stepping out of their way. They were a family, Andrew guessed, even though distinguishing between the sexes was difficult, given that everyone was bald. One wore an oversized, shapeless pink dress over clunky black boots, the other ill-fitting gray pants and shirt in the same bland style as Andrew's. Between them, a small child of indeterminate sex clung to their hands. "Excuse," the man kept saying. "Excuse, please."

They stopped in front of Honora and Andrew. "Excuse," the man repeated. His wife's smile widened, reminiscent of the terrified young singers Andrew had seen audition back at Tiger Media.

Honora stared at them for a few seconds, her eyes shifting from the parents to the child. The kid saw the hard look on Honora's face for a moment and cowed into his mother's baggy skirt.

"Excuse," the father said again. His eyes darted between Honora and Andrew's faces. The guy was just as scared as his wife.

"Honora." Andrew tugged at her hand.

"Zoo?" the kid piped up, looking at Honora fearfully.

Honora said something that wasn't in any language Andrew had heard before. Shock, then genuine smiles lit up the Nym family's faces as they began an exchange in that rapid-fire tongue. They must have asked her something she wasn't expecting, because she grew flustered and stammered a reply. The male narrowed his black eyes at her, and Honora's expression hardened before she snarled a reply.

Honora and the couple eyed each other in frosty silence before the female spoke quickly, maybe trying to smooth things over. Without letting the child relinquish his grip on her, she gestured wildly with her free hand and said something to her mate. The male growled a reply to his wife before turning back to Honora. There was another standoff, a few bystanders stopping to watch.

When Honora spoke again, she was calm and apologetic. She pointed up and kept speaking, her face finally breaking out in a tentative smile. She offered the hand that wasn't clinging to Andrew's to the male, in supplication, he supposed. The Nym looked at it, a little confused, until his mate nudged him and whispered something. The man shook it, a tense smile on his face.

Finally, the family bowed and kept walking, a little more confidently. More people had stopped to gawk at the exchange, but she didn't seem to notice them.

"What did you do?" Andrew asked. That she hadn't let go of his hand hadn't escaped him.

"I told them where to find the zoo," she explained simply. She looked numb, like she couldn't believe she had done such a thing. "It's probably the only place here I can direct someone to. Decks twelve and thirteen, section F."

"And?"

"They said they hadn't met anyone in the Commons yet who speaks their language fluently."

"And you do?"

She nodded. "It went with my job description."

Honora still hadn't let go of his hand, and he didn't move away. He sensed that she needed the contact; she had just done something she never thought she would do. She had confronted a prejudice she had never expected to meet head on. At least, he hoped she had. "What else?" he prodded. "Directions to the zoo can't take that long."

She paused. "He said the only humanoids he's met who speak the Nym language are Kurrans. He asked me if I was Kurran, and I said yes."

"Half-Kurran," Andrew corrected.

"Three-fourths," she countered, then continued. "The Kurrans and the Nym have been at war for centuries, but obviously that's changed. It's not like the Commons. They don't start wars. The Empire does."

"And?"

"He said... I killed the rest of his family," she gulped. "He had two brothers who died in a battle with the Empire three years ago. He said the Empire and the Commons let the innocents die when they needed help the most." She looked away at a vendor selling glowing fish in jars, but Andrew knew she wasn't really seeing them. "I said he killed my parents."

"Honora..."

"He said if I was a true Kurran, I would still be in the Empire." She wouldn't look at him. "His wife said we're in the Commons now, so it doesn't matter anymore."

"But it does."

Honora finally faced him, her eyes shining, oblivious to the crush of people around them. "It does. You know what it's like, the total loss of your identity. How you think you fit into your world and then you don't."

She was so fragile, so unlike the Honora Andrew knew, that it frightened him a little.

Her death grip on his hand had relaxed a little, but she still clung to him. Under normal circumstances, he would take this as a positive signal—the first ones being that she had allowed him to sleep in her bed and hadn't turned away when he stupidly planted that kiss to her temple—but her staying glued to him only muddled an already strange affection he felt toward her. *Affection, that's all it is*.

Yeah, right. Even he didn't believe that shit.

Instead, he simply replied, "Yeah, I do."

———

TWO DAYS PASSED before Mora stopped by the apartment. She flopped on the couch, oblivious to Honora and Andrew, who had been parked there for the last couple of hours watching a trashy soap opera-type show.

"I see she has you hooked on *Lightning's Luck*," Mora commented wryly. Andrew moved to the side to give her more room, squishing against Honora.

"I did not," Honora indignantly replied. "We're only watching it because this is the only serial you've saved on your vidscreen. And we were very comfortable until you came along."

Andrew was very comfortable right now. Honora smelled good, like that citrus soap he had noticed before.

"I'm here for Andrew, actually," Mora said. "Fleet wants to see him. Also, I need more clothes."

"No," Honora protested. "He's my responsibility."

"I am not a pet," Andrew pointed out.

"All they want to do is issue him identification and hear his side of the kidnapping story," Mora said.

"I didn't kidnap him," Honora snapped.

"She didn't kidnap me."

Mora threw up her hands and rose from the couch. "Well, they want to see you, and since you're on a Fleet station, staying in a Fleet nurse's quarters, you don't have much choice. Let's go."

At least he was dressed.

Andrew followed Mora out the door, giving Honora an

apologetic look over his shoulder. "See you later," he called, the door sliding shut before she could form a reply.

Mora was talkative as she led him through the station to its military base, asking him how he liked the Empire and the twenty-ninth century. When Mora had to stand still and let her retina be scanned at a set of doors, he began to feel nervous. The fears he had of disappearing in the Kurran Empire resurfaced as they walked through miles of grimy white-tiled corridors. Every now and then, they passed soldiers wearing navy blue uniforms who said hello to Mora and looked at Andrew curiously.

Finally, at the end of a hallway, she pressed a buzzer. The doors opened silently, revealing a nearly-empty room lined with windows on its opposite side. A long table ran down the middle, and Andrew recognized the pair seated at it: Honora's uncle and the man he had met his first day in the Empire. Some other Fleet admiral. He racked his brain for a name.

"Sit down," Admiral Kharn said. If he was angry about his and Honora's running away in the middle of the night, he didn't show it.

Mora and Andrew took seats opposite them. "You remember Admiral Kentz," Kharn said.

Kentz. That was it. "Sir," he said respectfully.

Admiral Kharn pushed an envelope across the table to Andrew, the first piece of paper he had seen since he left Earth. "Your identification and a few other essentials," Kharn explained when he saw Andrew eyeing the envelope suspiciously. Andrew picked it up and felt the material, actually some kind of thin plastic. He slid out the contents, most of them electronic, to the table.

"This is your ID," Mora piped up, pointing to a small metallic square. His name was written on it in tiny raised letters, his last name spelled with a K and missing the U and E.

There wasn't a picture, just a tiny black chip inset in a top corner.

"We've appended a basic résumé to your ID that you can adjust as you see fit," Admiral Kharn said. He pointed to another, larger metallic square. "Here's your credit chip. There are two thousand credits available on it."

"Enough to rent an apartment," Kentz added.

Enough to fend for himself. Andrew got the message, loud and clear.

Kentz tented his fingertips and looked at Andrew, one white eyebrow uplifted. "While the investigation into the Nym's time travel is officially closed, we would still like to hear your side of the story."

Immediately, Andrew's bullshit meter went off. "I'm sure the Empire has given you all of my testimony," he said. He told himself that this guy was nothing more than one of the pompous, self-important "representatives" of tiny hipster record companies, one of dozens he had to deal with during his time at Tiger Media. Or a sound engineer. Those guys were always obnoxious when a show took place at the West Queen West location, always complaining about the acoustics.

The admirals both looked surprised at his reply. "Is this about Honora?" Andrew asked bluntly. "She did everything she could to save my life. I've accepted that living here is part of the deal."

He hadn't really, but Honora was what made living here tolerable.

"We would still like to hear your story." Kentz's tone said he wouldn't argue.

Andrew closed his eyes and remembered sitting in his therapist's office, but he couldn't think of a single session that applied to his situation. So he told the entire story of the lab and the pair of strange doctors. He told them about his business and drug habit, and rehab. Mora listened to the last part more intently, and he already knew her well enough to guess that she would eventually want more details.

When he concluded the story with finding himself in the year 2868, he rose from the table with his old air of authority. *Gentlemen, I'm finished here.* "Is there anything else you want to know?" he asked.

Admiral Kharn shook his head. "You're a free man, Mr. Claybourne."

Kentz tilted his head. "No," he said. "I'm sure our paths will cross again."

Andrew didn't care about that. He just wanted to go back to Mora's apartment. To Honora. Who had hardly left the couch in two days, and that worried him almost as much as his own growing affection for her.

He and Mora left the room, weaving their way through the myriad of corridors in the space station's belly. "What can two thousand credits get me?" he asked in the elevator.

"More than the thousand they gave Lily."

"Yeah, well, they sent her to college, too, didn't they?"

"My father is working on that. He thinks you should receive the same help she did. And speaking of my father, it was really shitty of Honora to just take off like that. She hurt my father's feelings."

"I didn't have any say in that," Andrew said defensively. "And I'm sorry about your dad."

They boarded an elevator. Mora sighed irritably and ran her hands through her two-tone hair. "I know. We should be used to it by now."

Andrew steered the conversation back to the original subject. "Fleet doesn't see me the same way as Lily," he pointed out. "It wasn't one of their officers who found me."

"Yes." Mora's answer was clipped. She softened a little. "Look, I agree with my father. You're not a stupid person if you did everything you say you did. If you had some options, someone backing you, and if you weren't stuck in a galactic pissing contest, you could do whatever you wanted here." She offered him a bright smile.

Honora was freshly showered and dressed when they returned to the apartment, her hair damp. There were still shadows under her eyes and she looked a little ticked off, but Andrew was used to that. She had her datatab in her hand, her fingers deftly flicking over the screen. "How did it go?" she asked in lieu of hello.

Mora shrugged. "Fine," Andrew replied. "They just wanted to hear about how I got here, and they gave me some money." He held up the envelope. "I think. It's on some kind of high-tech credit card. Is two thousand credits a lot?"

"If you ration it carefully, it'll get you by for a few months, depending on where you live." Honora didn't offer any more information. He knew she was irritated at being left out of the meeting with the admirals.

Mora excused herself to return to the station's infirmary, and Andrew felt a stab of guilt over his squatting in her apartment. She had been so gracious, and he had noticed her excitement at seeing her cousin for the first time in over a year when they arrived. She really seemed to love Honora and was genuinely hurt by the continued rejection. It rankled him. Honora had quite a few people in her life who were waiting for her to at least acknowledge them.

She kept her focus on the datatab. To break the silence, Andrew said, "So, I have two thousand credits."

"I have savings, too. We'll be fine."

"We?"

"Andrew, I don't think it's a good idea for you to wander around the universe alone for now. I'm looking for housing for us. There's a two-bedroom unit on another part of Rubidge that will suit our needs."

"Do I get any say in this?"

Honora set down her datatab on the coffee table. "All right. Where do you think we'll have the best employment opportunities in the Commons?"

He sat down next to her. She was right. "So you're thinking of joining the Commons Authority?"

"Possibly. I've been looking at the job postings for you, too. There's a restaurant looking for a live server."

"As opposed to a dead one?"

She gave him a withering stare. "As opposed to a serving bot."

He thought for a moment. Serving was certainly within his capabilities here. "Sure, sign me up. I worked at a Starbucks for a few months after I dropped out of university, when I was starting up Tiger Media." Remembering his ID chip, he held it out. "That reminds me, I need help with my résumé." He looked at Honora, who had plucked the card from his hand and connected it to her datatab. "There isn't anywhere else you want to go? Another station or planet?"

"No, this is the only station I'm familiar with in the Commons. And I don't like living on planets."

Well, maybe after he was more acclimatized to the Commons, he could find a nice planet to live on, free from worrying about running out of air. But then he wouldn't be near Honora. The idea made his chest ache.

But her solution might be just as difficult. There was that affection he had for her. All of a sudden, he was very aware that she was only a few inches away.

She caught his stare, and instead of an obstinate "What?" she stared right back. There wasn't a trace of malice in her eyes; instead, there was something softer.

Or maybe she was eyeing his newly acquired scars. He hadn't had the time of the energy to feel self-conscious about them, but under her scrutiny, he felt it now. He resisted the urge to make a flip comment about something in his teeth.

Finally, he said, "I trust you."

She broke their eye contact and busied herself with her datatab again. A few more taps, and she announced, "It's rented. It's furnished, and there's even twenty minutes of water included for free every day. We can move in two days." Another tap, and she brought up the contents of his ID chip. "Let's put together a believable working history for you."

Well, that was a hell of a lot easier than trying to find somewhere to live back home. It had taken Andrew over a year to find a townhome that wasn't in dire need of repair and didn't have a near million-dollar price tag when he was house-hunting in 2016. "I haven't had a roommate in a long time," he admitted.

Instead of the dark look he expected from her, she merely offered a smile. "Neither have I."

CHAPTER 14

The apartment Honora rented was small, in one of the oldest neighborhoods on the station, one step up from a slum. The unit itself was clean, but that was where its amenities ended. Andrew quickly discovered that its replicator barely worked, and when Honora enquired to the manager, she was told that the building had plenty of back work orders. A malfunctioning replicator was not a priority.

Still, it beat most of the places Andrew had lived during his twenties. They were reasonably close to the commercial strip, and it didn't smell like a deep-fryer. He could turn off the kitchen light at night and not have to worry about cockroaches scrabbling out from under the cupboards to scare the shit out of him in the morning. His first apartment in Parkdale had resurrected his childhood fear of the dark for a couple of years.

He sat down on the faded couch, recounting what happened when they moved in a few hours earlier.

The lock to the front door was old-fashioned by Honora's standards, utilizing a small chip reader. Andrew had been examining his key under the harsh overhead light as they made their way down the hallway to the second-story unit when Honora stopped in her tracks.

"What's wrong?" he asked without looking up. The chip key felt like it was made of silicone and was smaller than his palm. "Hey, do you think this thing will be wrecked if it ends up in the laundry? I do that sometimes."

When she didn't answer, he looked up. There were a couple of Nym fumbling with their key at a door at the end of the hallway, speaking quietly in their disjointed, guttural language. Or were they *Nyms*? Andrew hadn't heard the name used in the plural yet.

He didn't want a repeat of the scene on the commercial strip. It really didn't do well to piss off the neighbors before they officially moved in. One of the Nym looked up to see Honora and Andrew staring at them. Andrew quickly looked around for their apartment number. "Twenty-eight," he said, a little too loudly. "Come on, Honora, let's go." They were at twenty-one. He tugged on her hand. "*Honora.*"

She stopped looking at the Nym couple long enough to follow him down the hallway to apartment twenty-eight. She held her key in front of the small pad mounted on the door until the lock whirred. The door creakily slid open, and they stepped inside.

"Is this going to be a problem?" Andrew immediately asked. "Because if it is, I don't have a qualm about using some of these two thousand credits and finding a place of my own."

"No, it isn't," Honora said in a small voice. "It'll just take some getting used to. I'm already getting used to it."

"Seeing people you don't like?"

"Not seeing them as the enemy," she corrected him. "I've never seen Nym in peace time, just in cruisers trying to blow me out of space." She squared her shoulders. "If it makes you feel any better, most of the Nym don't like Kurrans, either."

The apartment's bedrooms were on either side of a bathroom, all directly off the small living area. After that exchange, Honora had taken to hiding out in her bedroom with the door closed, and Andrew hadn't moved from the couch since he tossed his bag into his. She had briefly come out to get something from the replicator, and upon hearing from Andrew that it didn't work properly, had placed the call to the building manager.

Everyone needed time alone, he figured. He watched an episode of the show Mora had recorded in her apartment, that obnoxious *Lightning's Luck* melodrama, then tried his hand at ordering groceries. There was a wall-mounted tablet computer in the kitchen that he played around with, and he picked out a few things at one of the lower-priced grocery stores. Thank God there were pictures of the wares; he would have been completely lost without them. He charged everything to the apartment and hoped Honora wouldn't mind. He would pay her back as soon as he found the twenty-ninth century equivalent of an ATM.

He parked himself back in front of the TV and was so thoroughly absorbed in its ridiculous shenanigans that he jumped when the doorbell rang.

Andrew opened the door, and a tall male Nym held out his grocery order in a box. "Hello," he said in accented English. Or Commons. *Whatever.* "Delivery."

"Hey." Andrew offered a smile to hide his surprise. As he accepted the box, he realized he had no idea of the current etiquette surrounding deliverymen.

"You just move in?" the guy asked.

"Yeah, a couple of hours ago."

"You are not worried about *us*, then." The man smiled, but Andrew could tell it wasn't genuine. He wondered how many doors had been closed in his face these days.

"Uh, no, I guess not. Listen, this is going to sound weird,

but I'm not from around here, and so—am I supposed to tip you?"

The Nym's bald head furrowed. "I do not understand."

"Um, a gratuity. I give you something extra for bringing this stuff here." If Honora wasn't hiding out in her room, maybe she could have explained things in his language.

The Nym shook his head, confused. "I do not understand."

"You and me both." He set the box down inside the door and leaned against the jamb. "It's just a way of saying thank you for doing something I could have done myself. A couple of dollars. Credits, I mean."

Comprehension dawned on the Nym's face. "Oh! No, my position already pays me. Thank you." He quickly bowed and turned to leave.

"Wait!" Andrew called.

He halted and faced Andrew, curiosity in his lime-green eyes. "Have I missed something in your order?"

"No, I just wanted to ask you something."

The Nym cocked his head to one side. "Yes?"

"This is also going to sound weird, but I noticed you speak Commons pretty well."

"I speak several languages. I am still learning new ones."

"Well, you've got a good grasp on it. Do you live around here?"

A few seconds ticked by as the deliveryman considered his words. Translating them, Andrew figured. He should have been more specific. "I live in the next building," he answered. "First floor. There are lots of us. The station calls it the Nym District."

Andrew wondered if Honora had known that when she rented the apartment. "Like I said, I'm new here, too. Do you want to get a coffee or tea sometime? I'm trying to meet new friends."

There was a pause as the man stared at Andrew. "You want a friend with the Nym," he said flatly.

"Why not?"

"Commons do not like Nym." The man was matter-of-fact, like it was the Commons's God-given right to treat them like shit.

"Do the Nym not like the Commons?" Andrew countered.

His wide, skinny shoulder shrugged. "We want to live quietly."

"Does *quietly* mean you won't have coffee with a new neighbor?"

The Nym's watch beeped, and he glanced at it. Ignoring it, he looked straight back at Andrew. "You have weapons?"

Andrew held up his hands. "I'm completely useless with weapons. The first and last time I tried to take one, I ended up on my back with a boot at my throat."

The deliveryman kept staring at Andrew, or more accurately, just above his head. "Yes," he said finally. "Tash's, on the strip. They do not fear Nym there. Eighteen hundred hours."

"Okay." Before Andrew turned back to his apartment, he said, "My name's Andrew."

The Nym bowed again. "You may call me Verk. My real name is too long to pronounce."

"All right, Verk, I'll see you at Tash's." He turned back into the apartment, where he came face-to-face with Honora.

The door creaked shut behind him. "You know we live in the Nym District?" he asked. He lifted the box of groceries and deposited it on the counter.

"Thank you for getting food."

"Someone had to. What stuff goes in the fridge?"

"Andrew," she said softly. "I know we live in the Nym District. That's the reason the rent is so cheap."

Andrew felt around the box for the stuff that was already chilled and stuck them in the fridge unit built into the wall.

"I know I'm not good with people," she said.

His attraction to her notwithstanding, he wasn't up to hearing another sob story from her. "You should get out more," he suggested. "You could come with me when I see Verk tonight."

"You wouldn't mind?"

Andrew was surprised that she was warm to the idea. "No," he replied. "And if you want to interact with others a little more, you should see Mora."

"I will." She bit her lip and dug a few things out of the grocery box. "I keep wondering what to do. Following orders has been my way of life for years. I've never had my own space before. It's always been the barracks or the estate." She held a can of fruit and looked around the small apartment. "I like it here."

"You can do whatever you want with it. Do whatever you want with your life." Andrew didn't mean to sound like a high school motivational speaker.

When she motioned to put some cans away in a cupboard, the room around them seemed to shrink. The kitchen felt too small; she was too close to him. More than ever, he knew it was going to be difficult to live with her, and not for the reasons she might have listed. *Affection* didn't cut it. That was too platonic.

She stood nearly as tall as him, her eyes never leaving his. She took a tiny step forward, and her eyes briefly flickered on his mouth.

This is a very bad idea, a small voice warned him, although it didn't specify *what* the bad idea was. He stood very still, hardly breathing for fear of doing something stupid.

She leaned a little closer, and he saw indecision waver across her features, an echo of his thoughts.

He must be imagining things. Maybe she was trying to get around him. But no, she placed a hand on his arm. Through the fabric of his shirt, her touch sent a zing of electricity through his body.

He dipped his head slightly as hers lifted. Their lips met carefully and far too briefly in a chaste kiss that shouldn't have the effect that it did. Heat suffused his body and overwhelmed his senses, quashing that same little voice that warned him there was no going back if he followed what his heart told him to do.

His heart. Andrew would have scoffed at the idea if he wasn't completely under Honora's spell, if he wasn't putting his hands on her hips to pull her closer. If she wasn't twining her arms around his neck and he wasn't kissing her again.

Her tongue teased his lips apart and he stumbled back in surprise, landing against the wall. As his hands slipped around her waist and under the hem of her shirt, he could have sworn he felt sparks move along her skin. Her fingers danced along the back of his neck and he couldn't suppress a shiver. She smelled and tasted so *good*, and when she pressed herself against him, all thoughts fled from his mind. Time travel and living on a barge floating in deep space were no longer issues. It was only her.

She released her hold and stepped away. She looked as dazed as he felt. "Wow," she breathed.

Andrew couldn't think of a rejoinder.

She moved a little further away until her feet reached the living room's threadbare carpet. Andrew couldn't move; his feet were rooted to the floor. She reminded him of a wild animal, one that would approach people but never fully trust them. One false move and she would hide away in her room again.

"Um," he said lamely.

"Yeah." She looked away.

"Was it really that bad?" He didn't mean to be flip, but a piece of his heart would be forever destroyed if she said yes.

There it was—his heart again.

She shook her head. "No."

"We could do it again, make sure it wasn't a fluke." He held his breath, waiting for her answer.

Honora sighed. "Do you really think that's a good idea?"

"We're both adults." He didn't want to go into the pros and cons of... kissing. Was that all it was? Was he seriously having a conversation with a grown woman about a *kiss*?

"We are." But she didn't move towards him, was in fact now inching further away.

He waited for her to say "I should go." Even if it was just to wander around the station for awhile.

"I don't know if getting involved is a good idea." Her words were uncertain, like she was trying to convince herself.

"We're already pretty involved," he pointed out.

She lifted in an eyebrow at him, offering a half-smile. Some of the tension eased from the room. "You know what I mean."

"What's the worst thing that could happen?" he asked.

"I don't know," she admitted. "I'm not very good at personal relationships, as you've pointed out." She fidgeted where she stood. "I don't think we would want the same thing if we were involved."

Andrew's body finally relaxed. "What do you think I want?"

She looked away, embarrassed. "I don't do long-term."

"Oh." Those things happened. He pulled out a kitchen chair and sat down, facing her. "What do you do?"

"I don't do anything anymore, but when I did, it was strictly for..." She trailed off and Andrew didn't push it. She flushed to the roots of her hair. "It's been a very long time," she admitted.

This was singularly the most awkward conversation he had

ever had with a woman, with anyone. At a loss for words, he studied the dented metal tabletop, gathering his thoughts. "Okay," he said, meeting her eyes. "I'm not going to ask you for something you're unable to give." He ran a hand over his face, trying to scrub away the feelings she roused in him, collecting his wits. "I care about you, Honora. You're the strongest, most capable person I've ever met, and you don't give yourself enough credit for the things you could achieve on your own. Without the Empire or Special Ops behind you." Taking a deep, fortifying breath, he continued. "And I am really attracted to you, and if you want to try to make something between us work, you know where to find me."

He didn't want to hear any excuses or, God forbid, an outright rejection. He rose and brushed past her to go to his bedroom, but not before he saw the astonishment across her face.

———

THE RESTAURANT VERK had picked out was big and bright, with stools lined up against a bar and generously sized booths bouncing with children of all species. Andrew said it reminded him of a diner back home. The sign out front identified it as Tash's in several languages, with "NYM WELCOME" scribbled on the window in that tongue and a few Commons dialects.

Verk had saved them a table close to the bar, where replicators spit out drinks and small side dishes and a man with a Kurran shock of bright blue hair worked a grill. A couple of servers bustled around the restaurant, taking orders and occasionally peeling a small child from their legs.

"Hi," said Andrew, looking around. "Good to see you. Verk, this is my friend, Honora. Honora, Verk."

She nodded and slid into place next to Andrew. Verk

suspiciously eyed her across the table. "You look Kurran," he said.

"I am."

He stared a few inches above her head, and Honora realized he was reading her aura. She shifted uncomfortably on the hard plastic seat. "You *were*," Verk clarified.

She nodded. "That's one way of putting it." She changed the subject. "Your grasp on the local language is very good."

"Getting better," Verk replied. "It is not perfect yet. On Nym, I was chosen to be a translator for the Commons and Empire..." He waved his hand, searching for the word.

"Intelligence?" Honora suggested in Nym.

Surprise crossed Verk's face. Then his mask of suspicion fell back into place. "You know Nym?" he asked in Commons.

"Yes." Andrew gave her thigh a squeeze that was meant to be reassuring, but only made her more tense. That, and setting off reactions in her body that had nothing to do with facing an old enemy. "I had to for my former job."

"Kurran Forces?"

"Special Operations."

Verk considered this for a moment. "You did not want to be there?"

"I did, very much so. But things change, you know?"

"I do. I was still learning languages when the Nym were rescued."

"What happened?" Andrew asked gently. "If you don't mind my asking. I'd like to know."

Verk looked at them like they were crazy. "Most people do not care." He looked around the restaurant, but Honora could tell he wasn't seeing the customers. "Our planet was..." He fumbled for the next word. "Cracking?"

"Destabilizing?" Honora prompted.

"Yes, destabilizing," he agreed. "For many years. The Nym

hated what the scientists were doing, hated the way our society worked. We wanted to leave. We were tired and angry when our babies and mates were killed, whole families killed when they tried to run away. The *forcefield*," he spat bitterly. "The forcefield around the whole planet. No one gets in, no one gets out. No one could see how bad things were there. All we wanted to do was leave and resettle on a new planet. But our government said no. There was a lot of disease, no medicine to fix it. People were forced into army or intelligence." He nodded at Honora. "I wanted to be a botanist, but the government said no, you learn languages.

"The Kurrans breached the forcefield," he continued. "It was weakened. A virus developed on our planet and killed thousands of Nym. Scientists and government started dying first. When the Empire finally reached us, they saw we are no threat."

"Do you have a family?" Andrew asked.

Verk shrugged. "No mate anymore, no parents. They got sick and the government made them disappear."

A server with deeply tanned skin and white hair streaked with fading blue appeared, a datatab in her hands. "Sorry, Verk," she said apologetically to the Nym. "We're a bit busy tonight."

"No problem. Tash, these are Honora and Andrew."

Tash smiled at them, and Honora managed a small one at the restaurant's owner. She felt a slight probing at her temples, a sign that she was in the presence of a high-level Kurran telepath. She arched an eyebrow at Tash, and the probing stopped.

"Sorry, my dear," Tash said. "I didn't mean to do that. Just kind of happens when I see other Kurrans. I don't often around here."

"It's all right," Honora assured her. "May I have a tea, please?"

Verk and Andrew ordered the same, and Tash disappeared. "What was that?" Andrew asked.

Honora and Verk looked at one another knowingly. "Tash is a telepath," Honora explained. "Kurrans rarely leave the Empire, especially telepaths with that kind of ability."

"They're at the top of the class structure?"

Honora nodded.

"Tash is good," Verk interjected fiercely. "She was the first to welcome Nym. She likes everyone." To Honora, he asked, "You are not a telepath?"

"Absolutely no telepathic or empathic talent," she admitted. "I'm one-fourth Commons by way of my father. You?" She was curious to know exactly how strong his extrasensory ability was.

Verk shrugged. "Empath."

Andrew shifted the conversation back to Verk's story. "Your parents were killed?" he whispered. Despite everything he had gone through with the Nym, Honora saw that he really didn't believe what their rulers were capable of until Verk had divulged that.

The Nym nodded and bowed his head slightly. "They were sick. Lots of Nym were. We had three classes on the planet. The highest were the rulers, born into it. They did anything they wanted, and they wanted all of space. The Commons, the Empire, I think they even wanted the Hefronn Galaxy. Second class was scientists. Third class is everyone else. Most people were third class."

"But you said you were a translator," Honora pointed out. "What does that make you?"

"Third," Verk replied. "I was good with languages in school, so the government picked me for their projects. I did not have a choice. Translate or be killed. I know several Kurran dialects, better than Commons."

"What happened to your upper classes when your planet was liberated?" Andrew asked.

"This virus did not pick who it infected," Verk said simply. "The rulers and scientists were first to die. It started in a lab. Scientists were trying to make a weapon to weaken an enemy—I do not know which—and it spread to them first. Then the planet started to destabilize." He stumbled over that word. "The lower class could finally escape." He looked away, and Honora saw the pain reflected there. "Many escape ships were shot down by Fleet and the Empire before they understood we were not threats."

"But *you* were never a threat," Andrew ventured.

"No," Verk agreed. "Most of us never were."

Tash reappeared with their drinks, and Honora paid with a few credit pieces. Andrew curiously looked at the small black coins but didn't comment on them. Honora sipped her tea without tasting it; she was too busy looking back and forth between Andrew and Verk.

The Nym had brightened a little. "The Commons isn't bad," he said. "I have a job and a home. I would like to translate again, maybe for this new Authority. Find a mate," he added slyly.

Andrew chuckled at that.

"You two are mates?" Verk asked.

Andrew and Honora both tensed and exchanged a look. Why, she wasn't sure. One heart-stopping kiss that made her toes curl was hardly the basis for a relationship, let alone everything else they had been through together. "Roommates," Andrew finally answered. Honora let out a breath she didn't realize she had been holding. Verk was looking at them blankly, obviously groping for a definition. "We share an apartment," Andrew explained. "Two bedrooms."

Verk got it. "Oh."

Oh, indeed. Honora felt very awkward, sitting next to the

first man she had been attracted to in years and knowing that the person across the table could probably pick up on that. Never mind the high-level telepath who owned the restaurant and could pick up on that from twenty feet away. She forced her thoughts back to what Verk had said earlier.

"The virus," she said. "You don't know anything about it?"

Verk shook his head. "I did not find out much about it. I lived with the rest of the lower class on the surface of our planet. Highest class lived and worked underground. We did not know about the virus until they came out."

"You're positive it's eradicated?" Honora asked. The question came out a little harsher than she intended.

Andrew winced. "Honora," Andrew whispered. "The guy was a translator under duress."

Verk nodded. Whether it was to Honora's question or Andrew's defense of him, she wasn't sure. "Yes," the Nym replied. "Just a translator. Your Fleet says the virus is eradicated. I trust them more than the Nym."

Honora paused, choosing her next words carefully. "Verk, do you know how careful the Kurran Special Ops are? How cautious?"

"I know of your expertise, but you are the first Ops member I have spoken to."

"Former," she corrected, the impact of her discharge still hitting her like a sack of rocks. "I left recently. But my training and habits are still with me and they always will be. I may not have empathic or telepathic ability, but I do know how to judge someone's character. I wouldn't be alive without it."

Verk shifted in his seat, his green eyes wide. His lips quivered. Honora saw that she was scaring the guy. *He probably expects me to leap across the table and choke the living shit out of him*, she thought.

"I believe you're honest," she said quietly. "But I do not

believe for a second that this virus is really eradicated. I *can't*. I've dealt with the Nym for too long. I know what your government was capable of." She leaned forward and dropped her voice to a whisper. "You've lived under their rule. You know what the government was capable of, too. Do *you* really think the virus is gone?"

"Yes," Verk said, swallowing. Sweat beaded on his bald head. "I do. Fleet says it is; no one has been infected since we came to the Commons last year. Like you, I do not believe everything the rulers told me, but I believe Fleet. They are honest."

"All right," Honora said, nodding. She took another swallow of her cooling tea.

She turned to see Andrew staring at her, his jaw clenched in anger. She looked away, unable to face the judgement she saw there.

CHAPTER 15

"What the hell was that about?" Andrew demanded.

They had seen Verk off back at his apartment in the block adjacent to theirs. Their get-together with the Nym —something Andrew intended as a way to make a new *friend*, for the love of God—had been tense since Honora had damn near thrown the guy over their table and interrogated him. He had to double-check to make sure she didn't have a weapon at her hip.

A hip he had spent too few precious moments touching earlier in the day, but that was beside the point. He was *not* going to let himself be distracted right now.

Honora's eyes narrowed in a look that dared him to defy her. Something he had done repeatedly over their days together, and he wasn't going to start backing down now. "I trust Verk," she said. "It's his government I don't trust."

"Well, now we've moved past one of your prejudices. I'll count that as a victory." Andrew could have really used a cigarette right now. He breathed deeply and silently counted back from ten.

If this were a movie, or even back on Earth, Andrew might have made a move. But it wasn't a movie. No matter what they said about not wrecking their friendship, he was treading on thin ice here. They both were. It was one thing to get involved with a roommate, another entirely when he was 851 years out of his own time and said roommate was the only person he knew. If things soured, he could be shit out of luck.

If he did something right now, he had a feeling it would make things worse. He would be forcing it.

He needed to get out of the apartment, be alone for awhile.

He stood up. Honora's eyes never left him, but she stayed where she was. He dropped his credit chip and ID into his pocket and walked to the door.

"Where are you going?" she asked.

"Just for a walk," he said. "I'll be back in a little while." Noting the alarmed look on her face, he reassured her, "I'm coming back. I'm not mad or anything. I just need to get out for a bit." He flashed her a sincere smile, one he hoped conveyed that was he said was the truth.

———

THE GALAXY GRILL was exactly the kind of grimy, shady place Andrew used to go to for post-show drinks and meals. It was loud, boisterous, and reeked of fried food, stale coffee, and spilled beer. Best of all, there was a small stage at the back, a band pounding away at drums and guitars. He blinked in surprise at the sight of the instruments.

Punky-looking servers bustled between tables, pocketing small black coins and scanning credit chips. The bar was lined with customers perched on stools even at the relatively early hour of nine in the evening, quite a few in rumpled dark blue Fleet uniforms. The scene was so familiar, so reminiscent of his home and his old life—the one he had before he flushed it down the toilet—that it made his chest ache.

But they were *hiring*. Honora had been good enough to point that out when she was scanning her datatab before they moved.

At first, he rethought his notion to look for work here this evening. The place was clearly busy. But he wasn't ready to return to the apartment and Honora yet. He summoned his courage and walked up to the bar, where a server with cropped black hair was keeping her eye on the band as she shoved glasses under a replicator. The unit sputtered and spit out frothy green water, and the server dropped lime slices in them. "What can I get you?" she asked over the din.

"I read a help-wanted ad," he said.

"Yeah? We're looking for a server, not a manager," she said, eyeing his ensemble: a black button-down shirt and pants selected by Honora, who didn't appear to realize that there were other colors in the spectrum. "Part time," the server added.

"That's what I'm looking for."

The server pushed the drinks to a waiting couple and stepped up to the bar, sizing him up. "Seriously," she said. "You want to work at The Galaxy?"

"It's close to my apartment and you have live music, so why not?" Andrew held his breath, waiting for her response.

She tilted her head to one side. "Are you ex-Fleet? You look like an officer."

"No."

She thought for a moment. "Okay," she said finally. "Come around back with me." She called for another server to watch the bar for a few minutes, and led him through the crowd into an office at the back.

Like his own office back home, the room was windowless, full of boxes and cabinets, employees' belongings piled on a metal desk that had seen better days. The only major difference was the lack of paper.

"I'm Riel Waket," she said by way of introduction. "Part owner and unofficial hiring manager. What's your name?"

"Andrew Claybourne."

"You have your ID with you, Andrew Claybourne?"

He nodded and handed over his ID card, praying she wouldn't notice his trembling hand. He and Honora had managed to come up with a workable employment history using suggestions Fleet had written into his card's program, and Fleet would provide falsified references if it came to that. Andrew had never forged a thing in his life until now.

Riel picked up a small handheld device that resembled his cell phone and scanned his card. She read the data, scrolling over the device's screen with her fingers. "You have some club experience," she said.

"I do."

"Music and events management and bartending, too."

"A few years," he confirmed.

"It would be a hell of a downgrade, going from music promotion on Earth to slinging drinks on Rubidge Station," she said suspiciously, but she handed the card back to him. He tucked it in his pocket. "I have to ask you, why do you want to work here?"

"Earth's too hot," Andrew said.

Riel snorted. "I've never been, but that's what I usually hear about it. Really, why do you want to work here?"

"I want something simpler," Andrew replied truthfully. "I got sick of all the noise, all the attitude. I wanted to start over somewhere."

"And you picked *Rubidge Station*?" Riel said incredulously.

The lie came smoothly to him. "I followed my girlfriend here."

Riel started laughing. "Oh, gods, please tell me she was worth giving up that kind of career," she said.

He didn't give any indication of his offense to that statement, but he forced himself to smile. "You have no idea."

When Riel stopped laughing, she regarded him for a moment. She was deciding what to do about him, he realized. "You have a lot of nerve showing up here, looking for a job, at this time of night," she said.

"It's the best time to meet someone important."

"Well, I'll give you a point for that," Riel replied appreciatively. She leaned against the desk. "Okay, we're looking for someone to work two evenings and two afternoons a week. The nights are 1900 to 0300 hours, afternoons 1200 to 1700 hours. I can pay two credits an hour and you keep whatever tips you earn. Obviously, no drinking on the job, but employees tend to forget that in a place like this, which is why I'm hiring right now."

"All of that sounds reasonable," Andrew said.

"We have music most nights, not that you really want to hear most of it. Rubidge doesn't usually attract bands you actually want to listen to if you have any taste," she said. As if on cue, there was an ear-splitting wail of feedback and a singer screaming into the mic back in the bar proper. Riel winced. "You're *sure* you want to work here?"

Andrew nodded. "When can I start?"

WHEN HE RETURNED to the apartment, Honora was watching a news program on TV. She looked up when she saw him in the doorway, alarm written across her face.

"I found a job," he announced. "I start tomorrow night." He couldn't contain his excitement. "My new boss said there's live music most nights."

"Congratulations." She smiled, and as always, the sight struck Andrew temporarily mute. "I just need to find one of my own now."

He resisted asking her about the Commons Authority and recovered his voice. "Thank you for finding the job posting."

"It was the least I could do."

She was only a few feet away, and he couldn't guess what her reaction would be if he closed the distance between them. She must have noticed his apprehension—she must have been just as uncomfortable with the latest developments in their friendship, as well—but she didn't move either.

He finally broke the awkward silence. "I'll be in my room," he said uselessly. *Excellent, Claybourne, where else would you go?* "There's some stuff I want to look up."

Her chronometer told her the time was 2300 hours. It wasn't that long ago she would have been in bed, deeply asleep, at this late hour. In her new life, she was wide awake at this ungodly time, cross-legged on her bed and nibbling a cookie. Nighttime snacking was also a new habit. She idly wondered where the station's gym facilities were. She hadn't had a good workout since before she was discharged from Ops.

Andrew had been holed up in his bedroom with his new datatab since he had come back from the restaurant. She didn't take it as an affront that he hadn't touched her when he stepped in the door; he seemed as flummoxed as she about their newly discovered feelings for each other. Her heart thudding so hard she was sure he could hear it, she had prayed that he would touch her. When he hadn't, she berated herself for not giving it a try.

Andrew wasn't like Mal or the few lovers that had been

before him. This wouldn't be a strictly physical affair for her, the only kind she had ever known. Andrew was special. She didn't want to get involved until one of them got bored.

She didn't think she *could* get bored with him.

For the first time, she wished she had sat down with Mora and picked her brain over men. Her cousin would know how to handle this. Despite her tendency to see life less seriously for Honora's taste, Mora had a fantastic ability when it came to dealing with people. Honora, of course, didn't.

Mora would probably surprise a man by crawling into his bed naked. Honora made a face at the imagery, but the idea remained. It wasn't her usual method of doing things, but she doubted that Andrew would be receptive to sitting down and working out a schedule.

She heard the bathroom door close and the hard whine of the old-fashioned water shower's pipes as they ground into action. The water shower was one of the reasons she had rented the place. Its free twenty minutes of use per day was a cheap ploy by the landlord to entice renters; these units catered to families who would certainly use more than that. But Honora didn't care about that. She just wanted real showers.

And Andrew could get out any minute.

Pulse racing, she stripped off her clothes before she could lose her nerve. Spying a towel in her open duffel, she wrapped it around herself before padding out of the room on bare feet.

You've gone into battle so many times you've lost count. You kept going when you were injured. You accepted orders to go into a vortex knowing the chances of not making it out were high, she told herself. *And you're shaking like a leaf when you try to do something spontaneous like normal people.*

Like the bedroom doors, the one leading to the bathroom wasn't automatic. Her hand on its grip, she paused for a second. What if he had locked it?

Then you'll get in his bed instead. That decided, she tried the door. It slid open with only a minor creak. She closed it behind her as quietly as she could, wincing when it clunked into place on its track.

The shower stall's high frosted sides made him appear blurry, but he hadn't seen or heard her. She touched the small light control panel until the illumination dimmed to half.

"Huh," she heard Andrew mutter.

This was her last chance to leave. Any second he was going to turn his head and see her through the shower walls.

She tossed her towel over the commode and forced her feet to move forward. "Andrew," she said in an urgent stage whisper over the sound of water.

"What the..."

She opened the stall door a crack and held on to the glass to keep her hands from shaking. "Hi," she said. *Seduction, your name is Honora Kharn.* And, truth be told, he looked better naked and wet than she had imagined. She wasn't sure she could form words right now.

Andrew took in her equally unclothed state and swallowed. "What are you doing here?" he asked.

When she found her voice, it came out as a squeak. "Helping to save on the water bill." She didn't move, fearful of what he would say next.

"Get in," he said hoarsely.

Oh, thank the gods.

She stepped in as he took her arm and put her under the warm spray of water. She rubbed some out of her eyes and angled her head to meet Andrew's face. He brushed some wet hair off her forehead. "I wasn't expecting this," he said.

"Neither was I. I just..." She trailed off.

"I would never complain about you hopping in the shower with me." He twined one arm around her waist, closing the microscopic distance between them. Her nipples—

and other parts of her anatomy—were crushed against his body, sending an inferno burning through her.

She kissed him, at last letting go of all the tension and nervousness. He returned it eagerly, leaning into her until her shoulder pressed against the tiled wall, his body flush against hers. His hands explored her, touching and kneading her hips, her backside. She tensed and held her breath as his fingers found the networks of raised scars that crisscrossed her skin, remnants of her days as a soldier.

"Is something wrong?" he asked, and she realized she was frozen on the spot.

She looked into his hazel eyes and saw warmth and concern there. "No," she assured him. She pushed herself off the tiles, putting everything she had into the kiss. His erection ground against her thigh, and a wave of dizziness passed through her, high as she was on the fact that this man wanted her; was now kissing her neck below her ear, like he already knew her erogenous zones; was rolling his hand over one breast. When he bent his head and took one stiff nipple in his mouth, she couldn't keep a little cry from escaping her. She felt the sensation deep in the pit of her belly and her knees wobbled. She put her hands on the wall and shower door to keep her balance.

Andrew raised his head when he sensed her reaction and held on to her. Dimly, she was aware of the pinging sound that meant they had gone over their free water allotment, but both of them ignored it.

Instead, she let her hand her hands wander over his body, taking in the line of his hip, his backside, until she lightly closed around the rigid flesh between them. He sucked in a harsh breath, and emboldened by his reaction, Honora gently traced him with her fingertips, stroking a little harder.

"Stop," he said suddenly. "If you keep doing that, this is going to be over before it starts." He kissed her fiercely, his tongue tangling with hers, before backing her against the wall again and gripping her hips. She slid one of her legs around him and squealed when he lifted her against the tile, her other leg wrapping around his waist.

"You're very sure about this?" he asked.

She responded with a kiss and clutched his shoulders. "Yes," she whispered.

She felt him position himself at her entrance, couldn't keep her moan of anticipation inside…

The shower sputtered and shut off, the pipes groaning at a level that under other circumstances would have sent Honora scrambling to contact the building manager.

"Shit," they said simultaneously.

Honora was still wrapped around Andrew, her body screaming for release, and, to a lesser extent, the warm water of the shower.

Andrew silenced her with a crushing kiss, his tongue searching her mouth, a promise of things to come. "My room," he murmured against her lips. "Or yours. I don't care."

He helped her down, reluctantly unwinding her legs from him and helping her stay upright. She squeezed the water from her hair and watched as Andrew wrapped a towel around his waist. "Come here," he said and held out hers.

Feeling self-conscious would be silly right now, especially in the low light, but she couldn't help it. She resisted the urge to cover herself; her healed scars and burns, once points of soldierly pride, likely weren't what he was used to seeing. "Feminine" would never be a word to describe her.

Andrew must have seen her demeanor change, but he didn't drape the towel over her like she expected. Instead, he started a slow perusal of her body that started at her feet and worked his way up. Even though the bathroom was steamy, she thought she could see his color rise. When he met her eyes, he had a devilish look on his face.

"Andrew, I'm getting cold," she whispered. She wasn't, but she felt far too exposed.

He wrapped the towels over her shoulders and rubbed the fabric against her skin. "Honora," he said in her ear. "You're beautiful."

Honora never heard that word used in connection with her, and the compliment made her smile.

A few quick steps and they were in his bedroom, Andrew expertly ordering the lights to medium illumination. Their towels tossed carelessly to the floor, he gripped her hips and pulled her to him, all hard and hot male. He guided her to the bed and lay on his side, facing her, propped up one elbow.

"Andrew?" she said expectantly. What had made him pause?

He laced the fingers of his free hand with hers, resting it in the center of his chest. "Honora, I want you," he rasped.

The words sent a jolt of electricity straight through her, tingles radiating everywhere. She felt the same—she thought she might die if he didn't touch her again—but she didn't want to parrot the words back to him. Instead, she freed her hand and let it slide down his chest, past his abdomen, to one firm thigh, before taking him in hand, running her thumb on the underside of his cock. He closed his eyes and leaned his forehead against hers, like her simple touch could be his undoing.

For the first time, Honora possessed erotic power over a man. The idea made her feel headier than she already did.

"You're not playing fair," he said hoarsely.

She planted a light kiss on his cheek. "I'm not playing at all," she whispered in his ear, lighting nipping his earlobe. Confidence bolstered, she pushed him on his back and straddled him before he could blink, pinning his wrists above his head.

He looked up at her, his eyes hooded with desire. "I've

thought about this." He wriggled his hands, but she didn't release him.

"You've thought about this?"

"A lot more than you think. Do you know how difficult this has been? You're hot as hell. It isn't as if I haven't noticed."

He was twisting under her grip, trying to get away and gain back the upper hand, Honora knew. She wasn't going to let him have it just yet. "Yes, I know what that's like," she said. "And I know exactly how hard that is." She shimmied just enough so he could feel her skin against his but stayed ever so slightly out of reach. Her aching center brushed against his erection, and she didn't want to make either of them wait anymore. She released her hold on his wrists.

Instead of trying to roll her over, he stayed where he was, his hands stroking her back, his eyes never leaving her face. When his hands reached her waist, Honora instinctively raised herself on her knees just enough to help him position her before entering her with one smooth thrust.

They were still for a few heartbeats, the shock of him inside her making her breath catch. It went beyond the physical; she felt a deeper connection than that. Andrew's face was a mirror of her own, like he felt it, too.

She let him establish a rhythm, his hands on hips guiding her as he slid in and out of her. Already Honora could feel pressure building in the pit of her belly, growing stronger as he increased his pace, and she knew she wouldn't last long. Her back arched, and he took the opportunity to close his mouth around one peaked nipple. The first waves of orgasm hit her, her breath coming in harsh pants. Andrew let go of her breast with a gentle scrape of his teeth that sent her too-sensitized nerve endings on fire. He saw she was close and let go of her long enough to cup her face in his hands and kiss her. His thrusts became faster, more intense, and she knew he was close, too.

Her climax hit her with the impact of a star going nova, knocking the breath from her as it ripped a cry from her throat, muffled by Andrew's mouth. She didn't stop. She wouldn't until Andrew found his, too.

She could tell by the tensing of his body, the bunching of muscles beneath her, that it wasn't far off. "Andrew," she gasped. "Look at me."

He obeyed, his pupils dilated. He thrust one final time, his hands digging into her skin, her name on his lips.

CHAPTER 16

Honora woke up at 0700 hours, later than she was used to. Her first thought was how warm she was, comfortable with the man lying beside her, and then how much she didn't want to get up. She could stay in bed, make love with Andrew until he had to go to work in the evening, and...

Did you just use the term "make love"?

She shook herself mentally and silently slipped out of bed. No, she was not going to think of that new area of her friendship using that term. That's all they were, friends who had spectacular physical chemistry and mind-altering sex. That was all.

The shower was working and didn't cut out when she stepped into it this time. She thought about Andrew's initial panic after their coupling last night, his worry about birth control and stuttering that he had never been so irresponsible in his life, until she told him about the tiny implants under her skin that took care of such things. Then he had regaled her of what had passed for contraception in his time, and she shuddered recalling that conversation. She would have been doomed if they had stayed on Earth.

She quickly dressed and choked down a half-cup of bitter coffee spit out from the replicator. She sent a short note to Andrew's datatab in case he woke up before she returned. *Gone to see Mora. Back in a couple of hours. H.*

She sent another message to Mora's personal transmit address asking to meet with her, knowing her cousin would never be without her datatab. Immediately she received a response: *My apartment. I'll have breakfast waiting.* It was punctuated with bobbing smiley faces. For the first time, the sight of them didn't irritate Honora.

Honora had never seen Rubidge as it woke up, the corridors of her apartment block bustling with uniformed residents getting ready for work, small children en route to one of the two schools on station. She saw more Nym in her building than humanoids and found that the sight didn't bother her. She overheard snippets of conversation: admonitions from mothers to behave, fathers arguing with scowling children that candy was not an appropriate meal to begin the day. They were such normal scenes, one that could happen anywhere in the universe.

She made her way across the commercial strip to get to Fleet housing, the strip's flashing lights and loud music rather pathetic when there were so few people about. The strip's lighting never mimicked planetary night and day—specifically the planets in the Commons, where they tended to have suns —and more than ever, the sights and sounds in the absence of crowds struck Honora as cheap and tawdry.

That wasn't the case for Fleet housing. The neighborhood was a sea of dark blue uniforms as shifts changed. Honora felt wistful as she saw the officers striding purposefully, each with schedules to follow and orders to obey. She wanted to *belong* somewhere again.

Mora's apartment door opened before Honora could press the buzzer. "Hi!" Mora said cheerfully, the dark circles under her eyes betraying her exhaustion. At first, Honora thought she might have pulled an all-nighter at the infirmary, but then she spied the rest of her outfit beneath her bright pink robe: A very short, electric-blue dress that was cut dangerously low in front, paired with sparkly tights. A pair of boots with obscenely high heels had been cast off in front of the couch. Her two-toned, shoulder-length hair was mussed, and when Honora looked closer, she saw that the rings under her eyes were actually smeared eye makeup.

"Don't look at me like that," Mora chastised at Honora's look. "I went to a birthday party for my boss last night. This morning," she corrected herself.

"Are you still drunk?"

Mora gave her a look that questioned Honora's intelligence. "No. I wasn't drinking that much, if that's what you're getting at. I spent most of my night on the dance floor with a couple of ensigns who are probably young enough to be my..." She waved her hand, looking for the right relationship to a woman in her early thirties. "Little brothers."

"Where is Zak, anyway?" Honora asked, reminded of Mora's much-older brother.

"He's on a battleship posted somewhere near the Sorkan border." She was poking around her tiny kitchen, producing coffee from a replicator much newer than the one in Honora's apartment. "What do you want to eat?" Mora cut herself a slice of the giant cake on the counter and waited for Honora's answer.

In less than a day, Honora had stayed up way too late, eaten cookies in bed, and seduced a man. Despite her suspicions about the Nym virus, she was feeling a little decadent. "I'll have some cake, too," she said.

Mora's eyebrows climbed so high they nearly disappeared under her red-tipped bangs, but she cut another slice for Honora.

Seated at the small kitchen table, Mora took a sip of coffee and said bluntly, "I'm assuming you're not here because you want some girl talk."

Guilt gnawed at Honora again. "Not entirely," she confessed. "But some of it is." She hadn't planned on telling Mora about what had happened the night before, but her cousin had more experience in matters like these.

"Is it Andrew?" Mora asked.

"I'll get to that in a minute." A curious look came over Mora's face at this, but she didn't pursue the subject. She probably assumed there wasn't much to tell. "We've moved into an apartment in the Nym District," Honora continued.

"That's the term the less-bigoted locals are calling it."

"Last night we went out with a Nym man Andrew's befriending."

Mora interrupted her. "Please tell me you didn't put a weapon to his head."

"No!" Honora said emphatically. "Look, I've spoken to a few of them during my time here. I—and the Empire—have been wrong about some things."

Mora was temporarily stunned. She dramatically swiped at her eyes, further smearing her makeup. "The Empire is *wrong* about something?"

Honora sidestepped this and forged on with her story. "Verk was a translator back on his planet. He told us about the evacuation and the virus that killed so many of them."

Mora held up a hand, serious again. "I know where this is going, and you are *not* starting a war on Rubidge Station."

"Who said anything about a war?" Honora snapped. "I just want to know more about the virus."

"And you figured that since I'm a nurse and Mother works for Fleet Medical, I would know?"

"Yes. That, and you're a nurse on the station that has the largest population of refugees in the Commons, your father is the admiral of the Fourth Fleet, and the first time traveler showed up on the last ship you were posted to."

"Second largest population of refugees after Repub-4, I work on a station under First Fleet's control, Lily has nothing to do with the virus, and the *Defiant* was a piece of shit. Then there's the fact that the research team the *Defiant* was carrying to the Fringes before she was decommissioned is now being led by my mother," Mora countered. "Try again."

"Do you know anything about the virus?"

"Do *you* know how to hold a conversation without acting like an Empire interrogator?" Mora took another swallow of coffee. "Have you tried being polite? 'Hi, Mora,'" she said in a bad imitation of Honora's accent. "'I know this is a long shot, but do you happen to know anything about the Nym virus? Oh, it's been eradicated? Damn. Hey, do you want to go to the White Dwarf with me? There's an exotic dancer who can do the most amazing trick with his—'"

"I get it," said Honora icily.

"So, ask me nicely."

Honora suppressed a sigh and tried again. "Do you have any information on the virus that decimated the Nym world that you could share with me, *please*?"

"Not much," Mora admitted. "All that's available to me is what Fleet's told us, and that's pretty much limited to symptoms and treatment options. Fleet Medical is still studying exactly how the virus originated, and mere nurses don't participate in research. I don't have access to anything classified." She shrugged. "I *can* tell you with absolute certainty that this virus isn't on Rubidge."

"Do specimens exist anywhere else?"

For the first time, Mora's expression darkened. "I don't know. I'm one of the people who would like to know that. The whole infirmary would. I *do* know that it doesn't appear to have any asymptomatic shedding. One minute you're fine, the next you're bleeding out all the holes in your head." Seeing the expression on Honora's face, Mora added, "I guess your Nym friend didn't give you the gory details?"

Honora shook her head.

"I've only see vids taken by survivors," Mora stressed. "Never a live patient. I've seen a lot, Honora, and those vids were damn near the worst things I've ever seen. All of the Nym who landed on station were subject to physicals before they were allowed here. We do have a stockpile of medication that Fleet Medical swears is effective, but we've never had to use it. I hope we never have to test it out."

"If the virus has been studied enough to determine that there isn't asymptomatic shedding and determine treatment, there must be a sample of it somewhere."

Mora shrugged. "Who knows? The samples could have been taken from tissue. If I thought too much about that, I would lose my mind."

"There must be a way to find out."

"Besides breaking into classified medical files, there isn't one."

"What about Commons Prime?" Honora pressed. The small planet was the hub of Commonwealth space, home to high-ranking military personnel, the Fleet's officers' academy, and a few moneyed families.

"Possibly." Mora's voice softened. "Look, Honora, you've just been discharged from a position that was your life and exiled from your home. I think you have a lot on your mind, and digging into this is a way of coping. You're not used to making your own decisions." Honora scowled, but Mora didn't stop. "I'm a nurse. I read people well. My unsolicited medical advice to you is to find a new job. The Commons Authority could really use someone with your experience."

Ah, the Commons Authority again. Honora's least-worst option.

"So tell me about Andrew," Mora prompted.

Honora shifted uncomfortably in her seat. "Are you going to make a big deal out of this?"

Mora didn't ask what "this" was. "Yeah, probably."

Honora was unsure where to start. "Things have changed between us," she began slowly. "We've become very close since I rescued him."

"And you're feeling the sexual tension. I get that."

"Well, yes, I suppose." Honora felt her face grow hot. She reminded herself of who she was speaking to. "Things have become a little more complicated, and I don't know what to do."

"Complicated how?"

Honora chose her words carefully. "We spent the night together," she explained. "Last night."

She had never seen Mora open-mouthed and at a loss for words.

"It just sort of happened," Honora said hastily, and reiterated, "I don't know what to do next."

"Shouldn't you be having this discussion with him?" Mora asked when she found her voice.

"I don't know. I'm not very good at this."

"Neither am I, in case you haven't noticed. Remember Bailey?"

Honora did. Bailey and Mora had a whirlwind romance in their early twenties when they were in university, culminating in a very brief engagement before Bailey's parents intervened. "What happened to him, anyway?" Honora asked.

"Don't change the subject." Seeing Honora's narrowed eyes, Mora sighed. "Last I heard, he finished his doctorate in non-humanoid cultures and archaeology. I think he teaches at the First Republic University." Mora had finished a degree in a similar field before enrolling in nursing school, three years of her life that she now proclaimed to be wasted. She steered the conversation back to where she wanted it. "So, what do you want me to do?"

"Give me some advice."

Mora hooted. "Oh, that's good. Look, there isn't a lot I can tell you to do besides talk to him and tell him what you want from this. And *don't* treat it like an interrogation."

"I rarely participated in interrogations in Special Ops."

"You mostly just shot things and kicked people in the crotch, I know. You probably shouldn't do that, either."

Honora looked at the tabletop, where a little coffee had splashed out of Mora's cup. "I don't think we have the same wants," she began. "We told each other that we don't do long-term or marriage, and I'm not getting ideas now." She looked up. "There's also that issue of his going home. If he gets the opportunity, I think he'll take it."

"I don't think that will happen," Mora said gently. "When Lily was asked if she wanted to go back—"

Honora's stomach turned over. "What?" she yelped. "Fleet had a way to go into the vortex?"

Mora held up her hands. "I don't know the specifics, but she told me that Fleet asked her if she wanted to go back. She opted to stay here. Vortex activity is dangerous. You know that."

An awful possibility reared its head. What if Andrew was given that same opportunity? What if he took it? It had only been a dream to Andrew, and she thought he might be settling in given that he went out and found a job. All of that was insignificant compared to the life he had been torn from on Earth.

"Honora?" Mora asked curiously. "Are you okay?"

Honora forced herself to nod. "I'm fine. You were saying about what I should do with Andrew?"

"You could talk to him," Mora suggested again. "If this

was something that was in the heat of the moment, you could both laugh it off and then forget it ever happened."

"You speak from experience?"

"I do," Mora replied without a shred of shame. "It happens sometimes. Or you could just take it one day at a time, see where things go. Go on a date. You're not obligated to marry him or anything."

"True." Honora was actually glad she was having this conversation with Mora. "It's just that for the first time, I've met someone whose company I actually enjoy out of bed."

Mora laughed. "Oh, my gods, I never expected to hear you say that." Her mirth subsided, but there was still a smile on her face. "You like him," she interpreted. "I think you're worrying too much. You're not flying into battle. This is supposed to be fun." She leaned closer across the table, a conspiratorial cadence to her voice. "Was he any good?"

Once again, heat suffused Honora's face, and she knew she was blushing furiously when Mora started giggling again. Honora couldn't keep a smile from her face, and she tried to hide it with her hands.

Mora sighed. "I really need to find a time traveler of my own."

Honora recovered and turned back to the other reason she was here. "Wouldn't you like to at least put your mind at east about the virus?" she asked.

"I would, to be honest, and so would a lot of Fleet medics. But as far as I know, the only way to access that kind of information is through hacking, and that's not my area of expertise."

"It isn't mine, either."

"Didn't they teach you to do that in spy school?"

Honora didn't bother to correct her. "No. I learned a few languages and the care and maintenance of obscenely expensive fighter craft. Don't you know anyone who would know how to do that?"

Mora clasped her hands together on the tabletop, a sure sign that she knew something.

"Mora?" Honora prompted.

"Yes," she said tersely. "I know someone who may be able to help. But he's going to annoy the shit out of you."

CHAPTER 17

Andrew woke up as the bedroom lights slowly cycled into an imitation of daylight. He rolled over and saw that he was alone in bed. Honora's absence didn't surprise him, but he would be hurt if she had decided that last night was a mistake.

He threw on a robe and went to her room to investigate. She wasn't there either, and her bed hadn't been slept in. Reassured, Andrew went to the kitchen to slap at the replicator until it puked out some coffee, and turned on the TV.

The apartment door opened, and Honora walked in. At the sight of him, she paused. "Good morning," she said.

"Good morning," he returned.

"I went to Mora's," she offered by way of explanation. She was blushing to the roots of her hair, and he wondered exactly how much she and Mora had talked about. "I left you a note on your datatab."

She sat down next to him, and he breathed a sigh of relief when she didn't shy away from him. "I'm just wondering," she said carefully. "But what are we now?"

The question hadn't escaped Andrew, either. "I don't know," he admitted.

"Friends with an exclusive sexual relationship?"

"That's a little more technical than I was thinking, but it works." Relief coursed through him. For a moment he was afraid she would suggest they forget everything.

"I spoke to Mora about the Nym virus," she said.

His hackles rose. "Honora," he warned.

"I'm saying the same thing to you that I said to Mora: I'm not going to start a war," she insisted. "I just want to make sure it's really gone."

"And?"

"She wants to know, too. I don't think she's entirely convinced the virus is eradicated, either."

Andrew sighed. "So, is this your new mission?"

"Yes."

"Have you given any more thought to joining the Commons police force?"

"I *have*, and I wish everyone would stop asking me about it," she said petulantly.

"I think you should apply."

She sighed, and he felt a twinge of guilt about nagging her. "I will, when I'm finished with all of this."

Her datatab trilled from her pocket, and she removed it.

Andrew wasn't entirely convinced of her intentions. "You're not going to start a witch hunt, are you?"

"No!" she said forcefully. "I just received messages from a friend of hers who knows…" She paused. "Technology."

He knew that tone. "What kind of technology?" he asked suspiciously.

"Computers."

"You mean hacking."

She looked back at the datatab without answering.

"I knew it! Honora, you are *not* going to piss on the computer systems of the organization that helped out both of us." He stood up and ran his fingers through his hair.

"I won't be pissing on anything."

"Not you or this geek friend of Mora's. Did she actually agree to this?" Andrew couldn't fathom why someone so firmly ensconced in her career, with a family legacy no less, would do such a thing.

"She wants to know, too."

"What will happen if you're caught?" he demanded.

She thought for a few seconds. "Probably prison."

"Why are you so casual about this?" he asked, his voice rising.

"I'm not sure of the exact sentence, but breaking into computer systems isn't a capital crime. I wouldn't be subjected to a mind wipe," she replied calmly.

He was momentarily caught off-guard. "Mind wipe?"

"The erasure of a convict's memories and personality. Deprogramming, I suppose. It's a Commons practice that the Empire has adopted to keep the peace. The Commons has moral issues with executing prisoners."

"And it works?" Andrew couldn't help but be a little intrigued.

She shrugged. "As far as I know. I don't associate with criminals." She looked to find him glaring at her. "What?"

"You know you would be a criminal if you started hacking into Fleet systems, don't you?"

She smiled like she had the night before, explaining twenty-ninth contraceptive methods. Andrew felt the first stirrings of arousal thrum through his body at the sight—damn it—but he didn't let on.

"I spoke to Mora," she said patiently. "I trust her. The man she recommends once broke into the hardware of a Nym ship. He knows what he's doing." She looked at her tablet again and nearly snarled at the message there. "I've already received a transmit from him. I hope he's more professional than he sounds." She held it out for Andrew to read, or try to. It was a conflagration of consonants with a bunch of suggestive emoticons. *Huh.* Some irritating things never died.

"'Look forward to...meeting you,'" Andrew sounded out. "'Are you as adorable as Mora?' What the hell kind of hacker is this?"

"I don't know."

"One who's going to have his ass handed back to him a platter if he so much as looks at you the wrong way," Andrew muttered.

Honora's laughter rang out through the apartment.

———

Andrew ignored Honora's fashion advice when he got ready for his first night at his new job, even enlisting Mora's help via transmit to prove her wrong.

"Shouldn't you wear your suit on your first day?" Honora had wheedled.

"You don't go out to pubs or clubs much, do you?" He smoothed a non-existent wrinkle from his T-shirt.

"You know I don't."

Andrew's datatab pinged an incoming message. Mora was again siding with him.

Honora just liked how he looked dressed up; it wasn't common for her to see someone who wasn't wearing a bland military uniform. "Okay," she conceded. "Mora has an active social life. I bow to her expertise."

Andrew raised an eyebrow at her, and she knew what he was thinking: *Once again, former Lieutenant Honora Kharn has to admit she's wrong*. But he was smiling at her, and she didn't say anything.

Now, with Andrew gone, she wasn't sure what to do with herself. Part of her wanted to go to The Galaxy Grill and see what he was up to, but even she, with her lack of experience in relationships, knew it would be inappropriate. What would she do, sit at the bar and nurse tea all night? Did pubs even serve tea?

There was one thing she could do and needed to: There was a public gym in this neighborhood. A good workout would clear her head.

Well, she had had one the night before, she thought ruefully, and amended that to a workout that required her to wear clothes.

She changed into the appropriate gear and tossed her datatab and a change of clothes into a bag before making her way to the gym. It was staffed with a few humanoids and Nym, and she was pleased to find out that this was one of the few places on the station where she wouldn't be gouged. The facilities certainly weren't what she was used to back on Stappic, but the place was clean, if a little rough around the edges.

"Do you want a trainer?" the attendant asked from behind the front desk. He spoke with a Kurran accent, a Kortun one if Honora wasn't mistaken. The third planet in the Empire, two away from Prime. Honora's heart clenched at hearing the ghost of her first language.

She shook her head, more to clear her thoughts than a refusal to his question. She replied in Kurran, "I'll be fine, but thank you. Do you have a running sim?"

His forehead wrinkled slightly, his only betrayal at his surprise. He nodded and replied in kind. "Four credits for two hours."

"Thank you." She handed him a five-credit piece, a big chunk of silvery metal. "Where is it?" she asked, pocketing the black one-credit piece she received as her change. He slid a disc across the desk, her key to the sim chamber.

"Go to the back of the gym. The door's through there."

She thanked him again and stashed her bag in a locker before heading to the sim chamber. The room's simulations were better than she expected. It was a typical planetary scene set at dusk, probably for the benefit of the gym's Nym clientele. There was a dirt track, but when Honora looked closely she could tell that the images wouldn't shift at all under running feet. There were the twin Kurran moons peeking high in the artificial sky, and the walls were a little blurry in spots due to loose wires in the sim's hardware.

She took off in a run, hardly the sort of grueling exercise she subjected herself to in Ops, but running always felt good. Idly she wondered where she could find a sparring partner for hand-to-hand training. She might have to ask Mora about that, if her cousin knew anyone in Fleet who would be interesting in fighting with a former Ops officer.

Or she could join the Authority. They had to have decent gym facilities.

She guessed that she had run around the wide track at least twice when someone jogged up next to her. "Hi," said a familiar voice in Kurran.

She stopped for a moment to face the attendant from the front desk. "Hello." She knew she had plenty of time to run around the chamber and took off again at a slower pace. He followed.

"I'm Rori," he introduced himself.

"Honora," she replied curtly.

He started running alongside her. Change jingled in his pockets. "I haven't seen you here before. Did you just arrive on station?"

She increased her pace. "Almost a week ago. I thought you

worked here?" She deliberately placed emphasis on *worked*. She didn't care if she was being rude.

"I took a break. I don't see a lot of real Kurrans here."

"*Real* Kurrans?" she repeated without stopping. "There's one running a restaurant on the strip."

"You're obviously not from the Commons."

"Neither are you," she returned and chanced a glance at him. He had the very fair coloring of someone from Kortun, like Mora's side of the family, but he looked like he spent too much time lying in the sun lamps. Instead of the healthy look Andrew sported when she met him, this man's skin was a distressing shade of pink. The rest of him had the look of someone who spent too much time at the gym without putting his training into practice: a little too perfect for her taste. Sunburn aside, he was undoubtedly someone used to women fawning over him.

She didn't care about his backstory, she just wanted to get in a good run.

"I couldn't make it in the Forces," he confessed, answering a question she hadn't asked and didn't care about. "I wanted to try something new, so I came here. You?"

Her estimation of him plummeted another few points. "I'm ex-Special Ops," she said, forcing a hard look to her face, one that said *I eat nosy gym employees for breakfast.* "Fighter pilot."

Rori didn't seem surprised at that. "I could tell."

Honora inferred that if Rori had a shred of extrasensory ability, it had long ago fried under a sun lamp. If he knew what she was thinking, he would have trotted back to his post. She finally stopped and faced him. "Is something wrong?" she demanded.

He had the gall to look affronted. "No, not at all. I just rarely see Kurrans in this part of the universe."

She crossed her arms over her chest.

He looked at her with an avaricious glint to his eye. "Do you want to have dinner sometime?"

Sikiaka, now this pain in the ass was trying to pick her up? "No," she replied.

He tried again. "What about a vid?"

"No."

"What about..."

"No."

Her suspicions were confirmed: He wasn't used to being turned down. In the sim chamber's artificial dusk, she could see a flush creeping over his sunburned skin. "Why not?"

Why not? Aggravation colored her vision red. "I don't have to give you a reason," she snarled. "Now, if you don't mind, I'd like to get my four credits' worth of running." With that, she took off in a heart-pounding run, her shoes slamming against the unmoving dust of the track.

Heavy footsteps behind her told her that Rori hadn't given up. "Are you seeing someone?" he asked.

"I don't need to have an excuse to not date you," she shot back over her shoulder. Instinctively, she braced herself for a possible fight. She didn't know where his weak points were, and he had admitted that he had had some experience in the Kurran Forces but couldn't hack it.

Aim for the throat first, she decided. *Then go ahead based on his response.*

"I think I've seen you around the station," he called. "With some Commons guy."

Honora halted and whirled around. "I told you no!" she shouted. "Now I'm telling you to *fuck off*!"

Incredulity spread across Rori's face. "You left Special Ops to be with that guy?"

"Oh, for fuck's sake." She turned to the chamber door. "I want a refund."

"But you used the track!"

"And you harassed me most of my time here." She stepped into the bright lights of the gym and blinked at the glare. "I can either get my money back, or I can show you what those of us who can take it in Special Ops are capable of." She fixed him with a hard stare, her hands curling into fists at her side.

Even this idiot knew that a fight between him and a Special Ops soldier would be one-sided. "Fine," he mumbled.

Honora collected her things and met him at the front desk, where he shooed away a bored-looking employee and handed her back her four credits. She accepted them without another word and strode from the gym.

She was still fuming when she returned to the apartment and took a quick shower. The damn thing cut out again, just one more incident to annoy her. Then she remembered what had happened in here only a day before, and a warm, happy feeling spread through her. She wondered how Andrew was faring at his new job.

There was a message from Mora waiting for her on her datatab when she got out of the shower. *Be there in 20 minutes. I have my friend. HUGS!*

Instead of muttering to herself about presumptuousness, Honora simply dressed and waited, turning on the vidscreen to pass the time. Andrew had left it tuned to that ridiculous broadcast *Lightning's Luck,* and she didn't bother to change it.

She wanted to throw something at the vidscreen six minutes into the broadcast. Captain Trid—an obnoxious excuse of a man who reminded Honora of Rori—was crawling around the smoke-filled bowels of a starship, aided by a simpering first officer whose top had conveniently torn on a pipe. She complained about a strange smell in an exaggerated Kurran accent, and the idiot captain brushed her off.

Is this what my life has come to? Honora wondered. *Being pestered by men with more muscles than brains and watching* Lightning's Luck?

No, it hadn't come to that yet. Not as long as Andrew remained in her life.

The door alarm trilled, snapping her out of her thoughts. Mora and a tall, skinny young man waited on the other side. Mora's skirt nearly reached her knees, a length Honora hadn't seen on her since they were children. The young guy was blond-haired and had the lavender eyes common to the Hefronn Galaxy, a rarity in the Commons. He wore the regulation navy pants of Fleet and a dark green sweater with a hole unraveling at the shoulder.

He spoke first. "Hey."

"Hello," said Honora cautiously.

Mora and her friend let themselves in. When the door was closed, Mora said by way of introduction, "This is Ensign Taz Shraft, currently assigned to the *Fortunate Wanderer*."

He piped up immediately. "You can say it. It's the stupidest fucking name for a ship Fleet's ever come up with. Mora would know. We were posted to the *Defiant,* and that ship actually rattled when it hit hyperspace."

"Shut up, Taz," Mora muttered, elbowing him. "Taz, this is my cousin, Honora Kharn."

"Mora said you used to work with the Kurran Special Operations." There was a note of respect in his voice, and Honora felt herself soften towards him. "Fighter pilot?"

She nodded.

"Gods*damn*, but I'd love to hear about the specs on your ships sometime," he said appreciatively.

"Not now," Mora urged him.

Ensign Shraft's admiration sounded genuine. Honora let herself be flattered for a moment. "I'm not sure how much help I would be," she confided. "I only flew things and blew up what I was told to."

"I'd love to have that kind of job."

"Fleet has regulations to keep people like you from ever having that kind of job," Mora pointed out.

Shraft didn't seem to care that he had just been insulted. "Yeah, probably," he agreed. He removed a battered datatab from his pocket and plunked down on the couch without waiting for an invitation. "So, Honora, Mora says you need someone to hack into Fleet Medical about the Nym virus you're worried about." He looked around the apartment, a touch of disdain on his face. "Do you have any beer? Mora said there would be beer."

"You're the hacker?" Honora said, looking to Mora for confirmation.

"Don't let first impressions fool you," Mora explained.

"Do you have any idea what kind of story I had to come up with to get shore leave from the *Wanderer*?" Shraft said to them. "I think I deserve at least a drink for getting away with it. That, and doing something for someone I've never met that could get my ass kicked so hard I'd end up back on Vu'saar."

Vu'saar. That information made Ensign Shraft a little more interesting. Its galaxy, if one could call a pair of barely habitable planets a galaxy, was even more cloistered than the Kurran Empire.

Mora rolled her eyes. "Let me see what the replicator can bring up," she offered and went to the kitchen.

"Ugh," Shraft grunted at the mention of the unit. He patted the seat next to him, like he was in his home. "Sit down, Honora."

Honora fought the urge to roll her own eyes and obeyed. Taz held out his datatab.

"First of all," he began, "you know I could be looking at a dishonorable discharge for doing this, right?"

Honora nodded.

"I managed to break into Fleet Medical," he continued. "And guess what I found?"

She leaned over to see his datatab's screen. "What is it?"

Mora returned with a half-full glass of something that was more foam than liquid, with an ominous green tint. She held it out for Shraft, who scowled at the glass. "What's this?" he demanded.

"Beer."

"It looks like something beer threw up."

"Well, there's nothing in the refrigerator except for a bunch of healthy crap Honora obviously put there, so it'll have to do."

Shraft shook his head and sniffed the glass, making a face. "We should go to a bar."

Mora perched on the coffee table, facing him and Honora. "Are you still banned from the Solar Flare?"

"No, that was only temporary." Shraft turned to Honora to explain. "They really overreacted when I forgot to pay for a few drinks."

"You didn't forget to pay for a few drinks," Mora protested. "It was more like you remotely reprogrammed the Flare's replicator and made yourself a bunch of drinks."

"You had some, too!"

"I didn't know then!"

Honora couldn't take their bickering anymore. "The virus," she reminded them. As an afterthought, she added, "Please."

"Oh, *that*," Shraft said dismissively. "Well, after risking my ass to get this information, digging into the most encrypted files at Fleet Medical and Commons Prime, it turns out that everyone was telling the truth. There's no risk of the virus infecting the Commons. It's been eradicated."

All of the tension Honora had been holding on to the last few days evaporated, leaving a cold, hard ball of disappointment in her gut. "That can't be," she breathed.

"It can be," Mora said gently. "Look, I know you were

spoiling for a fight or a mission of some kind, but it's really gone."

And with it, Honora's sense of purpose.

Mora and Shraft exchanged a knowing look between them. "I did find something else," Shraft said.

Mora shook her head. "Taz, no."

"What is it?" Honora demanded.

"Shit," said Mora softly. "Honora, don't listen to him. It's not a good idea."

Honora looked at her cousin, and Mora flinched. They had never physically fought as children, but Mora was aware of the kind of training the Kurran Forces subjected its soldiers to. The way Honora was feeling now, she wouldn't hesitate to use force to get whatever information Ensign Shraft had his hands on.

"Tell me," Honora said flatly.

"The artificial vortex still has weak intermittent activity," Shraft explained. Mora buried her face in her hands. "The device the Nym used to create it is still active. Fleet isn't sure that it can't be dismantled without creating a black hole or something, so they're monitoring it until it stops functioning. Theoretically, you could bring your friend back to Earth, approximately around the time that he left."

Shock struck Honora mute, both at the news and that Mora had told him Andrew's story. When she found her voice again, all she could say was, "Andrew could go home."

Mora and Shraft gave her the barest of nods.

Honora shot to her feet and began pacing the room. She felt so small, like her body couldn't contain what she was feeling. The apartment—no, the entire station—felt too contained, that if she did what she wanted to do right now and let out a blood-curdling scream, she still wouldn't be able to unleash the utter rage and hopelessness that washed over her in dark, ugly waves.

Andrew would leave the Commons if he got a chance. He had been very clear about that. He would leave her.

For the first time in her life, Honora realized that she needed someone. She had found someone she could see herself spending the rest of her life with, someone she could love, was already beginning to love. And he would leave. For all of his idiosyncrasies and quirks, everything that made him endearing to her, he would go back to his own time, and she would be just a memory of some fucked-up time he spent in the future.

And she would help him go back. She already knew that. She didn't have the right to keep this kind of information from him, nor refuse him help to return. They were *friends*, she reminded herself bitterly. Just friends who had a physical connection. It had been a long time for either of them; they had been thrown together in a bizarre twist of time and space, and that *did* things to people. It screwed up their emotions.

He had told her he wasn't good at relationships. Neither was she. She had been foolish to hope for something more.

She had never wanted more, until now.

It was Mora's insistent voice that snapped her back to reality. "Honora!"

"What?" It came out harsher than she intended.

"It's a vortex, Honora. Even you can't be insane enough to try to go back in there."

"I can and I will," she replied harshly. "Look, I have to tell him that there may be a way back."

"These things have a way of getting out," Ensign Shraft said sagely. "That's why I told her about the vortex activity."

"He would hate me forever if—" Honora corrected herself. "When he finds out I didn't tell him," she finished bleakly.

"That's what I said," Shraft pointed out, shooting a glare in Mora's direction.

Honora had a crazy impulse to run to the restaurant. Not

to tell Andrew about this new development just yet—just to see him. But he would know that she was upset, and she wouldn't be able to hold anything in. She took her seat on the couch, feeling her heart and throat constrict, her world shattering to pieces.

CHAPTER 18

The hours had flown by.

Andrew had scarcely stopped to breathe during his first shift at The Galaxy Grill. The place had been nearly at capacity, full of Fleet uniforms, tourists, and fans of the band that had pounded away at their instruments on the stage. He had quickly figured out how to use the fancier replicators after coming up with a half-cocked story for Riel, explaining to her that they weren't used as much in the places he had worked on Earth and that he was a little rusty with the current models. She had bought it, and soon he was expertly slinging drinks and making small talk with the bar's patrons over the noise. The band wasn't bad either; a little louder than Andrew was used to, but they had given him a few albums on devices resembling tiny USB keys, gifts that damn near made him salivate.

They were small things, but they heartened him. He had found work, a job he liked so far. He had a home. He had Honora.

It wasn't making drinks and the meager tips that he liked so much—already he could tell that those black coins weren't worth a lot—but he had forgotten how much he had liked chatting with people, talking music and pop culture—even if he had to nod his head and smile a lot to his customers' conversations. In the years before he ran his life into the ground everything about him had been business. He hadn't gone to shows to watch the bands. He had gone to make notes on his smartphone and dig up the performers' contact information. He hadn't gone to restaurants with friends; it was always business associates or booking agents. There hadn't been any dates, let alone a girlfriend to speak of, nor had he so much as gone to a movie just for the entertainment value in years.

Andrew had been lonely. He realized that now, as the band's keyboardist threw a metallic-printed scarf into the audience and laughed at their drunken, half-assed response catching it. The loneliness had encroached upon him like the waning of daylight, until he hadn't noticed that he had been sitting in the dark.

He had found a friend in Verk, who he had run into on his way to work and invited to watch the show. Verk sat at a table with a couple of other Nym, nursing beers and occasionally waving to him when he caught their eyes.

It was Honora he missed right now, whom he was looking forward to going home to. The first person he had trusted in years, who had seen him at his worst, who had listened to his stories detailing his time as a coke-addled idiot, and who didn't judge him or run away. Who lost her job and her reason for existence because of him. A woman who was unsure of herself outside the realm of secret missions and blowing things up, who didn't think she deserved to be cared about.

When he let himself into the apartment at 3:30 in the morning, his body ached and his ears were ringing a little from the bar band's noise. As he walked down the hallway to their apartment, he jangled the USB keys in his pocket, next to his house key. All he had to do was figure out how to play them.

He was surprised to find that Mora and a scruffy young guy were in the living room with Honora, watching *Lightning's Luck* and, in the guy's case, playing with a small tablet computer. Honora sat on the couch, ramrod straight, and jumped to her feet as soon as Andrew entered the room.

Well, the presence of guests at this late hour certainly threw a wrench into his plans for the evening.

"Hi," he said. To the man, he held out his hand. "Andrew Claybourne. I don't think we've met."

He stood up and shook Andrew's outstretched hand, a surprising grip for someone who was so scrawny and punky-looking. His blond hair stood up in tufts around his head, like he had attacked it with a pair of scissors, and there were loose threads dangling from a growing hole in his sweater. "Ensign Taz Shraft," he introduced himself. "Communications officer, *Fortunate Wanderer*."

Andrew wasn't sure what a fortunate wanderer was, but this guy was clearly Fleet, even if his pants didn't match his shirt.

The exaggerated voices of the soap opera on the TV were the only noise in the room. Honora stared at a point behind him, while Mora and Ensign Shraft busied themselves checking their fingernails. It reminded him of when his grandmother had died and his relatives had gathered in a private room at the funeral home, not knowing how to communicate with one another.

Mora broke the silence. "Andrew," she said nervously, "Taz thinks he can get you home."

"No," Ensign Shraft quickly protested. "*I* can't get him home. But I know of a way to get there. We would need Fleet's help." He turned to Andrew. "I can do a lot of things when it comes to this." He waved around his computer. "But I can't do a vortex."

At first, Andrew thought this Shraft guy had been by simply to tell Honora that Fleet was right and there wasn't a virus to worry about.

Then it felt like all the air had been sucked out of the room, and he couldn't breathe for a few terrifying seconds. He felt like he had on that day so long ago when he discovered that Honora was telling him the truth, that he really was in the 29th century.

"There are a couple of Fleet officers who may be able to navigate a vortex," Ensign Shraft continued. "The former Lieutenant Kharn wouldn't be authorized, as she isn't military anymore."

He locked gazes with Honora, who had schooled her features into the same expression she wore when she was suspended from Special Ops: completely blank and devoid of emotion.

"Honora?" Andrew managed.

"I think you should do what you feel is best," she said neutrally. "You've said before that you had a life on Earth before you ended up here."

He had, hadn't he? He had been a respected businessman—at least, on his way to being respected again. He had a house and a car that didn't give him any trouble.

Here, he shared a cheap apartment with a disgruntled, suspicious former secret operative and had no idea what the credit pieces clinking around his pockets were worth.

But he was in love with that disgruntled ex-lieutenant. It was the first time he hadn't wondered about that emotion. He just *knew*.

He closed his eyes and counted back from ten, wishing away the most intense need for a cigarette he had ever had. He had hoped for a possible return home, and now an opportunity could be presenting itself.

He just wasn't sure he wanted it now.

"Honora?" he tried again.

"Yes?" She was still blank, a soldier waiting for orders.

"What should..." He drifted off. He didn't know how to phrase the question, or if a question should even exist.

"I can't make that decision for you, Claybourne."

So he was "Claybourne" again, was he? Disbelief gave way to anger. If Mora and Ensign Shraft weren't here, he would have raised his voice, tried harder to get a response out of her. *Talk to me!* he wanted to yell. *What should I do?*

Shraft didn't appear to notice his reaction, because he calmly explained, "I had to cover up my tracks—oh, and by the way, if anyone finds out I did this, I am *fucked*—but Fleet would probably be able to make an attempt to breach the vortex to get you back home. I'm not sure how they would do it or the probabilities of success, but the possibility is still there. You could probably even leave from Rubidge."

"Mora, Ensign—" Andrew began.

"Taz is fine, Andrew. I'm still insulted to be an ensign after seven years in Fleet, actually."

"We'll go," Mora said smoothly. Still, her eyes darted between him and Honora. "Taz, come on."

Neither of them said any goodbyes as Mora and Ensign Shraft made a quick exit. Honora didn't move from the couch, even as Andrew sank heavily into it. He found the remote between a couple of cushions and switched off the TV.

She kept her eyes fixed on that same point. "I think you should go," she said woodenly. There was an air of finality to her voice, like she was a commander and he her subordinate.

Well, that statement shot down any possible conversation Andrew could have with her. "You do?" he said, feeling his ire rise again.

"You belong on Earth. You've said so many times since I took you from there."

"Goddamn it, Honora, you didn't *take* me."

"I did." She turned cool eyes to him. "I brought you here, you were healed, and now you can go back."

"What if I don't want to?" he demanded.

"What is there for you here?" she countered.

"A lot of things!"

Her icy façade cracked. "No, there isn't," she shot back. "There isn't anything here for me, either. I am *not* enlisting with the Commons Authority or Fleet." She jumped to her feet. "I'm going back to the Empire. It's my home."

Andrew wasn't sure he could take another blow, but there it was. "When did you decide this?" he snapped.

"I've been thinking about it for awhile," she replied, her voice rising to match his. "I don't tell you everything."

"What were you planning to do with me?"

"You seemed happy enough here."

"You're one of the reasons I am!" he returned, then thought better of it. "*You're* the reason! I love you!"

His declaration was met with silence. Honora stared at him, shocked, then composed herself back into the frosty soldier he knew she wasn't. "No," she said, her voice low and dangerous. "I'm the first person you met here, that's all. It's not *me*."

Did she really think that lowly of herself, of him? He knew she had baggage—both of them did—but he thought they might have a chance at dealing with their issues together. "For God's sake, Honora..."

She stalked to the door, stabbing the button to open it.

"Don't leave," he said, hating to beg. But damned if he wasn't going to do that if it meant they could talk about this.

She didn't respond. If it were possible to slam the door, Honora probably would have knocked it from its frame.

———

Honora walked around the station for hours.

Part of her wanted to run back to the apartment, tell Andrew to damn everything and stay with her, but she couldn't do that. It wouldn't be fair for him to have that on his mind as well. If she were in his position, she would probably jump at the chance to return to her own time.

She had lied when she said she had been considering returning to the Empire, but the idea had some merit now that Andrew could go home. She could go into private business, running a freighter through the more dangerous areas of the Outer Fringes or colonies near the Sorkan border. A pilot with her experience would be welcomed at a shipping company. It would be a lonely life, but Honora was used to it.

When she finally began to tire, as the station started to wake up, she checked into a cheap hotel in the seediest part of the station. Rubidge prided itself on running a clean station, but there would always be a market for illicit business no matter the location. The area known locally as "The Docks" filled that need here. Here, in the lowest decks of the station, were the cheapest docks, services, and accommodations. When the desk clerk scanned her credit chip, Honora prayed that her bank accounts weren't about to be hacked and, on a whim, asked the desk clerk about the hotel's amenities.

"What are you looking for?" the greasy man asked, eyeing her figure.

In a station this large and in an area this transient, Honora could guess what this man thought she might be after and shuddered. "A bottle of something," she replied, recovering her composure. She thought quickly. "Um, a bottle of Kashaff whiskey."

"Twenty-nine credits."

It was outright thievery, but it was the only liquor Honora

could think of offhand. She nodded. "Have it sent to my room, please."

The clerk chortled and removed a bottle from under the desk. Its label was faded, and when Honora touched the glass, her hand came away sticky. "Here it is, love. We don't do room service here."

The bottle in one hand and a room key in the other, Honora made her way down the dank, darkened corridor to her room. She took in its furnishings with distaste: a patched chair, threadbare bedding, and a sagging bed, and she noted what looked like bloodstains that had been scrubbed out of the balding carpet.

She sat on the bed and uncapped the bottle of whiskey, taking a healthy gulp. Her throat and stomach immediately contracted, but she forced it down.

Two more swallows later, she felt like she was going to be sick and set the bottle on top of the scarred nightstand. While she was feeling a little dizzy, she wasn't drunk, and she doubted she could get to the point where she would forget her last exchange with Andrew and fall into a heavy sleep.

How can Mora do this on a regular basis? she wondered. It tasted awful and only made her feel worse, and she didn't think she had consumed even two proper-sized drinks.

She leaned back on the bed, ignoring the moldy smell of the sheets, and let her tears flow.

She had been a fighter pilot in the most elite squadron in this part of the galaxy and had gone into her career knowing she likely wouldn't live to see old age. Despite her occasionally seeking out perfunctory companionship, she had never needed anyone. Until she met Andrew, she had simply assumed that she wouldn't love anyone because she didn't have a heart.

She had been so very wrong.

She hurt more than she could remember. Even if Andrew

was willing to stay, she had botched their relationship so badly she doubted he would ever be able to look at her again.

Honora didn't know how to solve a problem if the solution didn't involve weaponry or evasive maneuvers in deep space. She was completely defective as a human being, unable to relate to anyone on anything deeper than a sexual level. It wasn't the loss of her parents when she was a child or her years in the military. It was *her*.

She wiped her eyes with a corner of the grimy blanket. *I'm broken*.

Even if Andrew stayed, she knew she wouldn't tell him she loved him. She didn't work that way. She couldn't. Love was something so alien to her, something she had never attracted and never felt she deserved.

Fresh tears gathered in her eyes. She burrowed her face into the pillow and cried until she drifted to sleep.

———

ANDREW SEALED his belongings inside his duffel bag. Briefly, he wondered if bringing stuff from the future back to his home wouldn't somehow screw up the space-time continuum, then decided that if Fleet didn't care, he wouldn't either. *I don't care about anything in this fucking universe*, he told himself, over and over. Maybe it would be true if he repeated it enough.

He had gone to The Galaxy Grill as soon as he woke up, after a short, fitful sleep when he figured that Honora wasn't coming home for the night. He came up with a bull-shit story to the manager on duty about a family emergency back on Earth and a promise that he would return as soon as he was able. The manager had accepted the excuse and paid him his previous night's wages, scanning his credit chip to deposit the amount. "Riel left a note," the manager told him.

"She said you did really good. Come back as soon as you can."

Andrew lied and said he would.

I don't want to come back. I don't want to work in a bar when I could be a partner at a radio station instead. I don't want her.

Honora had come home around eleven in the morning, her face puffy. She still wore the same clothes as yesterday. She was rumpled and looked sleep-deprived, and if Andrew hadn't known any better, he would have been sure she had gone out drinking. They stared at one another, facing off in the living room, neither sure of what to say.

"You're leaving." Her tone was flat, the finality in her voice breaking his heart. He knew she could tell that he wasn't just moving out to another apartment.

He let his eyes meet her and nodded. "Like you said, it's for the best."

"When are you going." It wasn't a question.

"I don't know what Mora's friend cooked up, but Fleet contacted me this morning a few hours after you had your temper tantrum, and someone's dropping me off on Earth in a couple of hours."

Her red-rimmed eyes widened. "So soon?"

He shrugged. "It's now or never." Somehow, he managed to say that without his voice cracking.

She bit her lip. "Andrew," she said carefully. "I...you've become very important to me."

If you say that you want me to stay, I'll stay. He couldn't voice the thought; he didn't want to tell her what he wanted to hear. It had to be her.

"I wish things could have been different," she finished quietly.

He took that as a sign of encouragement. "They could be."

She hesitated. "Andrew, I don't know. Things happen to people when they're thrown together in the kind of situation we're in."

"You have a lot of experience with time travelers, then?" His words came out sharper than he intended.

Her eyes flashed. "You know I don't. But I do have experience with refugees, and..." Her voice broke. "If things didn't work out—and I'm not sure they would have—you would have stayed here for a stupid reason."

A scathing retort was on the tip of his tongue, but he looked away. He didn't know what she was referring to as a stupid reason: her or what could have been between them. He knew if told her he loved her again, she would dismiss it. A lump formed in his throat, and with it, a humiliating wave of rejection washed over him.

"Okay, then," he said brusquely. He picked up his duffel and slung it over his shoulder. "Are you coming with me to lift-off?"

She wore an unfamiliar expression on her face, somewhere between horror and sadness.

Well, breaking up is hard to do. Even if they weren't breaking up because they had never really been together. "I'll see myself out." Against his better judgement, he pressed a quick, chaste kiss to her cheek. Without a backward glance, he let himself out of the apartment.

CHAPTER 19

No matter how assured Fleet was about going into a vortex, Andrew was still terrified.

He had guessed during his talks with Fleet's personnel that Taz Shraft hadn't tipped anyone off; Admiral Kentz prefaced the meeting by saying that Fleet had been looking for a way to return him since he and Honora showed up. Andrew didn't want to ruin another soldier's career, so he kept his mouth shut and pretended that all of this information was new to him.

The pilot was Fleet Commander Jax Darkel, an affable, easygoing guy who seemed too relaxed to be stuck in this kind of dangerous job. Andrew had spent the last hour in a top-secret meeting with Commander Darkel, Admiral Kentz, and a few other men in uniforms covered in braid and medals, reviewing the entire procedure and the odds of everyone making it out alive. According to the admiral, Andrew had an eighty-seven percent chance of ending back up on Earth in 2017, likely a couple of days after that fateful one in August.

"What am I supposed to say to people when I show up?"

Andrew had asked at the meeting. "The way Lieutenant Kharn described what she did to the lab, it was supposed to have been leveled."

Kentz looked irritated that Andrew was questioning this. "You survived the blast," he said in a voice that questioned Andrew's intelligence. "We've pinpointed a drop-off point that roughly corresponds to the area where the lab exploded."

"What do you mean, 'roughly'?" Andrew asked. "You know Toronto has a lake, right? I don't want to end up in the drink."

Commander Darkel had chuckled at that, but the smile was immediately wiped from his face with a warning look from Kentz. "It will be on land," the admiral assured him.

"So, you understand how this is going to play out," Darkel said to Andrew.

He nodded. "You fly into the vortex—said vortex has enough energy to suck us into it and bounce us around for awhile—and I'm ejected in a life pod."

"When you land, you activate the self-destruct sequence and then run like hell," Darkel finished.

"Yeah."

"The trip will take us less than a day," Darkel continued. "We're a little closer to the vortex than the Kurran Empire. You'll probably be in the life pod for an hour or two, tops." He spoke as comfortably as if he were giving Andrew directions to the nearest gas station.

He was so sure of this that it bordered on cocky, and if Andrew didn't know any better, he would have assumed the commander dove headfirst into volatile space phenomena on a regular basis. So unlike Honora, who spoke frankly about the dangers of a vortex.

"The shuttle you'll be using is here at the station," Kentz said. "We contacted Lily Stewart and asked if she would like to accompany you, but she said no. Again." He looked a little perturbed at this, and Andrew wondered what the Lazarus Cryonics receptionist had done to aggravate the admiral. "I even offered to send her lover with her," he finished. The admiral glared at everyone assembled. "That information doesn't leave this room."

Well, if that didn't make things a little more interesting. It was too bad that Andrew wouldn't find out the rest of that story. Commander Darkel caught his eye, and Andrew saw the message there: *I'll tell you in the shuttle.* That reminded him of something.

Shuttle?

"Are you sure a shuttle is secure enough to go through a vortex?" Andrew asked the people assembled. "Lieutenant Kharn has one, and it isn't sturdy enough to go into a vortex."

Admiral Kentz bestowed a condescending smile on Andrew and actually patted his hand. Andrew instinctively pulled away. "This is a *modified* craft, Mr. Claybourne. It's just as secure as the ship that brought you here, and your pilot is just as qualified."

Andrew hated to have to take the bastard's word for it.

Commander Darkel looked at the fancy wristwatch strapped to his arm and stood up, noisily scraping his chair against the tiled floor. "We need to be off," he announced. "If anything happens to me, tell my mother I love her." The few assembled around the table offered half-hearted titters at this.

"Nothing will happen," Admiral Kentz assured them. "Go to the shuttle. You're scheduled to clear out soon."

Now Andrew could see that the craft wasn't as impressive-looking as the one Honora had commanded on that hot summer afternoon 851 years ago, but the pilot Andrew would be traveling with assured him that it was in top shape. In the cramped cockpit, Darkel showed Andrew the life pod he was supposed to strap into when the time came. "How are you so sure it will work?" Andrew asked, trying not to let trepidation creep into his voice.

They were still docked at Rubidge Station. It wasn't too late to turn back, call everything off, and stay here instead. He desperately wanted to.

Honora doesn't want you.

Andrew had never sacrificed anything for a woman, and the one time he was willing to do so, she didn't want him. No, it was better to leave.

Darkel closed up the pod but didn't lock it. "Fleet used information obtained from the wreckage of a Nym ship and given by the Kurran Forces who brought you back here to study the vortex. They're very confident this will work."

"I thought the Nym were secretive before their planet collapsed."

"Oh, they were," Darkel assured him. "That Nym ship is one of the reasons Admiral Kentz wanted to send Commander Marska and his wife back to Earth. They helped destroy one of the Nym ships and embarrassed the admiral. I've met them a few times. His wife has bigger balls than half of Fleet. Marska's a lucky man."

Andrew would have been as well, if Honora hadn't shut him out.

He was obedient when he strapped himself into the seat next to Darkel's, a bittersweet reminder of all the times he and Honora had cruised through space and he wouldn't sit still. She had promised to teach him to fly, something that never came to be.

I should have told her I love her more than I did. Maybe things would have worked out differently if she could have come to believe me.

He dismissed that thought as soon as the shuttle hit deep space. Honora didn't do that sort of thing; she had been very clear about that. He had been an idiot to think she would change.

As the shuttle tore through space at a velocity far greater than Honora had ever taken, he told himself the moisture forming in his eyes was the result of the movement.

———

THEY WOULDN'T LET her in.

"Access denied, my ass!" Honora yelled at the locked doors. Some bastard wearing an ensign's insignia had refused to allow her into the Fleet-controlled docks. An *ensign*, for gods' sake! She settled for kicking the doors and pounding her fists against them as hard as she could, desperately hoping for a weak spot in the metal. She swore in every language she knew, cursing the ancestors and parentage of every Fleet officer.

Finally, the doors opened, and that obnoxious, incompetent fuck Kentz stepped out, disdain written across his face. The doors cycled shut with a heavy clunk. A spot gleamed on the top of his round head where his white hair was thinning, the only thing about his appearance that wasn't regulation and perfect. Honora had never hated Fleet and the whole gods-damned Commonwealth more than she did then.

"We've met before," he said.

Honora muttered a Kurran curse under her breath.

"I beg your pardon? I don't speak that language." He said it like it was beneath him, like the whole Empire was an aberration in civilized space.

"Where is Andrew?" she demanded.

"If you're referring to Mr. Claybourne, that's classified information."

All reason evaporated from Honora's mind, and before she could stop herself, she had pinned the admiral against the closed doors leading to Fleet's secret rooms, his lapels bunched in her fists. A medal broke free off his uniform and dropped to the floor, its clink echoing in the empty corridor. "Where. Is. Andrew?" she asked again, slowly and deliberately.

The admiral valiantly struggled to free himself and failed, and Honora realized that it had been a very long time since this man had been in any kind of hand-to-hand combat situation. She increased her grip, fistfuls of his uniform in her hands, and kept him pressed against the doors.

She was aware of the ensign in charge of door duty and ass-kissing yelling at her to let him go, and she released her grip.

Kentz bent down to pick up his medal. "I was awarded this for bravery in the Sorkan border dispute," he huffed and pinned it back to his jacket.

"That dispute hasn't ended yet," Honora snapped. "Now, tell me. I rescued him. I have the right to know. Where is Andrew?"

He ignored her question. "Oh, yes, we met back in the Empire." He adjusted his clothes. "Mr. Claybourne is returning to Earth as we speak. The shuttle cleared half an hour ago." He narrowed his eyes. "Kharn, isn't it? I will personally ensure that you will not be able to leave this station until we're certain Mr. Claybourne and his escort have reached their destination."

As if Honora could go after him anyway. She didn't have access to a craft that wouldn't break apart upon entry to the vortex.

She shook her head, torn between praying he was wrong and the knowledge that he wasn't. "No," she said.

A few Fleet security grunts had appeared and were braced to take her down. "This won't be necessary," she told them. "I'm leaving."

"Arrest her," Kentz ordered with a wave of his pudgy hand.

"Damn it," she whispered. If she was going to be arrested anyway, she should have rearranged Kentz's smug face.

She didn't fight back when she was handcuffed, and she cooperated when she was led through the maze that made up the station's military base. "Where am I going?" she finally asked.

"Brig," one of the grunts replied.

"You can't bring me to the brig," she protested. "I'm not Fleet. I believe protocol requires that I kept in the public jail."

"You assaulted a Fleet admiral, so you're going to the Fleet brig."

"I want to speak to someone about my rights," she demanded.

They turned down a corridor and into a white-painted, featureless room. One of the grunts unlocked her cuffs, while the other kept his hand on the laser weapon holstered to his hip. "Stand there," the guy who had unlocked her ordered. He pointed to a corner of the room. Honora did so, and immediately a forcefield shot to life. Its electrified orange bars stretched from floor to ceiling.

The grunt stood on the other side of the glowing bars. "I'm going to level with you," he said in a low voice. "There isn't anyone posted to this quadrant who wouldn't shake your hand after what you did to Admiral Asshole up there. If anything, they'd be pissed that you didn't take a couple swings at him. Is there anyone I can get in touch with for you? You're entitled to bail."

"What am I looking at?" she asked. "I have my credit chip on me."

"I'll have to ask, but this is probably going to be treated like a D and D, so I'd guess around four hundred credits. Maybe more, since you manhandled an admiral."

Honora nodded. Drunk and disorderly charges were common on stations with the kind of nightlife Rubidge had.

"Can you contact my cousin for me? Mora Kharn. She's a nurse at the Fleet infirmary."

A grin split the soldier's face. "You're related to Mora?"

"How do you know her?" Honora asked.

"You sure you want to know that?"

"No," Honora replied quickly. She sagged against the wall. "Could you just call her, please?"

The grunt nodded and left with his friend, who was smirking at the mention of Mora's name. Dear gods, what exactly did her cousin get up to in her off-hours?

She remembered why she was here and the colossal mistake she had made. It had been only hours since she and Andrew had parted in anger, and she missed him already. It was an unbearable ache that reminded her of when she lost her parents. The sense of hopelessness and lack of direction was almost overwhelming.

She should have begged him to stay.

Maybe she wasn't being selfless by insisting he return to his own time. She was only insulating herself against possible heartache, as she had her whole life. If she couldn't feel anything and refused to relate to anyone, then she couldn't be hurt.

Honora wiped away a few stubborn tears and slid to the floor. This loss was worse than her discharge from Special Ops. She wasn't sure she could ever move on. Every time she thought of her new life in the Commons, she pictured Andrew with her in some way.

She had left her chronometer in her duffel and wasn't sure how much time had passed when the door to the brig whirred open and Mora burst in wearing her nurse's uniform. Honora jumped to her feet and scrubbed at her eyes with her fingertips.

"Honora!" Mora shouted. To the grunt behind her, she

commanded, "Unlock the forcefield. I've already bailed her out."

The bars dematerialized, and Honora stepped out of her cell. "Thank you," she said. "What was the damage?""

"Eleven hundred credits."

"Insane," the grunt commented. "She should've been given her own ship."

Mora ignored him. "Honora, let's go." She grabbed her arm and pulled her from the brig. They kept up a brisk clip as they marched through the base's corridors.

"Eleven hundred credits?" Honora hissed.

"I talked them down from two thousand. Admiral Kentz says he has a lump on the back of his head."

"When I get back to my apartment, I'll transfer the credits to you." Honora jerked her arm from Mora's grasp. "Thank you."

"No, thank *you* on behalf of Fleet. I can't wait until I tell Lily. She'll think that's hilarious."

Honora's heart twisted at the mention of the other time traveler. "Andrew's gone," she said weakly.

Mora stopped and faced Honora. "What?" she yelped. "Already?"

Honora nodded miserably. "Kentz said he left this afternoon after I bullied it out of him."

Mora's face softened. "Oh, Honora, I'm so sorry."

Honora felt her face crumple, and she let out a sob that echoed off the corridor's walls. She looked away, knowing it was pointless. When Mora reached out a hand to her shoulder, she didn't recoil. She leaned into the touch and let Mora envelop her in a hug. "I screwed up so badly," Honora said through her tears. "I didn't want him to go."

Mora didn't ask any questions or chastise her, only saying, "I know you didn't."

"I'd so bad at this," Honora whispered. "I feel like I'm a cyborg in a lab and the doctors forgot to program me like a normal person." She sniffled and pulled away. "Mora, I love him."

Mora's face didn't register any surprise at this announcement. Nor did she appear put out that the first time Honora used that word it was about a person to whom she wasn't related. Instead, Mora hooked her arm through Honora's and said, "I kind of figured that."

MORA ACCOMPANIED Honora back to the apartment in the Nym District. The crowds were sparse there, and Honora was grateful she didn't run into any neighbors. Once they were there, Mora contacted the doctor on duty at the infirmary via her comm badge and begged off work for the rest of the day. She promised to do a 48-hour on call at the doctor's whim to make up for it.

"You didn't have to do that," Honora said, sinking into the couch.

"I did," Mora replied. "We're family. Families do that for each other."

Honora snorted. "I'm a really lousy family member."

"Yeah. Not to piss on your grief or anything, but you can be difficult." Mora fixed them cups of tea and took a seat next to her. "You know we love you, right? Me, my parents, and Zak."

Honora wasn't sure how to respond to that, so she didn't.

"I know we're not the Empire, and my parents weren't yours, but we always wanted to you to feel welcome," Mora continued. She looked into her own cup, at the floating shreds of tea leaves. "Things didn't pan out between us the way I'd hoped, and I feel terrible for you about Andrew, but maybe all of this—it'll change your perspective about people."

"My perspective?"

"A lot of people care about you," Mora explained. "I was so excited when you came to live with us when we were kids. I'd always wanted a sister, and Zak is so much older than I am, and my mother was always off doing research with Fleet Medical."

"And I disappointed you."

"Yeah, but it wasn't entirely your fault. I was *ten*. I didn't consider that you would be grieving for your parents and your home and you wouldn't want to live with us. I just saw you as a playmate and a confidant, and we'd play with makeup and talk about boys, and I was impatient and frustrated when that didn't happen."

"And I never grew out of that. That's the part where *I* fucked up."

Mora shrugged. "I don't know. It hurts that we don't know each other well enough for me to say that."

Honora felt a pang of regret as well. Mora wanted to look out for her, be her friend. "I thought about that last night," Honora admitted. "I mean, this morning. Me and Andrew had a fight and I spent the night in a hotel. I tried to get drunk."

"Tried?"

"It didn't work. Kashaff whiskey tastes like vomit. I gave up quickly."

Mora smiled at that, then turned serious again. "There's not a lot I can do to help you move past Andrew's loss besides being your friend right now," she said gently. "You just have to go through this one day at a time."

"It feels like he died."

"Well, he did, in a way," Mora replied. "You need to give yourself time to grieve."

Honora nodded dumbly and squeezed her eyes shut, wishing that everything had gone differently.

———

THIS VORTEX TRIP was definitely rockier than the last one Andrew had made. He had never been prone to motion sickness before, and right now he was fighting back waves of nausea. He declined Commander Darkel's offer of a transderm to take the edge off and instead gripped his seat's armrests, keeping his eyes straight ahead. Wasn't that what one was supposed to do for motion sickness? His stepmother had claimed to have issues with it, but what illness didn't Judith claim to suffer from?

At the thought of his father and stepmother, he made a face. He was going back to them, and he really didn't care one way or another.

It would have been better to stay in the Commons.

"Commander?" he asked nervously.

Darkel's usually smiling face was furrowed in concentration as he maneuvered through the vortex. "What?" he barked.

"Is it too late to go back?"

"Are you fucking crazy? Yes!"

Darkel didn't look as confident as Honora had been. The shuttle dipped dangerously to the left, and Andrew forgot which side it was. Port or starboard? Did it really matter?

"Commander—"

"Godsdamn it, Andrew, I'm trying to navigate a vortex here!" He slapped a flashing light on the command console. "*Fuck!*"

The shuttle lurched forward and Andrew had to brace his hands to keep from smacking his face into the console. He quickly checked and tightened the safety straps.

"We've only been here seventy-two minutes," Darkel said. "This shouldn't be happening."

"What?" demanded Andrew. Fear left a metallic taste in his mouth.

"It's just... this isn't working."

"I thought there was an eighty-seven percent chance of this happening!"

"That still leaves a thirteen percent chance of failure. Look, I don't think this is going to work. We've got to abort."

Hope surged through Andrew. "Okay," he automatically agreed.

"Damn it!" the commander shouted again. A siren began to wail as the reverberations shook the cockpit, causing a panel to fall off the wall in a shower of sparks. Outside, the vortex swirled around them in angry slashes of color, the stars dotting the black void of space visible through it like a filmy curtain. It hadn't looked like that last time.

Darkel snapped his straps and stood up, holding on to the back of his chair for balance. "I don't know what's wrong," he admitted. "All I know is that we're definitely looking at thirteen percent if we stay in this vortex. Get up, Andrew."

With shaking hands, Andrew let himself out of the seat.

"Get into the life pod," Darkel ordered. "I can configure it to dump you out of the vortex and back into space."

"What?"

"Just do it! The life support on here is going to die in less than ten minutes!" Darkel shouted. "Now!"

The life pod—a clear, plastic-looking thing that resembled a coffin—was strapped to the wall in a closet that could be sealed off by airtight doors. As Andrew stepped in, Darkel explained, "The shuttle's probably going to blow apart."

"What about you?" Andrew asked.

"There's an emergency pod below. Get in here and you might have a chance at staying alive."

Darkel pressed a transderm against his neck, and within seconds Andrew had to fight to stay awake. The shuttle lurched again, and he hit his head against the back of the pod.

"Wait," he tried to croak.

"No!" Darkel slammed the transparent cover into place.

Andrew tried to raise his hands, trying to reopen the pod door, but he couldn't lift his wrists high enough. He leaned back heavily and closed his eyes, the last image registering in his mind that of Honora.

CHAPTER 20

Two weeks of wallowing had been enough for her.

Honora couldn't do this anymore. She hated hanging around the apartment with its memories of her time with Andrew. She kept his bedroom door closed and had taken to eating her meals in restaurants with Verk or Mora. Her cousin pulled a couple of strings for her and got her authorization to work out in Fleet's gym. She did everything she could to avoid being in what used to feel like home.

Verk had accepted her story about an emergency in Andrew's family with some skepticism but didn't prod for details. He had found work with the Commons Authority as a translator the day Andrew launched out of her life. Over the last week, he kept urging her to consider applying.

"It's not bad," Verk said enthusiastically in near-flawless Kurran while they ate lunch at Tash's. "They're always looking for recruits with your experience."

"How long is the contract?" she asked, picking at her salad.

"Two years, with an option to renew at the end," Verk replied. "You get the advantage of military benefits, but you're not stuck with the minimum ten-year commitment. I know they're short on pilots. Most of the new recruits are retired Fleet officers looking to pad their pensions. I think you should give it serious consideration."

"What would they think about an ex-Ops fighter pilot who threw a Fleet admiral against the wall?" she asked.

"Why would you throw a Fleet admiral against the wall?" Verk asked. He set aside his spoon. He didn't ask about her dishonorable discharge; Honora guessed that he sensed it was a sensitive topic.

"He got in my way."

Verk laughed. "I'm sure you had a good reason. I know you well enough by now." He took a sip of tea. "Just think about it, Honora."

She shrugged noncommittally. "I will."

"Have you heard from Andrew?" he asked suddenly.

Her breath caught. "No."

"I was hoping he would stay in touch."

"We parted on bad terms. I don't think I'll hear from him again." She sighed.

"I wish I had known he was leaving. I would have given him my transmit address."

Verk was fishing, but Honora wouldn't take the bait. "It was very sudden. He had that family emergency to deal with, and neither of us handled it well. Especially me." She looked away, out the restaurant window at the bustle of tourists.

Verk didn't ask any more questions, but Honora knew there would be more. He was chipping away at her exterior, wanting to know more about her. That was what a friendship was, she supposed. That, and he missed Andrew as well.

They finished their meal in silence, and Verk laid his credit chip on the table. "My turn," he said firmly.

"You got dinner last night."

"Translators make more than deliverymen," he said, and his bright green eyes lit up in his smile.

She walked with him back to the Authority base on the opposite end of the station from Fleet's and downloaded an application to her datatab from an automatic kiosk. After repaying Mora the obscene amount for her bail, she knew she would have to get back to work and soon. She wouldn't be able to live off her savings much longer.

When she bid goodbye to Verk and left the Authority base, her datatab trilled from inside the frivolous little purse Mora had given her. She slid out the datatab and read a message from Uncle Tarek.

There's been an accident. Come to the base immediately.

Heart pounding, she bolted in the direction of the Fleet base as fast as her feet could take her.

———

THIS TIME there wasn't an idiot ensign who wouldn't let her into the base. Uncle Tarek was waiting for her at the door to a briefing room, the dark half-moons under his eyes stark against his pale face.

Her hands clenched around her purse, which was tethered around her wrist. "What does this mean?" she demanded. "An accident?"

She was only angry because if she wasn't, she would collapse in a fit of grief.

"Honora," Uncle Tarek urged. "Get in here."

He ushered her past the base doors into a conference room full of Fleet uniforms and one familiar face. *Commander Kakos!* He, too, looked ashen. Despite all of this, Honora couldn't help but salute at her former commanding officer. He replied in kind, but it was a pathetic salute.

Seeing the looks on the faces of everyone assembled, Honora asked, "What happened?"

Admiral Kentz shot one of his customary glares at her but didn't speak. Another man wearing far too many medals spoke up. "The shuttle Commander Jax Darkel was piloting to twenty-first century Earth couldn't withstand the vortex. Andrew Claybourne was on board."

Couldn't withstand... It took a moment for those words to make sense. When they did, she felt her knees go weak. Her vision blurred. Vaguely she was aware of chair legs scraping against the floor, of someone guiding her to a chair and whispering in her ear, "Breathe in... breathe out. In, out."

She leaned her head in her hands, forcing herself to follow the directions. When she looked up, Uncle Tarek and Commander Kakos were standing sentry on either side of her.

"They entered the vortex at the sixty-three minute mark," one of the admirals was saying. "Two weeks ago. We miscalculated its force, and the shuttle started to break up ten minutes into entry."

"Oh, gods," Honora whispered.

This was worse than Andrew simply going back to 2017. His death had been theoretical, too abstract to really ponder other than the reality that she wouldn't see him again. She still knew he would have been relatively safe back home. The stark reality of his death—his real death—was too much to handle.

She tried to stand up. "I have to leave," she said, but the words came out in a strangled croak.

"Lieutenant Kharn, wait," Kakos said softly in Kurran.

"This rendezvous is supposed to be conducted in Commons, Commander," Kentz spat.

No one paid any attention to the squat little man. "Mr. Claybourne's life pod was ejected into Commons space, fairly close to Earth," Uncle Tarek said.

Honora looked up, hardly daring to hope. "What?"

"His pod was picked up by a Fleet patrol ship two days ago," Uncle Tarek explained. "Commander Darkel's emergency pod was found yesterday, orbiting Earth. The ship was there to look for the remains of the shuttle when we didn't hear from Darkel."

"The vortex's activity is now negligible," said the admiral who had spoken up earlier. Honora strained to read the name embroidered on one of the medals he wore. Brynon? "It's gone. We tried to keep it going using the technology we gleaned from the Nym, and we can't."

"Andrew," she said urgently. "Where is Andrew?"

"That's classified," Admiral Kentz said smugly.

She looked to Kakos and Uncle Tarek, knowing they saw the desperation on her face. "It's classified, Honora," Uncle Tarek reiterated sadly. "I had to bend a lot of rules just to let you know he didn't make it to the twenty-first century."

"But he's alive, isn't he?"

"Dismissed, Kharn," Kentz said, the sneer evident in the man's voice.

Honora regarded the admiral, the useless sack of meat whose greatest military achievement was not getting killed in the line of duty. Who existed only to exert power when it wasn't necessary.

She jumped from her seat and vaulted herself across the table, intent on choking the living breath from the fucker. Before she could wrap her hands around his throat, she was pulled back, a muttered *"Sikiaka!"* telling her the hands belonged to Kakos. "Not now," Kakos said.

The admiral sputtered. "Did you see that? She tried to kill me this time!"

No one from the table moved or objected. Brynon lifted a hand to his mouth and uttered a strange cough.

"Not now, Kharn," Commander Kakos said quietly. Louder, he said to the group, "Allow me to escort Lieutenant

Kharn off the base." He nodded at everyone. "Admirals, always a pleasure."

She threw one last, venomous look at Admiral Kentz before following Commander Kakos from the conference room. When she opened her mouth to speak, he shushed her in Kurran, "Not here."

Once they were off the base's territory and in a lift heading back to the civilian area, he said, "I have to be brief." The doors slid shut and the lift began a smooth descent, not the direction Honora was expecting. "No one in Fleet is authorized to tell a civilian anything about this."

There was uncharacteristic mischief in his dark eyes.

"What are you saying?" Honora asked.

"I am not Fleet." He paused, letting the reminder sink in. "Andrew Claybourne is being treated at the Fleet hospital on Commons Prime. If you go to the civilian docks, you will find your dock fees paid and your shuttle ready to launch."

Grief gave way to hope. "He's alive?" Joy, then gratefulness, flared to life within her, and she threw her arms around Kakos in a hug.

He gently peeled her off. "I'll take that as a thank you."

"I can never repay you for this," Honora said.

The lift doors opened. Honora said a quick goodbye before she started a sprint down the chilly corridor to the airlocks. She turned back to ask Kakos one last question. "What about authorization?"

Kakos actually looked amused at the question. "It's a hospital, Kharn. You don't need authorization to visit a patient in hospital." Before the lift doors closed, he added, "I wish you well. Special Ops feels your loss acutely."

She ran for her shuttle, and once strapped in, she drummed her fingers against the controls as she waited for clearance to depart. One shuttle at a time, as inefficiently as possible. A ten-minute wait for the airlock to open felt like hours. "Come on," she said audibly into the shuttle's communicator.

"You have to wait," the controller groused. "Everyone else is in a hurry, too."

She tore out of the station as soon as the airlock's lights turned red, earning an expletive from the controller. She slapped off the communicator and tore through deep space, setting a course for Commons Prime. *An hour*. She could do this.

What kind of condition was Andrew in? Kakos would have mentioned if he was suffering from amnesia or was nonresponsive, wouldn't he?

More frustration mounted when she arrived at Commons Prime, a small planet that was a stark contrast to the pile of rusty metal that was Rubidge Station. She gritted her teeth at the myriad security hurdles, authorizing a scan of her shuttle for weapons and answering questions about her intentions on the planet. She docked at an adjacent spaceport and walked through a body scanner before she could be taken to the planet's surface by way of a transport beam. She was too nervous and excited to be irritated at this inconvenience and wasn't even nauseous when her molecules rearranged themselves. She rematerialized on a transport pad in the hospital's lobby.

Her datatab chose to beep at that moment, and a transmit from Kakos read simply: *Room 6213. Do not ask for directions from a doctor or nurse, just in case.* There was a lock override code written there as well.

She walked purposefully, blending in with a group of civilian visitors squabbling among themselves in a dialect she didn't speak. She felt tears gather in her eyes and impatiently brushed them away, terrified of what she would find in room 6213. How secure had that life pod been?

The shuttle couldn't handle the vortex; what if there had been a breach in the pod, as well? He had been drifting in space for over a week. What if he hadn't had enough nutrition available? What if he had been awake during his whole ordeal? The what-ifs roared through her mind.

She steeled herself outside of room 6213 and entered the override code into the lock, an old numerical one that was a couple decades out of date. For the first time, she was grateful for the Commons's anachronistic technology.

Andrew was in bed, lying on his side away from her, his light brown hair mussed. At the hiss of the door opening, he turned around. His eyes widened and he sat up.

"Honora?" he said.

He was coherent and in one piece. *Oh, thank you, gods.*

She crossed the short distance to the bed and threw herself on it. His arms circled around her, squeezing her ribs, but she didn't care. "You're alive," she said. "Oh, gods, I can't believe it. You're here." A sob caught in her throat.

He released her enough to cup her face in his hands and kiss her. It was harsh and possessive, and it thrilled her from head to toe. "I didn't think I would make it," he admitted. His eyes were moist. "Honora, I wanted to go back. I wanted to come back here and tell you I want to stay. I love you."

She wiped away her own tears. "I love you, too. I was so stupid—I was scared, and that's not an excuse, and..." She tried to smile. "I can't believe you're here."

He hadn't let go of her, like he was afraid she would disappear if he relinquished his hold. "I am," he said. "I'm not leaving. I'm staying with you."

"Good. I'm not letting you leave."

He sat up straighter. "I do. I want to get the hell off this planet and go home."

She laughed and touched his face, reassuring herself that she wasn't dreaming this. She saw the dark circles under his eyes, the deep bruises that crept under the pushed-up sleeves of his shirt. "What happened?" she asked.

"The vortex shut down, and Commander Darkel put me in the life pod and shot me out into space," he explained. "Darkel survived, too, through an emergency pod, but he's in rough shape. Worse than me."

"Will he make it?"

Andrew's expression darkened. "He will, but he has some new body parts. Something malfunctioned in his pod. He's here, too. I've spoken to him a couple of times, and he said that an emergency pod is designed to be retrieved from space immediately."

"They're not built to hold a person for days."

Andrew swallowed. "He lost a leg. It's been reconstructed with a bionic one."

Honora didn't know what bionic meant, but she nodded. She couldn't help but feel a little angry at Fleet on behalf of the commander.

"I owe Darkel a lot," Andrew finished. "He could've put me into the emergency pod instead. He didn't have to save me."

Honora considered this. There were a lot of imbeciles in positions of power in Fleet. But then there was Ensign Shraft, who had broken into classified files for her. Uncle Tarek undoubtedly had an idea of why Kakos escorted her from the base and permitted it. Mora had done more for her than Honora could say. And now this Commander Darkel had saved the man she loved, someone he didn't know.

She was still itching for a chance to clock Admiral Kentz in the jaw, however.

"When can you and Darkel leave the hospital?" Honora asked.

"Darkel's going to be here for awhile, getting used to the new leg. I'm just recovering from dehydration." He stroked her cheek with the backs of his fingers. "I want to go home with you."

He refused her offer to help him out of bed. The door slid open before either of them could activate it, and a nurse stepped in. "Hello, Mr. Claybourne," she said perkily. "You've been transferred to the infirmary at Rubidge Station. You live there, right?"

Andrew eyed Honora, no doubt wondering how she pulled that off.

"It's on the orders of an admiral," the nurse added.

Uncle Tarek. It had to be.

"You're free to leave," the nurse said cheerfully.

Honora picked up the duffel lying on the floor, a grin spreading across her face to match Andrew's. "All right."

———

"YOU PROMISED to teach me to fly."

"*You* promised to take me out when we got that suit."

They had departed the Commons Prime spaceport. Andrew had handled the transport beam like a pro, swaying only a little. Now he was hanging on to the back of her seat like old times, and Honora had never been more grateful for it.

"Aren't you going to tell me to sit down?" he asked as she navigated out of the main commercial lane.

"No. Just give me a minute." She made a few adjustments and brought up a list of authorized hover sites nearby, places where pilots could stop safely and run systems checks or conduct an exterior examination.

Or let someone inexperienced handle the controls.

She found a spot and set a short course for it, then stood up and gestured to the command seat. "Your turn."

Andrew grinned devilishly and sat down. His mirth faded when he saw the controls, their blinking lights and Kurran commands. "I don't understand any of this."

"When we can do this properly, the first thing you'll do

before requesting departure authorization is run a safety checklist." She brought up the screen, the list's points all green to indicate optimal systems. "Then you'll... oh!"

He had tugged her in his lap, his arms locking around her waist. "Continue."

"Well, after you've been cleared for departure, you set a course for wherever you're going, and that course has to be shown to any authority who requests it, and... Andrew, are you paying attention?" She couldn't suppress a gasp when he lightly nipped the soft skin under her ear. One hand slid under her shirt, caressing her waist.

"I am. I'm a multitasker. I can do two things at once. It's what makes me a good bartender."

Honora regained enough of her composure to stop the shuttle at the hover site and turn on the perimeter alarm before locking the console.

"What are you doing now?" Andrew asked as her fingers flew across the console.

"Giving us some privacy. Maybe you can multitask, but I can't." She looked at him and winced at the circles under his eyes. "That is, if you *want* some privacy."

He kissed her in reply, and Honora eagerly responded. He shifted her in his lap and took what she felt beneath her as a yes. She stood up, grabbing his hands to pull him with her, and he pushed her against the console until she was sitting on it. He broke their kiss long enough to ask, "Will this break anything?"

"I don't know," Honora admitted. While the console was secured, she wasn't sure what making love on it could do. It wouldn't do to break their means home in an embarrassing way, in a public place. She hopped off. "There's the sleeping area in the back."

It took some maneuvering to find a comfortable position on the narrow bed, and Andrew paused his hands' exploration under her clothes long enough to ask, "Are you sure this thing is strong enough?"

Honora dramatically sniffed. "It's Empire-built, Andrew. Of course it is."

"And no one's going to crash into us if we're parked here?"

"No, we'll hear an alarm before that happens. But it would be embarrassing to answer a Fleet hail and talk on the vidlink with them when I'm naked."

"I could do it."

Honora laughed, then tugged his shirt from the waistband of his pants. "Then you'd better be naked, then."

He shucked off the rest of his clothes and helped her out of hers. At the sight of him under the shuttle's unforgiving light, she gasped at the bruises along his body, at the small regenerators stuck to his shoulder and ribs. "Andrew, will you be okay to do this?"

His body slid over, the touch of his skin warm and welcome. She arched into him, his erection rubbing against her thigh. "Of course," he said. "You're thinking too much."

When he thrust into her, she couldn't keep back a cry, a climax already building as he moved harder and harder into her. She wrapped her legs around his hips, allowing him deeper access, until her whole body thrummed with pleasure.

He caught her lips with his own when she cried out, and she felt his body shudder in kind when he found his own release. He sagged against her, his head buried against her neck. They remained that way for what felt like an eternity, before Andrew softly said, "Honora, I love you."

———

THEY RETURNED TO RUBIDGE STATION, both alternating at the controls—sort of. Andrew kept Honora snuggled in his lap while she taught him a few things, both the controls that were universal to shuttles and a few words of the Kurran language.

When Honora requested authorization to dock at the station and they took their place in the queue, she said, "I'm going to apply to the Authority."

"Seriously? I thought you were going back to the Empire."

She cringed at that reminder of her monumental stupidity. "No," she said. "I'm staying here. Verk is working for them as a translator now. He started right after you left. It doesn't sound that bad." She paused. "It sounds pretty good, actually. Oh, and you might hear a rumor that I threw Admiral Kentz against a wall. That's true, just so you know."

"That's my girl."

She flushed with pleasure at this, then turned serious as she followed the traffic controller's directions to a waiting dock. For once, Honora wasn't displeased at the thought of the station or its queues or the Commons—not as long as she had *him* with her.

"Andrew?"

"Mmmhmm?" he said into her hair.

"It's good to be home."

ABOUT THE AUTHOR

Jessica Marting is a sci-fi and paranormal romance author, art enthusiast (not quite an artist, despite all that time in art school), an avid reader, and makeup collector. She lives in Toronto.

Sign up for her newsletter at jessicamarting.com/newsletter for pre-order alerts, sales, freebies, and more.

ALSO BY JESSICA MARTING

Magic & Mechanicals

Wolf's Lady

Sea Change

Bound in Blood

Dragon's Keep

Spellbound

The Searchers

Blood Ties

Blood Moon

Blood Virtue

Zone Cyborgs

Haven

Paradise

Oasis

Safe Harbor

Sanctuary

Refuge

The Commons

Supernova

Celestial Chaos

Standalone Novels & Novellas

Spindle's End

Trade Secrets

Neon Vice

Dead Ringer

Rapture

Escape From Europa 10

Castaways

Demon's Favor

Her Purrfect Match